BRIAN FLYNN

THE LEAGUE OF MATTHIAS

BRIAN FLYNN was born in 1885 in Leyton, Essex. He won a scholarship to the City Of London School, and from there went into the civil service. In World War I he served as Special Constable on the Home Front, also teaching "Accountancy, Languages, Maths and Elocution to men, women, boys and girls" in the evenings, and acting in his spare time.

It was a seaside family holiday that inspired Brian Flynn to turn his hand to writing in the mid-twenties. Finding most mystery novels of the time "mediocre in the extreme", he decided to compose his own. Edith, the author's wife, encouraged its completion, and after a protracted period finding a publisher, it was eventually released in 1927 by John Hamilton in the UK and Macrae Smith in the U.S. as *The Billiard-Room Mystery*.

The author died in 1958. In all, he wrote and published 57 mysteries, the vast majority featuring the super-sleuth Antony Bathurst.

BRIAN FLYNN

THE LEAGUE OF MATTHIAS

With an introduction by
Steve Barge

DEAN STREET PRESS

Where is the Queen of Herod's kiss,
And Phryne in her beauty bare:
By what strange sea does Tomyris
With Dido and Cassandra share
Divine Proserpina's despair?
The wind has blown them all away—
For what poor ghost does Helen care?
Where are the girls of yesterday?

Alas for lovers! Pair by pair
The wind has blown them all away.
The young and yare, the fond and fair;
Where are the snows of yesterday?

—VILLON.

INTRODUCTION

"I believe that the primary function of the mystery story is to entertain; to stimulate the imagination and even, at times, to supply humour. But it pleases the connoisseur most when it presents – and reveals – genuine mystery. To reach its full height, it has to offer an intellectual problem for the reader to consider, measure and solve."

BRIAN Flynn began his writing career with *The Billiard Room Mystery* in 1927, primarily at the prompting of his wife Edith who had grown tired of hearing him say he could write a better mystery novel than the ones he had been reading. Four more books followed under his original publisher, John Hamilton, before he moved to John Long, who would go on to publish the remaining forty-eight of his Anthony Bathurst mysteries, along with his three Sebastian Stole titles, released under the pseudonym Charles Wogan. Some of the early books were released in the US, and there were also a small number of translations of his mysteries into Swedish and German. In the article from which the above quote is taken, Brian also claims that there were French and Danish translations but to date, I have not found a single piece of evidence for their existence. Tracking down all of his books written in the original English has been challenging enough!

Reprints of Brian's books were rare. Four titles were released as paperbacks as part of John Long's Four Square Thriller range in the late 1930s, four more re-appeared during the war from Cherry Tree Books and Mellifont Press, albeit abridged by at least a third, and two others that I am aware of, *Such Bright Disguises* (1941) and *Reverse The Charges* (1943), received a paperback release as part of John Long's Pocket Edition range in the early 1950s – these were also possibly abridged, but only by about 10%. These were the exceptions, rather than the rule, however, and it was not until 2019, when Dean Street Press released his first ten titles, that his work was generally available again.

The question still persists as to why his work disappeared from the awareness of all but the most ardent collectors. As you may expect, when a title was only released once, back in the early 1930s, finding copies of the original text is not a straightforward matter – not even Brian's estate has a copy of every title. We are particularly grateful to one particular collector for providing *The Edge Of Terror*, Brian's first serial killer tale, in order for this next set of ten books to be republished without an obvious gap!

By the time Brian Flynn's eleventh novel, *The Padded Door* (1932), was published, he was producing a steady output of Anthony Bathurst mysteries, averaging about two books a year. While this may seem to be a rapid output, it is actually fairly average for a crime writer of the time. Some writers vastly exceeded this – in the same period of time that it took Brian to have ten books published, John Street, under his pseudonyms John Rhode and Miles Burton published twenty-eight!

In this period, in 1934 to be precise, an additional book was published, *Tragedy At Trinket*. It is a schoolboy mystery, set at Trinket, "one of the two finest schools in England – in the world!" combining the tale of Trinket's attempts to redeem itself in the field of schoolboy cricket alongside the apparently accidental death by drowning of one of the masters. It was published by Thomas Nelson and Sons, rather than John Long, and was the only title published under his own name not to feature Bathurst. It is unlikely, however, that this was an attempt to break away from his sleuth, given that the hero of this tale is Maurice Otho Folliott, a schoolboy who just happens to be Bathurst's nephew and is desperate to emulate his uncle! It is an odd book, with a significant proportion of the tale dedicated to the tribulations of the cricket team, but Brian does an admirable job of weaving an actual death into a genre that was generally concerned with misunderstandings and schoolboy pranks.

Not being in the top tier of writers, at least in terms of public awareness, reviews of Brian's work seem to have been rare, but when they did occur, there were mostly positive. A reviewer in the Sunday Times enthused over *The Edge Of Terror* (1932), describing it as "an enjoyable thriller in Mr. Flynn's best manner" and Torquemada in the *Observer* says that *Fear and Trembling* (1936) "gripped my interest on a sleepless night and held it to the end". Even Dorothy L. Sayers, a fairly unforgiving reviewer at times, had positive things to say in the *Sunday Times* about *The Case For The Purple Calf* (1934) ("contains some ingenuities") and *The Horn* (1934) ("good old-fashioned melodrama . . . not without movement") although she did take exception to Brian's writing style. Milward Kennedy was similarly disdainful, although Kennedy, a crime writer himself, criticising a style of writing might well be considered the pot calling the kettle black. He was impressed, however, with the originality of *Tread Softly* (1937).

It is quite possible that Brian's harshest critic, though, was himself. In *The Crime Book Magazine* he wrote about the current output of detective fiction: "I delight in the dazzling erudition that has come to grace and decorate the craft of the *'roman policier'*. He then goes on to say: "At the same time, however, I feel my own comparative unworthiness for the fire and burden of the competition." Such a feeling may well be the reason why he never made significant inroads into the social side of crime-writing, such as the Detection Club or the Crime Writers' Association. Thankfully, he uses this sense of unworthiness as inspiration, concluding: "The stars, though, have always been the most desired of all goals, so I allow exultation and determination to take the place of that but temporary dismay."

Reviews, both external and internal, thankfully had no noticeable effect on Brian's writing. What is noticeable about his work is how he shifts from style to style from each book. While all the books from this period remain classic whodunits, the style shifts from courtroom drama to gothic darkness, from plotting serial killers to events that spiral out of control, with Anthony Bathurst the constant thread tying everything together.

We find some books narrated by a Watson-esque character, although a different character each time. Occasionally Bathurst himself will provide a chapter or two to explain things either that the narrator wasn't present for or just didn't understand. Bathurst doesn't always have a Watson character to tell his stories, however, so other books are in the third person – as some of Bathurst's adventures are not tied to a single location, this is often the case in these tales.

One element that does become more common throughout books eleven to twenty is the presence of Chief Detective Inspector Andrew MacMorran. While MacMorran gets a name check from as early as *The Mystery Of The Peacock's Eye* (1928), his actual appearances in the early books are few and far between, with others such as Inspector Baddeley (*The Billiard Room Mystery* (1927), *The Creeping Jenny Mystery* (1929)) providing the necessary police presence. As the series progresses, the author settled more and more on a regular showing from the police. It still isn't always the case – in some books, Bathurst is investigating under-cover and hence by himself, and in a few others, various police Inspectors appear, notably the return of the aforementioned Baddeley in *The Fortescue Candle* (1936). As the series progresses from *The Padded Door* (1932), Inspector MacMorran becomes more and more of a fixture at Scotland Yard for Bathurst.

One particular trait of the Bathurst series is the continuity therein. While the series can be read out of order, there is a sense of what has gone before. While not to the extent of, say, E.R. Punshon's Bobby Owen books, or Christopher Bush's Ludovic Travers mysteries, there is a clear sense of what has gone before. Side characters from books reappear, either by name or in phys-ical appearances – Bathurst is often engaged on a case by people he has helped previously. Bathurst's friendship with MacMorran develops over the books from a respectful partnership to the point where MacMorran can express his exasperation with Bathurst's annoying habits rather vocally. Other characters appear and develop too, for example Helen Repton, but she is, alas, a story for another day.

The other sign of continuity is Bathurst's habit of name-drop-ping previous cases, names that were given to them by Bathurst's "chronicler". *Fear and Trembling* mentions no less than five separate cases, with one, *The Sussex Cuckoo* (1935), getting two mentions. These may seem like little more than adverts for those titles, old-time product placement if you will – "you've handled this affair about as brainily as I handled 'The Fortescue Candle'", for example – but they do actually make sense in regard to what has gone before, given how long it took Bathurst to see the light in each particular case. Contrast this to the reference to Christie's *Murder On The Orient Express* in *Cards On The Table*, which not only gives away the ending but contradicts Poirot's actions at the dénouement.

"For my own detective, Anthony Lotherington Bathurst, I have endeavoured to place him in the true Holmes tradition. It is not for me to say whether my efforts have failed or whether I have been successful."

Brian Flynn seemed determined to keep Bathurst's background devoid of detail – I set out in the last set of introductions the minimal facts that we are provided with: primarily that he went to public school and Oxford University, can play virtually every sport under the sun and had a bad first relationship and has seemingly sworn off women since. Of course, the detective's history is something not often bothered with by crime fiction writers, but this usually occurs with older sleuths who have lived life, so to speak. *Cold Evil* (1938), the twenty-first Bathurst mystery, finally pins down Bathurst's age, and we find that in *The Billiard Room Mystery*, his first outing, he was a fresh-faced Bright Young Thing of twenty-two. So how he can survive with his own rooms, at least two servants, and no noticeable source of income remains a mystery. One can also ask at what point in his life he travelled the world, as he has, at least, been to Bangkok at some point. It is, perhaps, best not to analyse Bathurst's past too carefully . . .

"Judging from the correspondence my books have excited it seems I have managed to achieve some measure of success for my faithful readers comprise a circle in which high dignitaries of the Church rub shoulders with their brothers and sisters of the common touch."

For someone who wrote to entertain, such correspondence would have delighted Brian, and I wish he were around to see how many people enjoyed the first set of reprints of his work. His family are delighted with the reactions that people have passed on, and I hope that this set of books will delight just as much.

The League of Matthias (1934)

"God alone knows why we took it into our heads to enter the place!"

THE young hero and heroine thrown together in peril is another stalwart of the Detection genre. Two strangers thrust headlong into danger, each hiding their own secrets and yet the reader can – one presumes deliberately – see that they are destined to fall in love. One particular practitioner of this was John Dickson Carr, in, for example, *The Case Of The Constant Suicides*, which starts with a pair of academics butting heads on a train, heading for a date with murder in a Scottish castle, but the reader is in little doubt about how their relationship will progress.

It is a similar state of affairs in *The League of Matthias* (1934), one of Brian Flynn's rare ventures into a significant romantic subplot, as Lance Maturin, in Antwerp as part of an international trip, is convinced by Philippa, a dancer at the House Of The Red Flare, to pretend to be her husband to fend off the intentions of the villainous De Verviac, only for the pair of them to find themselves on the run when a "famous English detective" is murdered in Philippa's hotel.

As in the opening sections of *The Padded Door* (1932), here Brian Flynn plays with the chronology of events, as after things have significantly deteriorated for Lance and Philippa, the clock turns back to days earlier in London, with Anthony Bathurst heading to Antwerp to investigate the murderous League of Matthias – another first for Flynn, a secret society of the sort only found in classic crime fiction. This leads him to Philippa's hotel and disaster! What follows is a rollercoaster of events, as Flynn ties together a multitude of plot threads with some significant skill, in particular maintaining a strong whodunit element within the plot.

It is in this book that we finally get some insight into one of the great mysteries surrounding Anthony Lotherington Bathurst

– what exactly is on his visiting card? Several times previously, Bathurst has been able to interview many a witness by flashing his card, but no real detail has been given about this seemingly magical device. Well, apparently, it consists of his name, the words "acting in conjunction with Scotland Yard" and the signature of Sir Austin Kemble, the head of Scotland Yard. How exactly this works is still a mystery – is the signature of the Commissioner of Police that well-known? It's a necessary plot device, as Bathurst does most of his work as a lone investigator, but probably ranks up there with the psychic paper from the modern Doctor Who series in terms of believability.

Do we read classic detective fiction for believability, though? No, of course not. We read it for surprises, plot twists and turns and to attempt to beat the author at his or her own game. *The League of Matthias* delivers on all those counts. On top of everything else it contains, in my opinion, one of the subtlest pieces of misdirection that I've ever read. I am delighted that after so many years, other people will get the chance to enjoy it as well.

Steve Barge

Chapter I
THE RED FLARE
(Told by Lance Maturin)

God alone knows why we took it into our heads to enter the place! But you do strange things when you're knocking round aimlessly . . . sightseeing . . . and just wandering on from one place to another . . . lacking a definite purpose or destination. In all probability, it was Hilleary who suggested going there. Most impulses that actuated our little party, foolish and otherwise, emanated from him, and I think that Fawcett and I were more or less satisfied and content that this should be so. After all, it saved us trouble, which was something for which to be devoutly thankful.

After a tour that had lasted over a couple of months, the three of us were in Antwerp. Had come in from Malines and been there a matter of three days on the night when this story of mine opens. We had put up at the Hôtel de Lutèce, and on the evening in question had strolled through the quaint old streets of Antwerp, past the quay and back again . . . along by the waters of the Scheldt . . . until we had come to this abode of the "Red Flare." During the previous days that we had spent in Antwerp, we had seen all the sights that attract the many. The harbour and docks, the old cathedral, the city's many artistic treasures, and the house where the Flemish master Rubens had lived . . . Fawcett rather fancied himself when it came to a discussion on art . . . and this evening, I suppose, the three of us had a craving for lighter fare in the shape of entertainment.

We had struck through the cathedral close and then on from there through Antwerp's high and narrow streets. This had brought us, of course, to the farther side of the city and to what, so we had been informed, must be regarded as its oldest parts. Until, as I have said, we had come to a halt outside this place of the scarlet flare.

It seemed to me, at first glance, to be half café and half inn; as we paused there, as one man almost, we heard, I think, when I come to look back, the strains of music drifting through the door.

It is my rigid intention to be perfectly candid, in the telling, about the entire affair—from the very outset. The place, as I first saw it, was the reverse of inviting. That is, to three healthy young Englishmen, as we were . . . fit, clean, and I suppose, taking all in all, moderately sane. There were signs of crumbling brickwork about the exterior, which were thrown up into greater plainness by the huge flare of red light that filled the doorway. Yes—I'm sure now that it was Dennis Hilleary who had mooted the idea of breezing in there, "For something else better to do." That was how he put it to us.

We nodded complacently when he projected the idea, and Fawcett and I trooped in, in Hilleary's wake. Through a kind of bar arrangement—into a good-sized room beyond. There was nothing remarkable about this room. It was of the usual sort. There were little marble-topped tables to accommodate, in most instances, two people; waiters, none too clean, flitting backwards and forwards in service of various patrons; and, at the end of the apartment, the inevitable stage or, to describe it more accurately, raised platform.

Hilleary and I collared a table close up to the stage. Fawcett seated himself at a table a few paces to the left of us. I mention these details in the light of what took place afterwards. The entertainment, if I embrace charity and call it such, was evidently well under way; the programme, I should say, being a little more than half over. We gave appropriate orders to the waiters who approached us, and began to take general stock of the situation. In about five minutes I was bored stiff. But the beer was good, so I decided to stay. The artistes, one and all, were pains in the neck to me. They were coarse, vulgar, and, without exception, untalented.

And then—just as the show had reached rock-bottom—something happened! A girl came on the stage. As she didn't open her mouth to sing, I presumed that she was about to dance. I could have sworn that she wasn't a day more than twenty. She was amazingly and startlingly beautiful. She had that peculiar lustrous duskiness of skin that belongs, perhaps, more to the Latins than to our own people. Of medium height, she gave me an impression, even in that first moment of seeing her, of having in reserve an unusual quality of nervous energy that for some reason or the other was more than ordinarily submerged at that particular moment.

Her eyes had flecks of green in them that made her infinitely more attractive to me . . . I must admit that there were definite reasons for this . . . and her dark hair swept in waves above her forehead. The throat of her rose straight and slim from firm shoulders, and, although dark, she was not sallow. Her face, on the contrary, was clear and clean and fresh. There was a soft sweet colour on her cheeks that I felt certain was not due to grease-paint, but which brightened and softened them as a peach is brightened and softened by its bloom.

She smiled as she faced the audience . . . and then, at that moment, although she smiled, I noticed something else. There was not only pain in her eyes—there was more than pain there. There was fear! Not ordinary fear, at that. But a deep-down, haunting, brooding fear. I looked across at Hilleary, over the table, and I saw that he was watching her too. Adrian Fawcett's back was to the stage and his nose was buried in a tankard, so that my instinctive glance in his direction failed to yield me very much that was instructive.

The girl began to dance. There was nothing whatever that was outstanding in her performance. I will admit that at once. It was neither very much better nor very much worse than many similar performances which it has been my lot to witness at various times in various places. You could put it down as average, adequate, and satisfactory—but no more than that. Right above the remainder of the programme, of course, but, judged by decent standards, just ordinary and commonplace. I probably numbered in my own acquaintance at least a dozen girls who could have done what she did.

She finished her dance . . . terrific applause from all the tables . . . and then I had what I will call sensation the second.

A man in the dress of an Apache slunk on to the stage L.U.E., in the approved manner of such people, and the ragtag and bobtail orchestra began to play and fiddle like demons in the heat of hell. I gathered the impression that they were just about to commence the real work of the evening, and that everything else that they had done previously had been accomplished simply to while away the time.

There then began the usual dance of the Apache kind—with all its attached exercises. The fellow, whom I instinctively hated like the very deuce, and into whose evil face I could have cheerfully pushed my fist, caught her, poised her, balanced her, embraced her, crushed her, and flung her away from him . . . all according to invoice, plan, and to the manner born. A greasy-looking waiter, sensing, I'm afraid, my exaggerated interest, thrust a programme into my hands and then stood impudently at my side . . . waiting for the riposte . . . for the inevitable *pour-boire*. I slipped a coin into his predatory fingers and glanced at the slip of paper that he had given me, for information.

Without a doubt, the number that we were watching was *"Danse Macabre."* De Verviac and Philippa. Cast aside for the last time, flung to the boards in that final fierce frenzy that is the usual and characteristic finale of this particular form of entertainment, the girl whom I watched, rose, caught de Verviac's outstretched finger-tips, and came forward to acknowledge her share of the storm of applause with which the pair was greeted.

And then, *mirabile dictu*, she looked me straight in the eyes and sent me a message from her soul. In the cold words of print, this statement may sound and read very much like a sloppy absurdity. You could argue, my dear reader, I haven't the slightest doubt, that I was seduced by vanity and overridden by imagination. That I was a ready and willing victim of a combination of atmosphere, emotion, and impressionableness. Were I in your place and you in mine, I should probably argue exactly as I suggest you would do.

Nevertheless, when that girl on that stage looked across at me through the nebulous curtain of smoke that hazed between us, I was as absolutely certain that she appealed to me for help as

I was that my name was Lance Maturin. I will candidly confess, too, which is a point in favour of my argument, that my first impulse was to take no notice.

For one thing, I hadn't the least desire to play knight-errant, and, for another, she had caught me (from her point of view) at an unfortunate moment. One of the reasons—the chief reason indeed—that had induced me to join Fawcett and Hilleary on this jaunt had been a girl's unfaithfulness. A girl who had succeeded in knocking the bottom out of my world as thoroughly and effectively as that time-honoured job of work has ever yet been performed. A girl whose eyes had looked love . . . whose lips had spoken love . . . who had used the ways with me that lovers use . . . who had sworn eternal loyalty and allegiance to me, but who, as I unexpectedly discovered one evening, had been admitting me, all the time, to what had been a mere shareholder's privilege.

If I lived many years beyond my allotted span, I question whether I shall ever forget the tempest of impotent anger that shook and shrivelled my soul when I came upon her in Paton's arms, looking up at him as she had so many times looked up at me. You can understand, therefore, that I was in little mood to don the costume of Sir Galahad that evening in the room of that house of the scarlet flare. Time and solitude are the only conditions that conquer a man's pain when he has been deserted by the woman he loves and who, so he believed, has loved him.

When I first caught this girl's mute appeal, I glanced again at Dennis Hilleary to see if he had spotted it as well. If he had, he gave no sign. Fawcett's face was still averted—as I said, his back was half turned from me—but the girl's eyes weren't moving in his direction at all . . . all the time they looked straight towards our table and into my face.

Well, the applause died down and the orchestra struck up again. The girl and her escort made their exeunt. The man appeared to me to pull her from the stage backwards, and then, curiously enough, I found myself wondering what the real relationship between them was. You can imagine the guess that I made!

It was just then that Hilleary leant across the table and spoke to me. "'Not too bad a turn, that, Maturin—after the stone-cold stuff that was put across before it. These two are coming on again, I fancy." He was right. The words had scarcely left his lips when the girl, whom I had come to think of as Philippa, came on to the stage again. She had changed her dress and now wore a pale green creation which, although enhancing the beauty of her, had the effect also of making it less overwhelmingly start-ling. This was due, no doubt, to the fact that I had become more accustomed to it. It had grown on me tremendously quickly, and, because of that, I accepted it in the light of an inevitable indication of what was right and proper.

The orchestra was now giving us a haunting melody.

The girl began to dance again. And de Verviac entered. Exactly as he had entered to her before. Watching them intently, as I was, a moment or so passed before I realised that the greasy waiter was standing at my side again. I was annoyed at what I considered a show of over-attention. I hadn't beckoned to him and I was in no need of anything. He had already had one tip out of me—why the hell couldn't he be satisfied with that? On the point of choking him off, I was suddenly prevented from so doing by his next action. Bowing obsequiously, with a rare click of the heels, I should imagine, for him, solemnly and with an excess of ceremony he pushed a folded piece of notepaper between my fingers. Extremely surprised, I unfolded it . . . wondering all the time who my correspondent could be. The message that I read was in the following terms. I will attempt to reproduce it here word for word as I remember seeing it in front of me then.

"Monsieur, I call you that, although I am almost certain that you are English. Help me, for I am in deadly peril. If you would save my life, please come to my dressing-room immediately this number is over. My room is on the right-hand side—behind the stage., Do not fail me—I implore you.

Philippa.

The sentence that immediately preceded the signature was heavily underlined.

I nodded to the waiter, who was still standing at my elbow, to get him out of the way, I think, more than with any other object. I remember that I did that first of all—before considering in any way what my answer to the appeal was going to be. The man's presence at my side irritated me, and, try as I would, I couldn't rid myself of the idea that his face wore a covert grin and that he was reading into this girl's cry for help a contemptible meaning. At any rate, look at it now how I may, there is one thing that I *do* remember clearly. That I badly wanted time to think!

When the waiter fellow had cleared off, I began to sort myself out, as it were. My first inclination, as I have said, was to have nothing whatever to do with the affair. Why should I allow myself to be dragged into a sordid domestic squabble such as this would probably prove to be? It would be incredibly foolish of me and almost unthinkable. It was a marvellous thing, I argued to myself, that a man was unable to come out for an evening's entertainment without being pitch-forked into a heap of trouble. Besides—women were the very devil. I knew that— none better, I swore to myself; and the girl whose message I held in my hand would assuredly prove no exception to the rule. Then I spotted Hilleary looking at me rather curiously.

"What's the game?" he demanded cheerily. "I didn't bring you in here this evening, young feller-me-lad, for you to get the 'glad' and start misbehavin' yourself. You're goin' to pull no stage-door stuff here."

I shook my head impatiently. "Don't be all sorts of a silly ass," I answered. "Can't you realise that men and women aren't all alike? Give me credit for some sense, Dennis, do." As I spoke, de Verviac and Philippa came to the finish of their second turn. In answer to the crashing burst of applause which greeted them, they repeated their previous performance and bowed themselves off the stage.

When that happened, my head seemed to clear suddenly, as though somebody had chucked a bucketful of cold water over me, and with a curt, "Don't wait for me," to Hilleary, I strode off to behind the old-fashioned staging where I imagined the girl's dressing-room might very well be. The words of the poignant appeal that she had sent out to me were burning themselves into my brain . . . "deadly peril" . . . "save my life" . . . "Do not fail me, I implore you."

I cursed softly to myself for a priceless fool . . . but something else stirred within me . . . the thought that a girl had implored me to help her . . . more than that, had deliberately picked me out from a company of men to help her . . . and that, as a Britisher, I couldn't possibly let her down. As I walked forward in search of her dressing-room, I remembered, with an uncomfortably chilly sort of feeling, that I hadn't a weapon of any kind with me, and that if it came to a rough house, as seemed highly probable, I should be forced to rely on my two bare fists.

I came to a door that was partly ajar, and again, for an inexplicable reason, I pushed it open a little more and slipped into the room. With nothing more than two bare fists and my brains to back me up!

CHAPTER II
PLAYING WITH FIRE
(Lance Maturin's story continued)

THE girl I was seeking was standing in the room, just behind the door, with one hand to her breast and the other to her lips, which were parted. When she saw who it was that had entered, she gave me the biggest shock of my life . . . and I've had a few, I can tell you, even in my short span. Coming straight up to me as I crossed the threshold, she threw her arms round my neck and kissed me passionately on the lips. "My darling," she cried in English, "why have you been so long? I thought that you would never come. Oh, my heart's darling . . . how have I lived through the days without you?"

Her eyes were shining and her voice was gloriously low and sweet to hear, and just as the thought flooded my brain that Hilleary's assumption had been the right one after all, I was destined to receive shock number two. She pulled me to her again . . . put her lips on mine again . . . kissed me just as passionately as before, and then in that low voice almost whispered . . . "Please play up to me, m'sieu! That is right, isn't it? Forgive me and understand my shame . . . but for God's sake play up to me . . . it may mean my salvation . . . somebody of whom I am desperately afraid may be close and listening . . . you are cold and distant . . . am I so unattractive, then?"

Although so perilously close to distress, she smiled coquettishly and provocatively, and the green eyes that I had seen grow dark with fear now changed to a wonderful and enticing brilliance. "Kiss me," she demanded imperiously, and, although I obeyed semi-instinctively, I fear that the effort was a poor one, for my mind was busy with a hundred and one other things. Fancies and ideas raced through my brain—each close on the heels of its predecessor.

She smiled at me a little ruefully, but patted my cheek and held me to her with an odd air of proud proprietorship. "When husband and wife meet like this . . . after weeks of separation . . . it should be the time for a second honeymoon, *n'est-ce-pas?* Which—who knows?—may be even sweeter than the first. My darling, I have ached to feel your arms around me." And then again she drew me close and whispered, "For mercy's sake, play up to me . . . Didn't you understand what I said to you just now? He is no doubt listening at this moment. Where are your endearments? Call me something sweet . . . other men have had no difficulty, believe me. If nothing else, call me by my Christian name."

I braced myself for a tremendous effort . . . I could have done so much better, I felt, if she had given me more warning and a few minutes' grace. "Philippa, my sweet," I murmured, in a kind of faltering desperation, "I, too, have ached to be with you again. I can't tell you how much. Every moment away from you has been but bitter emptiness and desperate waste. You're wonderful, my dearest. More wonderful to me than ever before, and I love you more than life itself."

She gave my fingers an ardent pressure and I found myself thrilling in response. Then I saw her raise her head suddenly and stand there listening. After a moment or so of this attitude, a look of relief came over her features. "I was right. I thought he was there. He's just gone." She whispered the words, and, as I looked at her again, her cheeks flamed flaunting scarlet. She dropped her eyes to the ground. I pretended to ignore both indications. Time looked as though it were going to be precious, and I had more important things to do than philandering. The obvious question sprang to my lips. "Who has gone?"

"De Verviac," she returned—"but he will come back. Oh, my friend, be assured of that." She went over to the door by which I had entered and closed it. But she stayed by it, with her hand holding the handle, and I could see that she was still listening despite what she had said. At length she shook her head slowly and came away. "Yes, I think that it is all right for the time being. He has gone. I heard somebody close the farther door." Her eyes met mine again, and for the second time a wave of colour flooded her cheeks. But I was impatient now and in no mood for further subterfuge or evasion. If it were possible, I was determined to bring her to the point of explanation.

"Mam'selle," I said, rather stiffly and pompously I'm afraid, "I should esteem it a favour if you would be good enough to explain. It would at least help me to understand something of the situation and—because of that fact alone—make things easier for me." The dark look of haunting fear shot into her eyes again. She came to me and held the lapels of my coat. "You will help me?" she implored. "You will not desert me now that you have come to me? You wouldn't do a thing like that, would you? I know that you wouldn't. That you couldn't! Buoy my courage up, and then—"

"Philippa," I interrupted boldly, "you are English. I am certain of that, now that I have heard you speaking. I thought at first, from your colouring—"

"You are right," she admitted with a delicious toss of the head. "I am English. And you are, too. That is why I asked you for your help."

"No," I cried hotly, "that isn't altogether true . . . because I had friends with me . . . men . . . English, too, like me . . . you could have sent your message to one of them . . . had you cared . . . and not to me. So, you see, what you say isn't altogether . . ."

She laced her fingers together for a fleeting second. The fear in her eyes had gone. "I know. I know. All that you have said is perfectly true. I saw the three of you . . . and I deliberately chose *you*, my friend. Oh, but a girl knows these things . . . the men that she can trust . . . don't ask me how she knows . . . I think God gives her the intuition, the instinct. If it were not so, my friend, I don't know what we should do sometimes when we are sorely troubled. I *knew* when I looked at you that . . ."

"That what?" I demanded.

"That I could ask you for help and that you would not misunderstand me or expect . . ." She paused for a moment before completing her sentence.

"Expect what?"

"Any return," she concluded in reply.

It may sound perfectly ridiculous, and I can't explain the reason altogether, but I found myself thrilling again at her words, and, for the first time for many weeks, I forgot that Dorothy had ever existed. I suppose that men are like that. "Feed the brute" may cut chunks of ice, but I'm not sure, when I come to assess the matter carefully, that "Flatter the brute" wouldn't be an even more successful injunction. When women tell us we're wonderful . . . and "different from other men" . . . and "not like that" (blessed trinity of words), we're all inclined, I think, to send for an extra size in hats and "strike the stars with an uplifted head."

Besides, I could feel the exquisite touch of her kisses on my lips. I was still conscious of her almost incredible fragrance, of her hair that held the scent of violets, of her bare young arms with their delicate odour of hyacinth, and at the moment (I was young, remember) I would have pulled down the very temples of the gods themselves, if she had asked me to do so. I caught her hands and pulled her towards me. She came willingly enough, and I said again, "Explain, please, Philippa. I must not and cannot, work in the dark. Of whom are you afraid? Of what are you afraid? And why?"

She nodded quickly and for the second time broke away from me and darted with swift grace to listen at the door. Apparently she was satisfied, for she came straight back to me and motioned me to a seat on a little green divan arrangement that stood at the side of her dressing-mirror. She seated herself beside me. "I need protection to-night as much as any girl ever needed it—since the world began. Not only a man's protection . . . but a *good* man's protection. There is a difference, you know."

She leant over to me and placed her hand on my sleeve. "Something tells me . . . I can't tell you what, but I am certain of its truth . . . that if you fail me it will mean that I shall lose my life. De Verviac is at fever-heat, and when he is thwarted of his purpose . . . continually thwarted, as he has been over this one . . . he is a devil that sticks at nothing. Hot in hatred and mad in malice. I fear him, and God knows I have cause to fear him."

She averted her face, but even so I saw that her eyes were fringed with tears. I put my fingers gently on her turned cheek and brought it deliberately towards me again. To my astonishment her face flamed scarlet again.

"Tell me," I said as gently as I knew how—"tell me all the trouble."

She shook her head slowly. "It's not that which is worrying me. It's what I want you to do for me."

"Tell me that, then," I returned; "if I can help you, why then—"

"But it is hard, my friend . . . ever so hard. I want you to come home with me now . . . because that is where de Verviac will come—as he has come before."

I rose from the divan where I sat. "Let us come now, then," I said softly. "It's quite an easy matter, surely."

"That is not all," she continued. Her voice was toneless and her scarlet cheeks were turned away from me once again. She was flying the flags of shame.

"Well?" I asked—"what is there else?"

"You must be prepared," she said, still tonelessly, "to play the part of my husband. . . . I am your wife, you must understand, whom you have not seen for months."

"Even that," I answered gallantly. "I hope that I shall do better than I did before in the role . . . I'm beginning to know my lines and pick up my cues more promptly."

She went to the door, and stood there for a minute or so with her back towards me. "You must understand, too," she said in that cold, matter-of-fact tone, "that any half-measures will be useless. There must be nothing left to chance if he is to believe. It will be necessary for you to come to my bedroom . . . and equally necessary for you to stay there with me for some time . . . perhaps even to seem to sleep with me." She blushed most deliciously.

Her words took my breath away, and before I could answer she had pushed open the door and was calling back over her shoulder to me . . . "Come quickly . . . please. We shall almost certainly be followed."

CHAPTER III
SLEEPING PARTNER
(Still told by Lance Maturin)

I WENT after her . . . a pace or so behind. And, once again, as I watched her gloriously lithe and lissom figure pass down the corridor in front of me, I was able to think of Dorothy in Paton's arms . . . kissing and being kissed . . . using the ways that lovers use . . . with comparative equanimity, which had been a thought that had tortured me and seared my soul ever since he had taken her from me! A thought that had made me writhe in the exquisite agony of lacerated vanity! Marvellously! A thought that had kept me lying awake night after night . . . in the nervous insomnia of its mere envisagement. Strange, wasn't it? I had known this girl, Philippa, for but half an hour. And here I was dedicated with almost fanatical zeal to her service.

Outside in the street . . . the street that I had come to call the street of the Red Flare, she stopped and silently waited for me. When I came abreast of her, she held her arm out to me for escort and I took it instinctively. We crossed the road. It was a dark, damp, murky night now and I soon heard the soft pad of footsteps behind us. Philippa caught at my arm and pulled me closer to her side.

"What did I tell you?" she said quietly—"he takes no chance, does he?"

"What shall I do?" I asked her.

"Nothing," she said . . . "it would be foolish to challenge him now . . . just come along with me as quickly as we can go. Take no notice of him. We haven't far to go. My lodging is near the church at the end of the next street."

I wasn't sorry to take her advice. Remember that I had no weapon of any kind with me. If this fellow were armed I was absolutely at his mercy.

"Let us run!" she whispered.

"Will he attempt to stop us getting in?" I asked.

"Oh no, no! He will watch us go in. That is what he has come to find out. But he knows me too well and he will still wonder. That is what I want him to do. Wonder and wonder and wonder again."

"All we have to do, then," I said between breaths, "is to get to your place and slip inside. Then we shall be safe—if what you say will happen is true." I was holding her arm, and I saw her shake her head sadly as though she were sorry for my lack of understanding. When she spoke again, she spoke curtly and authoritatively.

"He will come back—I told you so. Don't doubt me for an instant, my friend. That is as sure as anything ever will be in this world . . . in this transitory life of faith, hopes, and fears. Cross over here."

I obeyed her—and gradually our running slackened to normal walking pace.

"Look—there is the church of which I told you. It is the Church of the Sacred Heart. We have only a little way to go now. Turn round and see if you can still see anybody."

I turned as she had ordered me, and away in the distance, almost a block away, I saw again that low, crouching, slinking, slithering figure. "Yes," I said to her. "He is still there." I made no further announcement; it seemed to me that what I had said was enough. A further hundred yards brought us to a house before which she stopped and caught at my arm impulsively.

"Here," she said. "I have a key with me. So perhaps has de Verviac. Even if he hadn't, he would know how to get in."

I waited while she fumbled in her bag. I could see that it was a high, gaunt-looking house of white walls and shuttered windows like many of those I had seen on French soil—in places like St. Malo for instance. A quick mental calculation gave me the conclusion that it was a house of at least six and perhaps seven storeys. The windows, as I have said, were shuttered. I knew the kind. I had come across too many similar windows in France not to know them when I saw them.

The casements don't open as our English casements do, but they are constructed lattice fashion. I will explain what I mean by that statement. When they are thrust outward, the two sides in the middle open as swing-doors will do, and then fold back almost flat against the wall. Thus, when the window is opened to its fullest extent, a large open space is always left—as large a space as there would be if the glass itself were cut or removed clean out of its frame.

Philippa went to the door, key in hand. It was a massive affair—iron-studded—but it opened easily at the movement of her key. We slipped into the house. It was dark in the passage there and, to my surprise rather, smelt musty. The smell reminded me of the countryside in early autumn—of decaying leaves and dank earth. We had gone scarcely a few steps when an old crone, haggard and blepharitic, hearing the sound of our feet, no doubt, came forward and barred our way. She shuffled right up to us and at once poured forth a flood of Flemish punctuated by an embarrassment of gesture. Scarcely a word of it was intelligible to me, but Philippa evidently understood something of the old hag's meaning, for she answered her. I caught a name and the general gist of her reply, for she spoke slowly and deliberately.

I was her husband, she told this blinking, blear-eyed apparition whom she called Rasmussen . . . . the husband for the coming of whom she had been waiting for weeks. At any rate, the Lily-maid of Astolat who listened seemed more or less satisfied with Philippa's explanation, for she shrank away from us and gave us the right of the staircase. Another tall, grim-faced and grey-haired woman in a reddish dress lurked in the shadows below us as we set our feet on the first steps of the staircase.

At that moment I heard the chimes of the church clock clang out. I listened to them carefully. The first quarter! It must be a quarter past eleven. I followed my girl companion up three flights of stairs.

As far as I could tell from my present position, the house, save for the two hags I had seen downstairs, was deserted. At the head of the third flight of stairs, she stopped.

"This is my room," she said. "This back-room here. Come in, please."

We entered a bed-sitting-room, poorly furnished. Philippa found a box of matches and lit the gas. I walked to the window and looked out. At once, although it was dark, I could see the relative situation of the room in which we stood. It was at the back of the house, and the dark mass that I could see in the comparatively near distance was the remains of an old wall . . . a wall with a top so thick that, in places, it afforded a fair stretch of promenade. In all probability, it had been one of the walls that had encircled the old town of Antwerp. I remembered having read about them.

They dated back to the eleventh century, when the Margraviate of Antwerp had been held by the counts of the Ardennes and Bouillon, one of whom had been the famous Godfrey de Bouillon. This piece of wall that I could see as I looked out was doubtless a part that had remained of those historic walls . . . a part of those old ramparts that had given way in the course of time to the boulevards. Its highest point, I should say, was about six feet below the window-sill of Philippa's room. Only the narrow gulf of an intervening street separated us from the top of that ancient wall.

I turned from the contemplation of it to Philippa. "Well," I queried, "what's our next move?" I spoke with a jauntiness that was far from feeling.

"It is twenty minutes past eleven," she said, with a touch of weariness, "he will not come back until after midnight. I know his habits. And he will kill me, he said, if I don't give in to him to-night." The girl shivered as she spoke.

"Philippa," I said desperately, "I'm not afraid—don't think that—but I have no weapon of any kind. My fists are at your service. Beyond them . . ." I shrugged despairing shoulders. Without answering, she walked to the dressing-table and from a top drawer took something which she came and put straight into my hands.

"If my plan succeeds," she said, as my fingers closed on it, "there will be no need for you to use this. If I had not seen you to-night . . . God knows how I might have used it. Be careful. It is fully loaded."

It was a small revolver—pearl butted at that, and a careless glance told me that there was a monogram of sorts round the butt. But I knew that this aristocrat of revolvers could spit fire as effectively as any of its democratic relations.

"What do you mean?" I demanded, with a cold fear at my heart. "That you were going to use it on yourself?"

She looked at her watch again and shook her head. "For a time, my friend, let us sit and talk. There is at the worst a quarter of an hour that can be spared: There are things, you see, that I must tell you. At least, I owe that to you. Come and sit here, Gamaliel, and I will sit at your feet." She smiled artlessly. "Literally, I mean—not figuratively."

After putting the revolver in my pocket, I took the low chair that she had indicated, and she came and sat on the strip of faded carpet in front of me. As she snuggled herself against my knees and clasped her hands in front of her, the thought flashed through my mind as to what Fawcett and Hilleary were doing in the Hôtel de Lutèce and when I should see them and it again. If ever!

"No, my dear," she said simply, "I should not have killed myself . . . although many's the time, during these last few months, that I have been tempted to do so. But I have learned things, you see. Taught them to myself, would perhaps be a truer thing to say." She paused and looked up at me . . . straight into my eyes. And as I looked into her eyes, I realised for the first time how like they were to my own. A hint of green, a hint of russet, and a hint of a deeper brown. Her hair, too, was not unlike mine, if one studied the shade of it closely.

"Tell me," she said, "have you ever been in love? *Really* in love, I mean. Not just liking somebody . . . not being attracted by somebody . . . or pursued by somebody . . . but loving somebody with every fibre of your being and being loved . . . as you though . . . just like that . . . in just the same way . . . by that somebody in return?"

Merciful heavens! . . . the question brought back my pain and sorrow in full flood. "Yes," I said, "I have. Just as you say."

"What is it, then?" she asked of me . . . "*this love?* How would you describe it, you who assert that you have known it?"

"Describe it?" I echoed after her.

She nodded. "Yes . . . to convey all that it means."

I hesitated for a moment, but then found words. "Giving someone else the power of hurting you like hell," I answered brutally.

Again she shook her head. "Oh, but you're wrong. There's something else, too. Listen. Let me try to show you another side of love. Isn't it having somebody in your life that's more important to you . . . *much* more important to you . . . than yourself?"

I shrugged my shoulders. "Perhaps. It comes to much the same thing in the end, though, if you work it out to its logical conclusion. When you lose that person . . . who's so important to you . . . you're *finished*. You yourself, having been submerged, aren't important enough."

Her eyes held dissent. "Again I think there's something else. There are always your own feet for you to stand on. Don't ever allow yourself to forget that. That's one of the things that you should have learned from your love. Courage and sanity and . . . you know . . . cleanness."

She looked ahead of her, almost unseeing. "I think life's meant to be like that," she proceeded. "We meet and love . . . we give to others . . . they give to us . . . and perhaps—who knows—we are destined to pass on . . . having benefited by what we have given to others . . . and by what we have taken from them. We mustn't lose heart," she concluded passionately, "when our loved one leaves us and we are left to carry on alone. If we haven't learnt to stand on our own feet we haven't learnt anything. We mustn't do dreadful things . . . I've come to see and understand that . . . it's just like a child who kicks the stumps down when he's been bowled out."

But her words had brought Dorothy back to me and Paton . . . and all the burning torture that I had suffered . . . and I was moodily dissentient. "What is there else to do," I cried . . . "When your loss is joined by a bitter sense of unfaithfulness and disloyalty? There's love *and* love. Some people—so-called lovers I mean—are passively content to be *satisfied* with another. I can't put it higher than that—I wish I could. They *accept* each other—complacently—like one lives in a house or wears one's clothes. But for others—why, it's tremendous! The biggest— the *only* thing in life."

"I used to believe that the sun rose and set for—for somebody. That dawn brought her to me and that sunset took her away—until the next morning, I think that I interpreted everything through her and even perhaps because of her. Certainly all beautiful things! My mind and thoughts were saturated with her. I would have gone through hell for her . . . and I thought that she would have done the same for me.

"I think that to champion her . . . I would have contradicted God. When I knew that I had lost her, I felt like a tree stripped of its foliage . . . gaunt, scarred, and deserted . . . like a shuttered house of a vanished happiness . . . and then, slowly and gradually, all my feelings turned to dreadful bitterness . . . bitterness which I carry about with me every day . . . and from which, I sometimes have thought, there will never be any escape."

She nodded.

"That hurts, my friend, I know. Hurts dreadfully. Stifles all one's life and stings till one could scream. But that is the time when one has to fight so hard to keep brave and clean and sane. But even then—allowing for all that—there is something else."

"What?" I demanded. "I confess I'd like to know."

She smiled at me bravely through tear-fringed lashes. "Blessed memory. That exquisite sense of what has been. The good times that the two of you have had together. That nobody can ever take away from either of you. The perfect understanding and brave comradeship that, at least, *have* been yours for a time. The unselfishness of your love. The better parts of it. The parts of it that will last for ever. The little helps that you have been to, and brought to, each other. All the blessed intimacies and sweet secrecies that come from love such as we have been trying to talk about.

"After all, you can't give anybody anything *equal* to love. Simply because there isn't anything! Sometimes people snatch at other things and try to substitute them for love. Fame, power, or even simple things—such as home, comfort, pleasure. It's wrong of them and I think they always 'live to be sorry' for it. Do you remember your Swinburne? I've just loved this ever since I can remember. Listen." She looked up at me as she recited:

> "Ask nothing more of me, sweet;
> All I *can* give you, I give.
> Heart of my heart, were it more;
> More would be laid at your feet:
> Love that should help you to live,
> Song that should spur you to soar.
>
> "All things were nothing to give
> Once to have sense of you more,
> Touch you and taste of you, sweet,
> Think you, and breathe you and live,
> Swept of your wings as they soar
> Trodden by chance of your feet.

"I that have love and no more
Give you but love of you, sweet:
He that hath more, let him give;
He that hath wings let him soar;
Mine is the heart at your feet
Here, that must love you to live."

She repeated the last two lines ever so softly, and I loved the personal pronouns as I heard them.

"Philippa, my—"

She caught at my hand and pressed it. "My friend . . . can't you see and understand this . . . things of the spirit are imperishable . . . they can never die . . . and underneath, too, all the time, remember . . . are the everlasting arms."

The last words were almost whispered to me, and there was a little catch in her throat. She rose from the floor where she had been sitting. "Will you please put out the gas?" she said quietly. "We mustn't delay any longer. I'm going to undress and get into bed."

As she turned away from me and moved towards the dressing-table, I saw her face redden again in the realisation of her embarrassment. Deep in wonderment, I turned out the flicker of gaslight that had lighted the room and walked away from her—to stand by the door.

"You haven't told me much about yourself," I flung to her over my shoulder. As I half-turned I could just see the curve of her uplifted arms and the bunch of dark hair that crowned her head. I could see, too, the glorious set of her head upon her lovely neck . . . it had been the work of a supreme artist—that fashioning . . . some women have given me the impression that their heads have been pushed on to their shoulders by blind men working with the shapeless mechanism of mutilated hands. Her reply to my last statement came quietly across the room to me.

"When there is time, my friend, I will tell you all my story. All, that is, that I can tell you, without betraying confidences or hurting others. But I wonder—" She stopped suddenly.

"What?" I asked—almost desperately.

"If there ever *will* be time," she answered sadly. There was no answering this. Truth to tell, I felt very much as she did. I stood at the door, therefore, and waited. The interval was short. I heard the soft lapping of the water of her washing and then her voice came to me again, and the words she used were flat and dull.

"Will you please undress now and come to bed? I wouldn't ask you to do these things . . . but I know how cruel and suspicious he is . . . and it is so difficult to deceive him. The least little thing missing from a picture—the tiniest detail—and he is all suspicion . . . he becomes like St. Thomas himself . . . that saint of the shortest day . . . he will not believe."

Chapter IV
A NEW USE FOR BEDCLOTHES
(Lance Maturin's story continued)

THE knowledge that she was in deadly earnest both startled and shocked me. Those of my readers who find that statement difficult of belief should try—in my vindication—to visualise the swift subtleties of the situation. But I had promised to see her through to the limit of my power, and see her through, I would. I slipped off my coat and waistcoat, therefore, removed my tie, and took off my collar. Then I pulled off a shoe. I was just on the point of kicking off the second shoe, when the remembrance came to me that I had no sleeping-suit. I think that the first awakening of this thought pleased me rather than otherwise.

The room was dark, it is true, but I hated this comedy business while tragedy, very possibly, stalked outside the door. My relative pleasure, however, was short-lived. Philippa's voice, coming from near the pillow farthest away from me, butchered it ruthlessly and I was left to survey the bleeding pieces.

"If you want pyjamas," she said, "you will find a pair on a shelf in that little cupboard over there. I think that they will fit you reasonably well. Leave the door open . . . don't lock it, I mean. It will mean less noise when the time comes."

And, marvel of marvels, I raged at her opening words. To whom did these clothes belong? If there were a man who lived here with her . . . or visited her at times . . . why the hell couldn't he face her trouble instead of me facing it? If he had known the wonder of her surrender why the devil couldn't he spend himself too in the scrum? For moments, I was silent and sullen. Then a thought came to me. He might be dead or ill . . . unable to exert himself on her behalf. Instead of chafing childishly, I should be grateful for the privilege . . . for the honour of her selection . . . for the tang of the adventure. Ridiculous and conceited ass that I was—harbouring jealousy of a woman who was absolutely nothing to me and whom I had known for only two hours.

I found the pyjama-suit and shut the cupboard door. Then I fumbled with my other clothes, knelt on the floor of the bedroom rather shamefacedly and, in some clumsy way that I am unable to describe now, clad myself in the borrowed plumes that were neither "tasselled silk nor epaulette." Philippa had been right in her assumption. They fitted me splendidly, and the man to whom they belonged must have been about my own size. My own discarded clothes I folded neatly into a heap and laid them on the low chair upon which I had sat when Philippa had nestled at my knees. Then I remembered the revolver which she had handed to me some time previously. I considered that the best place for this would be under my pillow where it would be ready to hand. So I put it there, turned the coverlet down just a little and got into bed.

My companion propped herself on to an elbow and whispered to me. Her face, beautifully distinguished in the comparative darkness, was close to mine . . . her lips at that moment were in exquisite peril. The scent of her was clean and sweet and fresh . . . so daintily fragrant and delicately delicious that I murmured something to her of the truth of it. The green eyes flickered with gratification . . . I could see that plainly in the semi-darkness, but she shook her head again and put a hand lightly upon my cheek. The clean, clear coolness of it seemed to me almost miraculous. She whispered more.

"Don't tell me that . . . I fear that others may not think as you do. I should be disturbed if I thought that there might—"

She stopped suddenly and I sensed immediately from the manner in which she glanced round that every nerve of her was taut and tightened . . . she listened. I could hear the seconds of my wrist-watch ticking on . . . many of them, so it seemed . . . before she spoke to me again. And again in that low rich whisper to which my eager ear was already becoming so attuned.

"We are only just in time, my friend. I don't think he's used a key. He is below. Mother Rasmussen has let him in. He has a secret way of knocking . . . so that she always knows who it is. For money she would sacrifice her own flesh and blood."

She listened again. "He is coming up. You will protect me, won't you?" Her fingers caught in mine convulsively, but I disengaged them and felt for the revolver that lay beneath my pillow. Then I turned over, away from her, propped myself on my left elbow, revolver in other hand, and faced the door . . . and him who would come through it.

I waited some time . . . there were those dreadful staircases to be climbed . . . I had almost forgotten them, in my eagerness and anxiety. Then I saw the door of our room slowly opened as though the agent of the opening were being excessively careful, and a slight panther-like figure slink across the threshold and edge towards the bed. I pushed Philippa down a little with my shoulder, shivered at the sense of her lithe warm body and supple softness, and waited . . . God knows what for . . . I can't possibly tell you what it was that I was expecting to happen. The slinking figure came towards the bed—step by step.

"Philippa," I heard the man whisper . . . and there was a silky, seductive note in his voice that made me loathe him intensely. Still I waited. He spoke again in English.

"Philippa I am here. As I promised you. As I warned you." There was no movement from the girl beside me. This gave me the cue that I had awaited.

"So am I," I said, "and I don't know that I promised you anything. Of course—if you stay long enough—I may be able to remedy the omission."

I have never seen the face of man or woman change so suddenly. The concupiscence in it changed to black anger. "Who are you?" he cried malevolently, backing a couple of paces away from where I lay. I swung myself very neatly to the edge of the bed with my feet on the floor.

"Your question answers itself, Monsieur de Verviac," I replied to him; "if you will but consider the position in which you find me, it must be obvious to you that this lady is my wife. Any other contingency would be unthinkable." I fingered the pearl-butted revolver menacingly. "Also, Monsieur de Verviac," I continued, as bold as brass now action had come to me, "I find you most appallingly *de trop*. Get out, you scum."

If nothing else had given me courage, the look of frozen fear on the face of Philippa would have done so. De Verviac's face twisted into a greater hatred . . . parented by thwarted rage and mortification. The words he muttered were inaudible to me . . . they failed to reach me from the distance that he was away. From the facial expression that accompanied them, I judged this fact to be a matter for self-congratulation. I waved my weapon aggressively and he commenced to back towards the door. Even then, he nearly cheated me. For no sooner had he reached the door than he whipped his hand to his pocket and before I could realise what he was about to do, had fired twice in rapid succession at the bed.

I heard the first of the bullets whistle past my head and then the crack of splintered glass almost immediately behind me. I felt the second give me a red-hot stab in the region of the shoulder. Then I fired deliberately and viciously. Candidly, I shot to kill! Too late, I was afraid. For de Verviac turned like lightning and ran from the room. We heard his flying feet on the staircase. Philippa gave a sob of relief and I turned to her a little vainglorious and triumphant, I fear, that the encounter had ended as it had. "Now, perhaps, he will believe what I told him," she half whispered.

Before I could reply to her, however, a most surprising thing happened: I heard a challenging voice from behind. A voice which seemed to call out something peremptory—dictatorial. It was a voice, too, which I was unable to place. For it sounded like the voice of authority. Obviously, it didn't belong to either of the ancient crones whom we had encountered on our way up. The voice, about which I wondered, stopped suddenly . . . then there was a shot . . . another shot . . . followed by a dreadful scream and the slamming of the front door . . . after that, silence! A silence that was almost oppressive.

"What was that?" cried Philippa, clutching my arm. "I am afraid, my friend. Oh—look. Your arm! You are hurt! You are bleeding. It's your shoulder, I think."

I glanced down at my sleeve and saw, from the red stain that was gradually tinging it, that my wound was more serious than I had at first anticipated. But I shook my head, making light of the injury, and went to the door. Somewhat to my surprise, there was a glimmer of light burning somewhere below. I walked to the edge of the banisters that ran round the landing and looked over. What I saw there gave me a start. Stretched across the bottom stair of the lowest flight was a dead man.

I was absolutely certain he was dead, notwithstanding the height from which I looked down at him. He was huddled and helpless . . . arms flung open in that pitiable and yet simple way that the dead affect. I had seen men and women before like it and felt sure of the truth immediately my eyes rested on him. Also, he was a complete stranger to me. It was a man whom I had never seen before.

And, as I watched, something happened! The taller of the two crones came from somewhere and looked at the body on the stairs. Tried to pull it into a sitting posture. There was something excessively strange about her that I couldn't understand . . . couldn't mentally describe. I saw her shake her head, as though in doubt about something, and then suddenly look up to where I was leaning over the banisters. An inherited instinct urged me to withdraw my head and dodge back . . . if I hadn't, it is probable that this history would never have been written.

For a couple of minutes, I suppose, I stood there and did a job of hard thinking. Then I went straight back to Philippa. It seemed to me that there was only one course open to us. She was sitting up in bed, her hands clasped together, her fingers lacing and interlacing in nervous apprehension.

"Tell me," she said anxiously, "what is it? Whatever has happened? What did those shots mean?"

I replied with as much calmness as I could muster. "There is a dead man on the stairs. One of those wretched old women has just found him."

"De Verviac?" she inquired breathlessly—hand to cheek.

I shook my head. "No. No such luck as that. His kind live long—to annoy us. No—it's somebody else. A stranger to me. You may know him—I don't." I went on almost at once. Before she could answer—certainly. "Alas, Philippa, I don't like the look of things. In fact, the situation seems to me to be full of distinctly unpleasant possibilities. Probabilities, rather. For you and me, that is."

She seemed uncertain as to my meaning. "I'm sorry. I don't think I quite understand. Why?"

I pointed to the wound in my shoulder. I held up the revolver. "If that ancient crone down there—Mother Rasmussen—has taken it into her venerable and ugly head to send for the police, I shall probably spend the night . . . or rather the morning . . . in a nice comfortable cell—securely housed and with a charge of murder hanging over my head. Candidly, Philippa, as I look at things, I'm in a hole. The truth would hardly be believed if it were told to anybody. And, my dear, last, but by no means least . . . I have you to think of."

She shook her head. "You are too generous to me, my friend. You are heaping coals of fire on my head. For it is my fault that you are here. You are in this trouble because you were ready to come to my help. What are we going to do?"

The words had hardly left her lips when I heard the first sounds of official commotion below. There floated up to me the sounds of many voices. The identical sounds for which I had been waiting. I resolved upon immediate action.

"Philippa," I said to the light figure in the bed, "help *me* now. Otherwise it will be too late. Lock, that door, and stick a chair under the handle. Wedge it. You know how I mean, don't you?"

She slid out of bed instantly, to obey me. I walked to the window with its hole that de Verviac's bullet had made, and looked out across to that wall that I had seen before. A thought had come to me. The night now was pitch dark, and, as far as I could see from where I stood, there wasn't a soul this side of the shuttered house. At that moment a plan was borne in my brain. Its difficulty of achievement lay in the matter of time. How much of this valuable commodity had I at my disposal? I was pretty certain that the hag who had seen the man's body on the staircase had also seen my head craned over the banisters, and would put the police on my track as soon as ever she could get her obscene say in and make them understand. Therefore, it behoved me to fill the unforgiving minute and get busy as soon as possible. For I had determined to get away from this house of death and horror by means of that wall—the dark blurred shape of which, I could see six feet below the window of Philippa's bedroom.

I pushed the window open quietly and cautiously. The shutters folded back against the wall of the house itself. Then I remembered that I was in my pyjamas—or rather in the pyjamas of a friend of Philippa's. As I have said, it was still dark. "Stay where you are, Philippa," I called to her.' I slipped off the suit, crossed to the low chair where they were and threw my own clothes on me—stuffing tie and collar into my pocket in my haste.

"What are you going to do?" asked my companion as she watched my preparations.

"I'm going from here," I said, "by the window. On to that wall out there." I lit the gas . . . to a faint flicker.

"Then I am coming too," she said simply. "I can dress in three minutes. Don't you think that I can't. You learn to dress quickly when you are on the stage and can't afford a dresser." She gave me a wry little smile.

I made no reply. For one thing, my shoulder was hurting me like the very dickens—there was blood almost everywhere now—and, for another, I was busy with the sheets that had covered Philippa's bed. There was more noise from below, and, although the fear was father, probably, to the thought, I fancied I could hear footsteps on the stairs already.

"It's not going to be too easy," I muttered, "but I'm absolutely determined not to be taken like a rat in a trap. De Verviac alone would swear my life away. But I'm afraid you can't come with me, Philippa, much as I should like you to. It's impossible."

"I am coming, my friend. There is no doubt of it. I cannot stay here. I will not stay here. Don't worry. I am nearly dressed, as it is."

I looked at her curiously . . . at her deft fingers at work on clothing herself . . . and she crimsoned again under my gaze. Becoming practical once more, I accepted her view of the situation and pushed the heavy brass bed close to the window. I know that I must have worked with amazing speed.

"When you are ready, my dear," I said to her quite calmly, "come and help me."

Within the space of a few seconds, she was at my side. We took more of those sheets from the bed, ripped them into shreds, knotted the ends of them together, tied one end of our manufactured rope to a leg of the heavy bedstead and flung the other end out into the space that separated shuttered house and ancient wall. As I did so, I heard footsteps immediately outside the door and an attempt made to force the handle. Then the footsteps retreated. I wasted no time in argument.

"You are going first, Philippa," I said decisively. "Take hold of the stronger part as firmly as you can, lower yourself, kick hard and swing out. Have you the nerve?"

She made me no answer but her eyes shone with determination. I helped her on to the bed and pulled the rope up again. She stood on the window ledge and I put the rope of sheets into her hands.

"Don't be afraid," I said to her. "I've made it strong and sound. It will hold me. You need not fear, therefore. Let yourself go and hang on. When you feel it quite taut, kick firmly at the side of the house with your legs and start yourself swinging. If you get across, let go, and then the other end of the rope can come back to me."

She nodded and swung out into the black abyss. Once, twice, thrice, four times, I saw her kick herself into an impetus. Then I saw, too, how I could help her. When she was swinging just a little more freely, I took the part of the rope near the leg of the bedstead and used my own strength that it might swing with still more freedom. At last, with a mighty heave that almost tore my wounded shoulder in two, I swung her dangling body on to the top of that blessed wall below me. Without my help she would never have accomplished the task. I had made the rope of sufficient length to slacken as she stood there, and there was little chance of her being pulled away again. She released her hold, threw the rope off, and it fell back towards me, dangling in the depths. As it came, my eyes went to, the discarded suit of pyjamas that I had tossed on to the bed. Perhaps it would be better, I argued to myself, if I took the two pieces with me. To leave them behind would do no good to Philippa's reputation, and I could easily dispose of them somewhere, if we were fortunate and managed to get away.

I tossed the revolver on to the bed, tied the trousers round my neck and took the jacket between my teeth. As I did so, I could hear the noise from below getting nearer and clearer. The police and their assistants were returning to the attack. So I took the sheet-rope in my hands, lowered myself and kicked out as I had told Philippa to do. Without assistance, it was a herculean task, and, had the wall been a foot farther away, impossible of achievement. My weight anchored me so to the side of the shuttered house.

"Help me," I cried like a fool, as I swung towards her. "Pull me on to the wall." The pyjama-jacket with its bloodstained sleeve dropped from between my teeth into the opaque darkness of the street below. With all my strength I literally flung myself at the wall on which she stood. Philippa thrust out her two hands towards me and, stumblingly, I fell on to the top of the wall of salvation, where she grasped me and held me until I could stand with strength upon my own feet. The rope, freed from my grasp, fell back to the window.

"The pyjamas," I gasped. "'I dropped the jacket. But it doesn't matter much. They can't identify me from that."

She looked startled at my news, but shook her head and gazed across the intervening space at the room from which we had just escaped.

"I don't believe that they have got in yet," she said; "Perhaps our chair is doing its duty."

I took her by the arm. "Philippa," I said, "much as I should like to think otherwise, this is no time for lingering. The primrose path of dalliance is not for yours truly at the moment. In a quarter of an hour, at the most, the hunt will be up and we shall be . . ."

"We shall be what?" she demanded breathlessly.

"The hunted," I answered dryly. "Come on. Can you run?"

Chapter V
A MAN RUNS FOR A TRAIN
(Lance Maturin's story continued)

I stuffed the pyjama-trousers under my coat and we ran along the top of the wall. Luckily for us both, Philippa seemed to have a good idea of where we were.

"We're at the back of the Rue du Sacré Coeur. There should be a flight of steps not far from here," she gasped between breaths.

"Leading where?" I asked curtly.

"To one of the large archways that will take us into the town."

"Good," I grunted—"it might be worse, I suppose. I fancy I've heard the expression—'underneath the arches'—but I shall be glad when we come to them. Good job it's so dark. From one point of view, that is. For it cuts both ways."

"How do you mean?"

"We shan't attract so much attention. Running, I mean. It's rather too late for legitimate exercise, and the Olympic games are over."

"There they are," cried Philippa—"the steps, I mean. We shall be in the street in two minutes. Where then? Your hotel?"

I came to a quick decision. "No," I returned emphatically. "There is just a risk in that, I think. Who knows that I may not have been traced to your lodgings? De Verviac followed us there, remember, and he might be able to describe me. If that's so, the first place they will go to will be the Hôtel de Lutèce. As it is, two friends of mine are there, and they may tell them more than I should like. They were with me at the 'Red Flare,' remember. No. It will have to be somewhere else."

We reached the flight of steps that she had indicated and ran down them hand in hand. Philippa was brave and attempted to brighten the situation.

"On the other hand, they may not be able to connect you with the affair at all. Considering everything, that seems to me to be far more likely."

I nodded. "Yes, I know. That's what I'm really banking on, too."

We were now in a street. "Which way do we go now," I asked her, "to come to the main part of the town?"

She pointed to the left. "This way. But where shall we make for?"

I looked round. In every direction the place was still and deserted. The early hours of the morning found nobody about.

"Let us run again," I said to her, "for as long as we can keep it up. The farther we get away from them, the better. To one of the railway stations. We'll get away from the place, and then, even if there's a hue and cry for us, we'll double back on our tracks."

"Where will you go?" she queried breathlessly.

"Brussels," I said, on the spin of the moment, "and then double back again for the evening's boat from the quay. They'll never dream that we'd do anything like that. And you're coming with me."

She made no answer to this for some time, but continued to run on, in sharp little bursts of speed. "Then let me tell you something," she jerked out at length. "If that's your settled plan, don't make for the Gare Centrale. Or for the South Quay station, either. Take my advice and go to the Gare du Sud. I think it will be a lot better."

"Why?" I returned. "What's your idea?"

"I've two reasons for saying what I did. Firstly, the tram for the Harwich boat starts right outside the Gare du Sud; secondly, the earliest morning train for Brussels goes from there. In case you have to remember it, the train for the boat is number thirteen."

"It would be," I returned satirically. "I think I should have guessed that had I been asked."

She stopped in her running and laid a hand on my arm. Her face was proud and a little disdainful.

"Does monsieur feel, then, that he has been so unlucky? Has he had no compensations?"

"Such as?" I queried.

"To have rendered me a service? To have saved my life? Perhaps to have saved my honour?"

Her grand simplicity stung me into apology. "I'm sorry," I said. "Come. We mustn't waste time. Where are we now?"

"In the Rue van Geert," she answered. "Soon we can strike through to the long avenue that will lead us almost straight to the Gare du Sud."

We were now beginning to meet people. Not many, it is true. Just a few, here and there, but sufficient of them to cause me to change my tactics and to alter the manner of our progression. I told my companion what I thought of things. As a result, we gradually slackened our run to a walk. In a way, I was by no means sorry for this, for the wound in my shoulder was giving me a considerable amount of pain. Every now and then I threw a quick glance over my shoulder to see if there were any signs of pursuit. But, as far as I could tell, all was quiet behind us.

Suddenly I was almost startled out of my wits. A roar sounded in my ears that suggested to me, keyed up as I was by the events of the night and morning, all the evil and cruelty held by hell. Candidly, I was almost frozen stiff with horror and stopped still in my tracks. Philippa saw my distress, laughed softly and pulled me along again.

"You silly. It is all right," she said. "Although I can very well understand how you feel. I have been frightened, in the past, when I have heard them. Don't you know where we are? We're close to the Zoological Gardens. You could hear the lions. They've been uneasy for the last two or three nights. It's like that sometimes. People say the weather disturbs them."

I grinned feebly at Philippa's explanation and understood immediately. It was the Jardin Zoölogique, of course. I had seen the public announcements of it placarded in many places of the city. The wound in my shoulder was growing more painful and discharging more blood at almost every stride, but I plugged along determinedly, and eventually Philippa and I came to the Gare du Sud. Much to my relief, we passed into the station without comment or challenge from anybody. I will admit that I was as nervous as a kitten. I gave Philippa the money for the tickets, thinking that it would be better for us if she purchased them. There was the wound in my shoulder to be considered.

The Brussels train, I discovered, didn't leave for another three-quarters of an hour, but the train was already at the platform, by a stroke of luck, and we were allowed to take our seats soon after Philippa had purchased the tickets. We found an empty compartment—in the rear of the train—I shrank from walking the length of the platform—and immediately we got inside, Philippa turned to me anxiously.

"Your shoulder, my friend. It must be seen to at once. Let me attend to it for you."

I shook my head. "Not now, Philippa. To do so here would be too dangerous. We must wait until the train has left the station. Then you can fix me up before I put on my collar and tie. Use my handkerchief for a bandage. That's the best I can do for you."

This time she shook her head. "No . . . I have come prepared. I did not forget. See—I tore a piece from one of the bed sheets and brought it with me. Here it is."

She pushed her fingers down the front of her dress somewhere and, as she did so, blushed deliciously.

"Thank you, Philippa," I returned. "That was very sweet of you. When the coast is reasonably clear you shall see to my arm."

She looked at me—examiningly and critically. "Tell me," she said very deliberately—"and the truth, please. Do not deceive me.

Wouldn't it be better if we separated? If they search for me, they will search for a man and a girl travelling together. Is it not so?"

"I've thought of that," I said, and—God forgive me—I lied. "But I'm not sure that you're right—you know. They may not find out my identity—I don't see how they can, really. They will probably think that I was—er . . . a chance acquaintance of yours . . . and that we shall almost certainly have separated directly we got away from the house. Anyhow, it's too late now to alter our plans. We'll stick together and hope for the best."

I put as much resolution and finality into my voice as I was able to summon. Philippa's colour was now flaming scarlet, and I realised the *faux pas* that I had made in the description that I had given to myself . . . what damned silly things one can and does say without thinking. I don't know whether she was convinced by anything that I had said, but, to ease the situation somewhat, I executed some mental gymnastics and proceeded to other matters.

"On the way to Brussels, Philippa," I said, "you must tell me all about yourself. The plans I make for you, and what we are going to do with ourselves, depend on so many things. You understand what I mean, don't you?"

She nodded her acquiescence, and many minutes went by as we sat there in silence. Knots of people were now hurrying down the platform. There were men and women, young and old . . . some children . . . but none came to the door of our compartment.

I was just beginning to congratulate myself that in a minute or so we should be away and in comparative safety for the time being, when a man came running down the platform. For one wild, swift moment I thought that he was hunter and I his quarry. I panicked and shrank back, therefore, from the window of the compartment in case he should turn, see me, and recognise me. But I was wrong in my idea. He ran for the normal reason that he might catch the train, in a compartment of which Philippa and I sat.

To my chagrin and annoyance, he stopped when he came abreast of us, seized the handle of our door and swung himself into the compartment just as the train started to move. Then

I received one of the greatest shocks of my life. To my utter consternation, I saw that it was none other than Alec Paton . . . husband of Dorothy Paton . . . a man who knew me almost as well as he knew his own kith and kin. I made a frantic sign to Philippa that she might understand that an unexpected development had occurred . . . pulled my hat down right over my face . . . slumped into the corner, half-closed my eyes and pretended to be asleep.

Paton passed between us without giving either of us a glance, and took his seat in the farthest corner. Our luck had held so far! What we had to do was plainly indicated. Philippa and I must change compartments at the first stop . . . that would be Malines in all probability . . . but in the meantime another problem had presented itself. What the blazes was Paton—of all people—doing in Antwerp, and why had he been in such a devil of a hurry to catch this train?

CHAPTER VI
PHILIPPA'S DISTRESS
(Lance Maturin's story continued)

I HUDDLED myself into a shapeless heap in my corner seat . . . praying fervently that Paton wouldn't see the bloodstain on my shoulder. It seemed to me, as I crouched there, that my wound was fated *not* to be bandaged. With my face almost completely covered, I feigned sleep as hard as I could, but every now and then I took a furtive peep at Paton in his corner, through half-opened eyelids. To my relief, he hardly even so much as glanced in my direction; so I took the opportunity, when it came, to signal to Philippa that things were a bit better and there was nothing to worry about desperately for the time being.

My third glance at Paton convinced me that he was distinctly uneasy—if not downright agitated. He was a big, beefy fellow, dark and, in his way, handsome. He had broad shoulders and a powerful frame. I had never been particularly friendly with him, even before the affair with Dorothy was on the way, but he had for years been terrifically chummy with my cousin, who lived only a few miles from my father's place in Essex. Paton and my cousin had been thick at school, and the intimacy had continued ever since. As my cousin had said to me, at the time when I was so badly hipped, with all the cynicism of which he was so thoroughly capable he could hardly be expected to drop Alec Paton, whom he had known for so long, because Paton and I worshipped at the same shrine. When I pointed out that this description scarcely fitted the case . . . that Dorothy had been mine and mine absolutely before Paton infatuated her . . . the reply had been the time-honoured one concerning the conditions that appertain to love and war. God . . . that some people should ever have the word "love" upon their lips!

All the panorama of the past flashed through my mind as I took my fugitive glances at Paton from my seat in the corner of the compartment. As I wrote previously, he scarcely favoured me with a glance. Alternately he looked at his watch and out of the window at the countryside as it rolled past. Even so, I decided to adhere to my original decision . . . to change our compartments as soon as the train arrived at Malines. It was a fairly fast train, and I calculated that with ordinary luck we should reach Malines in about forty minutes. I waited until we crossed the valley of the Nethe before I made a move of any kind.

Philippa had played up to the situation splendidly, sitting absolutely silent all the time, but watchful and alert, in case an emergency should arise that demanded quick thinking and equally rapid action.

We had flashed through Contich, the junction for Lierre, and Duffel, and when we came to Wavre-Ste-Catherine, I made a quick sign to my companion which she interpreted aright. Gradually the train slackened speed, and we had no sooner drawn into the station at Malines and stopped than I was out of the compartment, Philippa on my heels, and into another empty compartment which we were lucky enough to find but a short distance along the train.

Out of Malines, Philippa became practical and I explanatory.

She bandaged my shoulder as best as she could with the strip of linen that she had brought with her from that sinister house which we had left with such scant ceremony. She made the neatest of jobs of it. Nothing untoward showed externally.

"Who was it?" she asked me fearfully, as I took out my collar and tie. I told her. His name . . . where he lived and all that I thought was good for her to hear of him.

"But why is he here? What is he doing on this train at so early an hour?"

I shook my head hopelessly. "I have asked myself the same question, Philippa, at least a dozen times since he turned up on the platform at Antwerp—and I can find no satisfactory answer."

"He was not seeking you?"

"Hardly. Otherwise. . ." I paused, and she was quick to take advantage of my hesitation.

"Otherwise . . . what?"

"Well—if he were—he didn't look very far—did he? He scarcely looked at me the whole time he was in there with us."

Philippa produced a safety-pin from an apparent nowhere and nodded primly as she adjusted my bandage. "Yes, I know. But that doesn't mean a lot, if you come to look at it carefully. He had no idea that it was you in the train and therefore didn't think of looking at you. Do you see what I mean? Had he known or even thought that such a thing was a possibility—things might have been different. At least, that's how it appears to me. Perhaps I'm not so easily satisfied as you are."

It was an idea, certainly, and after she had helped me with my collar and tie I was still thinking it over when we ran into the Gare du Nord, Brussels. Everything there went off smoothly for us, and I was just in time to see Alec Paton hail one of the taximeter horse-cabs that abound there and drive off.

"What about breakfast?" asked Philippa.

"Don't forget," I said, "that we are going to double back in our tracks. They'll never suspect us of intending to do that. All the same, we are not going to make ourselves unduly conspicuous in this city of Brussels. I'll buy some rolls at one of the smaller *pâtisserie* shops and we'll eat them in the Parc. The one in the upper town, I mean. I think that we shall do well to give a wide berth to café and tavern. It's not too bad in the Parc, either. It opens early and a band plays in there. For one thing, I want to talk to you very seriously, Philippa."

She nodded. "I know. It is only fair to you that you should know things. My whole life seems to have changed since last night. It is almost as though I had become a different person. As though, by some wonderful and secret process, I had become somebody else."

I found a little *pâtisserie* shop in the Rue de la Montagne, made appropriate purchases therein, re-joined Philippa, found the junction of the Rue de March-aux-Herbes and the Rue de la Montagne, and ascended by a very modern street to the Parc. This large formal garden lies between the Royal Palace and the Palais de la Nation. There on a seat by the round pond, and close to Grupellos' "Diana," I gave Philippa her breakfast and asked, at the same time, my first question.

"Who are you? Please tell me the truth."

Her answer took my breath away. "I am Philippa Castleton," she replied unaffectedly.

"What?" I queried in amazement. This was a facer and no mistake. "Not *the* Philippa Castleton, surely?"

She nodded. "Yes. None other. *The* Philippa Castleton. I'm famous—or should it be infamous? Daughter—only daughter— of the Right Reverend Harvey Eastwood Furneaux Castleton, Lord Bishop of Longbarrow. I can see that you remember the excitement caused by my disappearance three months ago."

I was still staring at her. "I should think I do. Who wouldn't? The papers didn't give you much respite those days. You got more headlines than de Valera, Bradman, Amy Johnson, and D.R. Jardine put together. Only Herbert Chapman held his own with you. Your father's position, I suppose, made things worse than they otherwise might have been. He'd always been pretty much in the public eye, you see, and when the yellow press got a chance to snap at his heels they took it with a vengeance."

She nodded again. "That's only too true. Do you remember what the papers said about me?"

I gave her more food, which she accepted eagerly. "Many things. Most things. Almost everything. I don't think that I can recall anything that they didn't say. Disreputable—that is."

"I know. Let me see if I can remember the various escapades that were attributed to me. I had run away with one of the curates. I had become a drug-fiend. I had been film-struck and fled to Hollywood. I had taken the veil. Been stricken with leprosy and been hidden in a special private hospital. Stolen bazaar funds. I had done everything . . . everything that I hadn't done. Do you remember the ultimate conclusion to which they came?"

I tried to remember. "No," I answered at length. "I don't think I do. What was it?"

She shrugged her shoulders and laughed in spite of herself. "That I had committed suicide. To hide my shame. 'I was only a bishop's daughter and my baby's clothes were in pawn.' Well— they were wrong. I ran away to get married. I was to meet the man I loved in Antwerp. I was under age at the time, and my father simply wouldn't hear of the idea of my marriage when I put it to him. He wouldn't even listen to hear the man's name; and he doesn't know it to this day. I came to Antwerp . . . met the man I was to marry . . . he was all ready and arrangements were complete. He left some of his things with me, in fact . . . to meet me on the following morning . . . when we were to have been married."

She stopped and I saw tears come into her eyes.

"Well," I said a little roughly and impatiently, "what happened?"

"He never came. I have never seen him again. Sometimes, I think that I never shall see him again. That he is dead."

The words that she had used to me burnt into my brain. "The man I loved." Not "the man I love." The past tense spelt Paradise to me. Good God—why did I worry over such things?

"You have no word from him?"

"Not a line."

"He's deserted you. Probably not the first girl he's served in the same way."

She shook her head. "I don't think so. I know him better than you do."

"That's obvious—since I don't know him at all. What did you do?"

"I stayed in Antwerp. For one thing, I felt that I couldn't possibly go back to Longbarrow . . . to my father . . . I would die first. For another, I hoped against hope that my lover . . . that he would come back for me. He had made me promise that I would never betray his identity to a soul until after our marriage. That promise I have faithfully kept and will keep if I can, for ever. I had a little money with me and I was able to stay on at my hotel while it lasted out. When I was spent out I found work. At the place where you saw me last night. I had always been a fairly good dancer, and I was fortunate enough to be able to turn this little gift to financial account. If I hadn't had that chance, God knows what would have become of me. I have managed to keep my job . . . the money I earn from it is enough for me to keep body and soul together and to retain my self-respect. With regard to that . . . in a place like where you met me . . . I have been ever so lucky."

She shivered and I saw the look of fear come into her eyes again. "You understand me, don't you?"

I nodded. The pathos of her face enhanced her beauty. "Tell me this man's name," I demanded.

"Don't ask me that, please. For I cannot tell you."

"You can tell me. It's ridiculous of you to talk like that. What earthly reason is there why you should—"

"Very well, then. I will amend what I said. I *will* not tell you."

She laid her hand on my arm. "Forgive me. You must. I may seem ungrateful . . . believe me, I am far from being that. But please don't ask me this man's name."

"Very well," I answered churlishly, "if you want to shield him, no doubt you will. I suppose the worse he treats you the more affection you'll give him. That's the world as it seems to me. Most girls have little to return for loyalty, and faithfulness counts for next to nothing. It's your business though, of course. Your past belongs to you and I have neither part in it nor claim on it. Therefore I will not presume to interfere. Let me point this out, however. Besides your past, there is the present to consider and also the future. What do you intend to do?"

She shook her head helplessly and tears possessed her again. "Oh—I don't know. I don't think I've had time to think yet. It's all been like a horrible dream."

"One thing stands out, though, from everything else," I declared with deliberate emphasis.

"What is that?"

"You can't go back there."

"Where? To Antwerp?"

"Not exactly to Antwerp. I meant to that house that we left last night . . . this morning rather . . . and also you can't go back to that place of the scarlet flare . . . to that charming friend of yours—de Verviac. If you have doubts—ask yourself. How can you?"

"I know that you are right. But what can I do?"

"You are coming home with me," I asserted, with fine courage and finer optimism. "If it can be managed. If we are lucky enough to get through this present trouble. Which won't be, I assure you, for want of trying on my part."

"You are angry with me . . . you who have been my friend and so good to me. I think, too, that I know why you are angry."

She looked me right into the eyes and once again tears were the tenants of hers. She was about to speak again when a newsboy, crying the morning papers, came along a path and passed close to us. The name "Anvers" on his news-bill caught my eyes. His news sheet, if I translate its contents into English, held a mine of interest for us both.

MIDNIGHT MURDER IN ANTWERP LODGING-HOUSE

FAMOUS ENGLISH DETECTIVE SHOT DEAD IN PASSAGE

MURDERER ESCAPES

I bit my lip but otherwise, I hope and think, betrayed no sign of personal disturbance, for the boy's eyes were on me.

The news-vendor averted his glance and passed on . . . he scarcely heeded us again . . . we might not have been there. He had no doubt seen many of our like before and made the usual allowances. I rose from the seat. We looked at each other—Philippa Castleton and I—white-faced and anxious.

"The announcement on that bill, Philippa," I said to my companion whimsically, "makes Lance Maturin more determined to get back to England, home and beauty than ever."

Philippa Castleton looked at me, wide-eyed and wondering; then, without the hint of a word, she slid pathetically from the seat and tumbled in a dead faint on to the grass.

CHAPTER VII
THE LEAGUE OF MATTHIAS
(From the MSS. of Anthony Lotherington Bathurst)

MY CHRONICLER has set me a most difficult task. He has requested me to furnish the public with the full details of the circumstances that took Rawlinson and me to the city of Antwerp somewhere about the time that this history has opened. The task is difficult from more than one point of view. My hands are tied with regard to certain of the more intimate matters ... more tied than they have ever been in the past, and certain necessary reticences are imposed upon me, because the affair, in its genesis, fringed upon "Intelligence"—that most marvellous branch of our own Secret Service. My readers, therefore, must be content, in the first place, to know this and little more. Later on, perhaps ...

Rawlinson—he was a Chief-Inspector at the time—and I had journeyed to Antwerp to deal primarily with three matters. Detailing these—they were two disappearances ... and the sinister activities of the League of Matthias. The disappearances were diverse. They embraced a Miss Philippa Castleton, and a distinguished member of our Diplomatic Service, a young man named Maturin. Miss Castleton had been missing for a matter of three months; Maturin, for a period nearly as lengthy. The details of the case of the missing lady are almost too well known to the general public to need any repetition here from me. Daughter of the Rt. Reverend H.E.F. Castleton, Bishop of Longbarrow, Miss Castleton's disappearance had excited a tremendous amount of interest throughout the entire country. Despite the activities of the family, of Scotland Yard, and of various private investigators whom his Lordship of Longbarrow afterwards employed unbeknown, I believe, to Scotland Yard, no traces of her had been discovered. Substantial rewards that were offered by the Bishop of Longbarrow were offered in vain. And gradually, as is invariably the happening in cases of this kind, the general excitement subsided; the hubbub died down and Miss Philippa passed more or less into oblivion.

Maturin's affair was an altogether different basis. And the trouble with him, as far as the job of investigation was concerned, was that it was a most difficult matter to *date* his disappearance accurately. I have already stated that he was a distinguished member of the Diplomatic Service. It would not be overstating the case if I asserted that he already had his feet on the rungs of the ladder of fame. For he had carried out, in spite of the comparative brevity of his service, two brilliant missions—each of which concluded with a coup and consequent personal aggrandisement. The Turkish concession in the matter of the Apostolides machine-gun, and the withdrawal of Ephraim Leveson's financial interest from the Bulgarian Government at an intensely critical moment . . . well-informed people consider that war was averted thereby by a hair's-breadth . . . were each regarded as flaming feathers in his diplomatic cap.

It will be seen, therefore, from this short account of young Maturin's operations, that his whereabouts at times were . . . if not altogether unknown . . . at least uncertain! The result was that it was quite possible that Maturin had been missing for some days before his own personal H.Q. took unto itself any degree of anxiety. At any rate, it can, I think, be safely assumed that when the "Yard" was requested to interest itself in the case, and to take a hand, much valuable time had elapsed and the scent had lost a great deal of its original aroma. And, let it be remembered—two months previously, a colleague of Maturin in the Diplomatic Service, by name of Erskine, had disappeared in much the same way and was not heard of again until his dead body was taken from the Scheldt.

When Sir Austin Kemble, the Commissioner of Police, requested me to confer with Chief-Inspector Rawlinson, very little had been gleaned that could, by any stretch of imagination, be termed informative or instructive. The only rumour that had been at all persistent was that the secret of Maturin's disappearance had been a love-affair, and the old adage—*cherchez la femme*—was once again supposed to be justifying itself.

Rawlinson, however, was a comparatively young, but zealous and efficient, officer. There isn't the slightest doubt that he had a great future in front of him. It was an unlucky fall of the cards for him that brought him into touch with the Maturin case, the Castleton disappearance case, and, lastly, the League of the Thirteen Apostles, or of "Matthias," as it came to be called.

This last-mentioned organisation had entered the arena of Continental crime about eighteen months prior to the disappearance of Philippa Castleton. By that statement, please don't misunderstand me. The League of Matthias had not entered the crime arena with any gesture of publicity or with any fanfare of trumpets. But the underworld, that dark forest and secret city of lust, passion, vice, and violence, knows strange gods and pays homage before strange altars to a strange decalogue. Something new will enter the forest and a thousand eyes will watch that something. . . . will watch it unsleepingly and unwaveringly. A thousand ears will listen . . . unceasingly. For a long time, may be, there will be an uncanny silence in response to these sensible exercises. It is difficult to say whether that silence is a silence of approval or of sullen acceptance. The flitting figures of the underworld, with its sombre shades and eerie echoes, seem to meet and to hold conferences . . . credentials, perchance, are called for and meticulously examined. Then, usually, there are whispers . . . hints . . . vague, nebulous. These whispers are succeeded by rumours no bigger than a man's finger . . . but when the rumours begin to take definite shape and the fingers assume the size of a man's hand, law and order simultaneously have their first chance to take part in the game with any hope of success.

This is exactly what happened with regard to the League of Matthias. Rawlinson's knowledge of the Continental underworld was marvellous and invaluable. That is the reason, of course, why the case had been given into his hands.

The first whisper of the infamous and notorious league had come from Brussels. From a restaurant in the Rue des Harengs—by name, "Restaurant à la Sirène." And there was this about it. It came two days after the murder of Svenhardt the banker, who had absconded from Christiania and successfully concealed his identity for over two years. The whisper yielded nothing tangible; it was carefully noted, filed, and reserved by the powers that be for future reference, That is the usual procedure when these legends from the underworld rise from the depths like shadowy bubbles and attach themselves to the light of day. This Svenhardt murder had happened about a year and a half ago. The doctors who performed the post-mortem on his body came to the opinion that his veins had been opened by jagged glass. There was little doubt that this opinion was sound.

For a considerable period of subsequent time there was a second silence. A silence, though, which, I have been informed, was regarded as ugly and ominous. As an unmistakable indication that the abhorred powers of evil were slumbering in the calm that precedes the inevitable storm. Then the words, "The Matthias League," had been whispered again. Note, too, in what connection. The whisper came about a week after the discredited Parisian actor, Etienne Busigny, was found hanged by the cord of a dressing-gown in a disused barn near Malines. This fact meant a greater official action. The police force busied itself generally. The representative of Authority mingled with many of the wastrels and wantons of the great cities, seeking more knowledge of this league . . . mingling stealthily in the gulleys and sewers of crime with covert purpose. With, however, but little success!

At length, from an unsuspected quarter, one more shred of information filtered through the network of immoral barrier and criminal caution. That shred was a number. Nothing more—nothing less. That number was 13. And again came a period of silence. Heavy, pregnant . . . almost oppressive. Broken yet again by the cremation of Dr. Whitsbury in a baker's oven in the Quai Van Dyck at Antwerp. Now the name of this Dr. Whitsbury should awaken memories . . . unpleasant memories possibly, but memories must be taken all round . . . the bad ones amongst them can be aroused as well as the pleasant. The evil that men do lives after them, but the good, thank God, is not always interred with their bones.

This Dr. Whitsbury had been a convicted abortionist. After having been suspected of the practice for a considerable time, Whitsbury escaped from one prosecution by the skin of his teeth, to be ultimately brought to book at the Winchester Assizes and sentenced to five years' penal servitude . . . a stretch which he served and from which he had been released about twelve months before he was found dead, as I have just stated, in the oven of the shop in the Quai Van Dyck. *And again*, within a week of the finding of his body, there came the sibilant whisper of the "infamous league," this brotherhood of blasphemy (if I may use the term) known to some of the more knowledgeable as the "Apostles."

The whisper was much more persistent and persevering on this third occasion . . . it seemed to have gathered strength and volume, to have amassed more certainty, to have taken unto itself an accumulative force. Enquiries came through to the "Yard." In connection with Whitsbury's death—naturally. He had been a New Forest man and had an uncle who moved in comparatively high places. You will observe that the three people whose deaths had aroused these whispers were each of a different nationality. Svenhardt had been a Norwegian, Busigny, French, and Dr. Whitsbury, British.

The job of looking into things generally—more as a safeguarding of public interest than for any other reason—was given to Rawlinson. That is to say, the "Yard's" own particular section of it. When we put our heads together, he and I, we were able to knock one or two interesting facts out of the business. One very simple . . . the others, perhaps, not quite so elementary. The simple fact was the "Belgian" thread that ran through the warp and woof of the pattern. The three towns of the three deaths had been Brussels, Malines, and Antwerp. Now Brussels is a mere matter of twenty-eight miles from Antwerp, and Malines almost equidistant between the two.

"Headquarters, Antwerp," said Rawlinson to me emphatically—"that's my opinion, Mr. Bathurst."

"Why Antwerp and not Brussels?" I demanded of him. I wasn't seeking argument—don't think that—I had no fixed opinion on the matter, at that particular moment—I was merely curious as to his reasoning. He produced his reason immediately.

"A port, Mr. Bathurst. Not only the great commercial port of Belgium but also one of the chief ports for the Continent generally. A town of quays and docks and sheds and warehouses. My experience of the seamy side of life teaches me that towns such as this are the towns of shadows and dark patches. There's something about them . . . I don't quite know what it is . . . that seems to attract the crooked and the—"

"Yet Brussels is but a stone's throw away, Rawlinson," I argued. "Still, we won't argue about it for the time being. A better way would be to start, I think, by assuming that your contention is the right one."

He nodded. I think that he was pleased by the way I had taken things generally. Another feature that emerged from our conference . . . one of the features that I alluded to as the less elementary . . . was this. Each of the three victims was a person of *distinctly* bad odour. Strongly "suspect," as a cross-examining counsel would say with unconcealed satisfaction . . . and "of questionable credit." Which is but a mild and generous way of putting things. Let us consider the facts as we had them, even more closely.

Here we had Whitsbury, a convicted abortionist; Busigny, a discredited actor with a charge of forgery hanging over his head; and Svenhardt, one of the most audacious embezzlers of modern times, a man who had ruined and despoiled literally thousands of homes in the Netherlands and the more Northern countries.

We left the pondering over this point and turned to something else. To the closer consideration of the number "thirteen," which, as I have said, had attached itself to this league of infamy and evil. One of the most extraordinary facets of the whole affair was the fact that none of the "big" criminal names (of all countries, mark you) could be traced to it.

"But why 'thirteen'?" queried Rawlinson of me.

"Why not?" I answered mischievously. He shook his head at me. I shook my head at him. "It's a dozen, you know, Rawlinson. What could be more appropriate than a dozen for the Apostles?"

"A dozen?" He wrinkled his brows in interrogative perplexity.

I explained to him. "A baker's dozen—surely."

Rawlinson grinned and rubbed his nose. "I see your point, Mr. Bathurst. I was a bit slow. Sorry and all that. All the same—I don't—"

At that moment there came the tap on the door which was destined to mean so much to us.

"Come in," cried the Chief-Inspector, and a man entered whom I recognised as being on the staff at the "Yard." He handed Rawlinson what was apparently a decoded message. Rawlinson read it, and although he spoke to me immediately afterwards there was a far-away look in his eyes.

"Now this is damned funny, Mr. Bathurst, say what you like," he said. "Either a marvellous coincidence or the working of Fate."

"One has a long arm, Inspector, and the other, I believe, a long finger. What's the spot of bother now?"

"Maturin, our missing diplomatist—and the second of his kind, mark you—is rumoured to have been last seen in—now, where do you think, Mr. Bathurst?"

I smiled. "I select Antwerp, my dear Inspector, with every possible confidence."

"Yes, Mr. Bathurst. *Antwerp!* And I'm going over there. I can't explain it, but something tells me that I'm on the track of something big."

He was right, poor devil. But not in the way that he meant. Without knowing it, he was on the track of the Greatest Adventure of All—he was to ship with Admiral Death!

Chapter VIII
RAWLINSON STRIKES THE TRAIL
(Told by Anthony L. Bathurst)

"Coming with me?" he confined, turning towards me.

"You tempt me, you know, Rawlinson, most assuredly. There is a Rubens triptych in the Southern transept of the cathedral, of the 'Descent from the Cross,' that I have always been led to believe is a masterpiece of its kind. To say nothing of the Cordovan leather hangings which the Waterhuis—"

He broke into my rhapsody. "Seriously now, Mr. Bathurst—will you come along over with me? I mean it."

"Seriously, Rawlinson," I answered . . . "I will."

Well, to push the history on, we went over to Antwerp together. Rawlinson's home was in the Thames Valley, and, to suit him, we went by a British India boat from London—a vessel of between nine and ten thousand tons. Rawlinson tried to engage me in conversation on our three problems, but I resolutely refused to talk about any of them and promptly closed all avenues of discussion. I have always found that to rest the brain, in affairs of this nature, is by far the best course that an investigator can pursue. The result was that, when our train steamed into the South Quay station, I was feeling better mentally than I had felt for some time. The brief holiday had done me a vast amount of good, and I felt equal to tackling almost anything.

We went to the Grand Hotel, in the Avenue de Keyser, and got fixed up very comfortably. Rawlinson—as ever—was for work at once, but I told him frankly that I wasn't having any until I was convinced that there was a definite programme to be attacked. After all, for all I knew, Rawlinson was chasing the rainbow, and as far as I was concerned he was going to chase it on his own for a day or so at least. Ploughing the sands is an exercise that has never held any appeal to me. I told him this and he grinned at me genially . . . "Right-o, Mr. Bathurst," he had said to me, "*you* carry on and *I'll* carry on."

"Understand, though, Rawlinson," I replied to him—"when you feel that you really want me, that you've something definite for me to get my teeth into, sing out and I'm your man."

Well, for some days, things jogged along pretty quietly, and I was able to do myself distinctly comfortably. Rawlinson flitted backwards and forwards from the hotel to the police and from the police to the hotel. The industry of the man was amazing. It was phenomenal. To say that he worked like a horse is but a positive statement. Find me the superlative of horse and I'll be able to convey to you a much greater degree of truth.

About a week after we had been over there, I fancied that I observed a change in Rawlinson's demeanour. Slight perhaps, but nevertheless noticeable. I was always taught, however, not to rush my fences, so I gave him a run before I asked him anything. I suppose a couple more days went by with nothing doing . . . and then things moved.

We were at dinner when Rawlinson decided to unburden himself. "Doing anything special tomorrow, Mr. Bathurst?"

"Hallo," I whispered to myself. "I'm going to hear something. At last." I put on a terrific look of unconcern before I answered him. "No—not that I know of. Nothing very particular. There's an old Flemish house in the Rue du Saint-Esprit—but why do you ask? Are you on to anything?"

Now Rawlinson was never a man with a gullet full of optimism. Rather the other way, in fact. Just a wee bit pessimistic. Always wanted to be very sure before he would take an extreme step. He had been born somewhere in the North of England. As I said, I never had rushed him, and I didn't rush him now. There was an appreciable interval before he replied to me. He looked carefully at his veal cutlet and then very carefully round the dining-room. What he saw—or better still, I suppose, what he didn't see—satisfied him, for he lowered his voice and began to talk to me.

"Have you ever, Mr. Bathurst, during your career, looked for something and found something else?"

I grinned. "I could answer that, my dear Rawlinson," I said half jokingly, "in several ways. Some of which, I fear, would disgruntle you. Still, I think I know what you mean. You've climbed a tree for an apple and found a pocketbook caught on one of the branches, that has been dropped there by a—well—anybody will do!" I gestured my indifference. "That suit you?"

He nodded briskly. "That will do as well as anything."

I was now thoroughly interested. "What have you been working on and what have you found?"

He was still hesitant, held back by his North-country caution. Eventually the words that he wanted came to him. "You know that I've been in close touch with the Belgian police all the time we've been over here, don't you? You haven't worried me and I haven't worried you—but you know what I've been doing and where I've been going. So I needn't explain the preliminaries. *Re* young Mr. Maturin, I must confess that I've accomplished absolutely nothing. I'm no nearer to him than I was when we set foot on the steamer at King George's Dock. But in regard to the 'League of Matthias'"—he almost whispered the last three words—"I think I've made a little progress. Just a little. Not much."

I realised that, for Rawlinson, this was an admission of some significance, so I sat up and took notice. "I'm listening, Rawlinson," I said cheerfully; "tell me the worst."

He crumbled a piece of bread on the tablecloth. "There is a dancer-fellow at a cabaret place on the farther side of the town, named de Verviac. That's the man's name, not the cabaret's. The Belgian police have had about two-thirds of a 'squeak' concerning him, and they've been good enough to pass the fraction on to me."

He paused . . . as I've indicated, he always had to fight an excessive caution . . . and on this occasion there was no exception to his general rule. I prodded him with a "prompt."

"Well? What are the words of the chorus?"

Rawlinson looked at me intensely—and then split an undoubted mouthful. "That this dancer, de Verviac, knew Svenhardt, corresponded with Etienne Busigny, and had actually been seen with Dr. Whitsbury in the Quai Van Dyck."

This was interesting with a vengeance, for the Inspector had worked to his climax most artistically. "Go on, Rawlinson," I said. "Tell me the extra verses—I could bear to hear the whole hymn."

That far-away look of his came into his eyes again. "Well, Mr. Bathurst, now comes the strangest part of the whole business. It worries me every time I think about it. You missed me at dinner last night, didn't you?"

I nodded. "I dined alone, Rawlinson. Disconsolate. Life had lost its radiance."

He smiled. "Where did you think I was? Where *do* you think I was?"

"I can give two answers to that. I thought at the time that you were hob-nobbing with Belgian bobbies. But now I know differently. Obviously, you were at the cabaret of de Verviac. Yes?"

Rawlinson nodded. "O.K., Mr. Bathurst. I went down there to have a look at this 'gigolo' fellow."

He leant forward. "And now, Mr. Bathurst, I'll ask you another question. For here enters your story of the apple and the pocketbook. What do you think I found when I got there?"

Rawlinson leaned still farther across the table to me. His eagerness and suppressed excitement interested and fascinated me . . . told me unmistakably that he had stumbled across something pretty big. So I drew a bow . . . just a little, shall we say, at a venture? But not altogether, for I reasoned in this way. He had already confessed to failure with regard to Maturin . . . I naturally attached myself to the alternative.

"I'll tell you *whom* you found there."

Rawlinson smiled with just a touch of conscious superiority. "Step on it."

"The daughter of the Right Reverend Bishop of Longbarrow," I answered. "Miss Philippa Castleton."

When it came, Rawlinson received it rather badly, I'm afraid. I had taken the wind out of his sails properly. Having shorn the lamb, I made haste to temper the wind. "It was a bit of a guess," I explained. "But you see, I knew that it couldn't be Maturin from what you had told me. So I naturally went for the other one."

"Well, you're right," he assented gloomily. "Unless I'm very much mistaken, the young lady we've been looking for all this time is de Verviac's dancing partner. Professionally, I mean." Rawlinson's gravity had its effect on me. I became serious.

"Congratulations, Rawlinson. You deserve all the success that you've had. Every bit of it. Your 'hunch' *re* Antwerp has turned up trumps and no mistake. You only had a series of facts, made up of tiny indications and cross-bearings, and yet you have managed to find the L.C.M., as it were, of the whole thing. My sincere congratulations on a splendid piece of work."

Rawlinson flushed under the battery of my praise.

"Thank you, Mr. Bathurst," he said quietly. "I appreciate that—coming from you."

I found myself liking him more than ever. "I always like to think—and try to think—of my job in terms of art." He flushed again as he said this. I think he was acutely conscious of self-revelation. "Do you understand me when I say that, Mr. Bathurst? It may sound a bit highfalutin, but . . ."

I essayed to help him out. "I think I understand you very well, Rawlinson. As I see it, all art must be a direct recording of Life. It must be *en rapport* with Life. Even inanimate objects have a violent surcharge of Life. Let me put it like this. There is a perfect span, and a perfect stream, of Life, with Beauty and symmetry flowing from the Creator and travelling back to Him."

He nodded eagerly. "Yes. Nature doesn't invest in technique. She is more practical. The planets move in symmetrical orbits. That's how I see things."

I, too, became practical. "Now, Rawlinson," I said. "Don't hesitate. Even though there was a cow with a crumpled horn, don't let that fact throw you out of your stride. Let me know how I can help you. I'm your man, you know, from now onwards." He seemed glum. I rallied him. "Don't forget my promise. We shall return to the 'Yard' bearing our sheaves before us, crushed under the weight of our blushing honours."

Rawlinson shook his head. "You're looking a bit ahead, Mr. Bathurst. I hope you're right, but I'm going to wait a bit longer before I become quite as confident as that. I like to be absolutely sure of things. Now listen, while I tell you more."

I nodded. "Nothing would suit me better. Go ahead, Rawlinson."

"De Verviac lodges in the Quai Van Dyck . . . near where he was seen with Whitsbury . . . and not a hundred yards from the baker's shop where Whitsbury's body was found. Miss Castleton's lodging is at the house of a Mother Rasmussen—not very far from this cabaret where the two of them dance. It's a place—the cabaret, I mean—that you couldn't possibly miss. A big red light—like a great torch—burns outside. Mother Rasmussen's house is in the Rue du Sacré Coeur."

Rawlinson paused. He looked at me, across the table, very deliberately. "Now—this is where you come in, Mr. Bathurst."

"Well? Tell me what you want."

He rubbed his chin—regarding me curiously. "I think I should like your advice first, Mr. Bathurst."

"On what?"

"My next step."

"Where to attack—do you mean?"

He nodded. "Yes—I suppose that would be one way of describing it."

I waited till the waiter had left us before I replied. "On the whole, Rawlinson, I think that your way is clear. Mine would be, I imagine, were I running the show. Miss Castleton represents something certain . . . something *definite*. De Verviac and his presumed association with the League of Matthias belong much more to that realm of good old conjecture. The intelligent attack, therefore, is obviously on the Castleton end of the tangle. Don't you agree? Surely?"

I watched his face as I put the questions to him. I could see that he had a bigger problem to solve than I had anticipated. That he was facing a bigger dilemma than would have confronted me. Minutes passed before he spoke.

"I realise all that you say, Mr. Bathurst. Every word of it. Both my sympathies and my sentiment incline me to the course that you advise. On the other hand, though, there's another point of view to which I can't shut my eyes. One, I think, that it's just possible you may have overlooked."

"Perhaps," I said. "What is it?"

"The relative *sizes* of the two jobs. Their relative proportions, if you like the word better. That's my particular snag. Miss Castleton's is an individual affair, as you might say. Touching, at the most liberal estimate, one family only. But this 'League of Matthias,' for all I know, may have what is nearly an international flavour."

He lowered his voice again—almost to a whisper. "It may be one of the biggest criminal organisations ever known. And, in going for the smaller, I may let the bigger slip through my fingers. That's how the general situation appeals to me."

Rawlinson rubbed his brow. "I'm rather worried, Mr. Bathurst, if you only knew."

I argued with him. "Granted all that, and admitting that there may be a big element of truth in what you say, your first duty is to Miss Castleton. And to her family! There's another point, too, to which I would call your attention. Your own point in relation to the League can't be forgotten. The point that you made to me before we left England. I will remind you of it. It's this. That not one of the murdered three has meant any loss to the general community. So long as these gentlemen of the League continue on their original lines of destruction, we may reasonably hope to escape anything like a national calamity. Has that fact occurred to you?"

As I spoke, an idea came to me, but I decided to keep it to myself. After all, these were early days and . . .

Rawlinson seemed to accept my view of the situation very reluctantly. "I suppose that what you say is right, Mr. Bathurst. I've always tried to do the right thing, and it's up to me to do it on this occasion as much as ever. All the same . . ."

"All the same—what?" I questioned.

He shrugged his shoulders. "I don't quite know how to put it. I've got a feeling about me that I can't shake off, that if I attack at the Castleton end of the problem I'm not going to pull the job off successfully. It's not that I'm over-anxious, and it's not due to depression. It's something bigger than either. It's no good asking me to explain it to you—because I can't. Call me 'fey,' if you like. I may be! Candidly, Mr. Bathurst, I don't know."

When they are written, Rawlinson's words may seem bare and unconvincing, but you must remember that the man was sitting opposite to me and that I could see every feature of him. Quite truthfully, his demeanour impressed me. He was absolutely sincere, I felt certain, and meant every syllable of what he had said.

"May I make a suggestion, then, Inspector?" I asked him.

He nodded eagerly. "There's nothing I would like better. That's what I was hoping you would do."

"Good!" I pushed away an inconvenient plate. "Let me on it with you. Divide forces. Let me work one end while you work the other. It isn't as though we couldn't call on reinforcements, if we should want any. There are the Belgian Police, for instance. They'll be at hand, if needs be."

Rawlinson nodded. "Thank you, Mr. Bathurst. I thought that you'd suggest something of that kind. I appreciate it." He stared moodily at his glass. Then he continued. "But I want you to understand, Mr. Bathurst, that I have no cut-and-dried plans, ready, as it were. That's one of my troubles. So that I'm unable to give you anything tangible . . . yet awhile. Understand?"

He looked at me quizzically. I signified my acceptance of the general situation. "Of course I do. No need to worry about that."

"There's something else, though," he proceeded, "that I ought to tell you. I'm waiting for something that may come along at any moment. When it comes—you will be ready?"

"Rely on me, my dear Rawlinson. Call to me wherever you are—I'll come to you."

As I had hoped, my reply brought a grin to his face. "Good. Where will you be to-morrow when you are away from the hotel? You started to tell me, I fancy, at the beginning of this conversation."

"You'll find me," I told him, "at Number Sixteen, the Rue du Saint-Esprit. You can't mistake it. It's an old Flemish house adjoining the Plantin Museum. It's called the Musée de Folklore Flamand, and it's well worth being visited. The poet Max Elskamp was responsible, I believe, for a good many of the presentations. There is a section devoted to Flemish criminals, which—with my well-known passion for colourful crime—I'm particularly keen on sampling. If you want me, come round or send round for me."

He pushed back his chair from the table. "That's O.K., then, Mr. Bathurst, and understood between us. You won't mind if I put you on the Miss Castleton end, will you? Rather than on the 'Matthias League?'" His voice was almost wistful.

"My dear Rawlinson," I replied, "I'm not a ladies' man, as you've probably observed by now, but I'll take the risk on this occasion, if only for your sake. Let us hope, though, that no objection will come from Miss Castleton."

The stare with which he favoured me came to me as an immediate reward. Poor old Rawlinson . . . he was always so deadly serious.

CHAPTER IX
THE HOUSE OF MOTHER RASMUSSEN
(Told by Anthony L. Bathurst)

As IT happened, I was in the Musée de Folklore Flamand early after *déjeuner* on the following morning. I had inspected the collections of furniture and food; I had seen the marionettes; I had just begun to get interested in a collection that had to do with mediaeval sorcery, when a small boy sidled up to me and pushed a note into my hand. I knew what it meant at once. It was Rawlinson's rally—his call to action. The youth disappeared as silently as he had come, and I opened the Inspector's message to read it. Rawlinson hadn't wasted words.

As we arranged—at the house of Mother Rasmussen. You will find all you want at the hotel. Developments expected any minute from now. Will communicate again.

"H'm," I commented. "Very nice of him. So this is the end of my round of pleasure."

I packed up from my museum meanderings and made my way back to the Avenue de Keyser.

When I got to my room, I found that to which Rawlinson had referred in his brief communication. For there, on my bed, was my costume—with accessories—for wear at Mother Rasmussen's according to a plan upon which the Inspector and I had agreed on the previous evening. The police authorities had been sounded on the matter—so Rawlinson had informed me—and the Rasmussen woman had been forced to toe the line.

I surveyed the costume with which I had been provided, with some degree of amusement. When I tell you that I was about to attire myself in a dress that would not have been inappropriate for one of Macbeth's witches, you will appreciate that last remark of mine to the full. There was one thing, however, for which I knew I could be devoutly thankful. Rawlinson had seen to the intricacies of the business as was his wont—that is to say, with the utmost thoroughness. Thick, coarse stockings—misshapen boots—of the type known in the trade, I believe, as "spring-sides"—grease-paints—white, carmine and brown "liners"—and dishevelled wig, were all there, in addition to the tattered and shabby red dress itself.

I took great pains over the niceties (if I may use the word in such a connection) and the more trifling details of my make-up. When it was completed, and I had clad myself in the red rags, as I silently styled them, I consider that I had made a very fair job of it. It seemed to me that I was fit for the barricades of the revolution—true companion of the Defarge. My most difficult task, I knew, would be to get three or four inches off the appearance of my height, and I noticed with a strong sense of satisfaction that the atrocious boots with which Rawlinson had furnished me, were both flat-soled and excessively low-heeled.

Looking into my mirror, I grinned malevolently at the repulsive image that I saw reflected there. As the world's haggiest hag—the crone of crones—I stood unrivalled and unchallenged. The stoop that I endeavoured to give to my shoulders was deucedly uncomfortable, but, by letting my muscles relax rather than stiffen, it gradually became more endurable.

Grey wisps of bedraggled hair hung over my fore-head, round my ears, and curled in a coy senility on the nape of my neck. Although I am tall and pretty solid with it, my feet, for my stature, are not unreasonably big. I have a long foot, it is true—but not a particularly broad foot, and the boots from the Rawlinson emporium fitted me quite comfortably considering that he had had to take a guess more or less at the size of 'em. I found one of the back staircases of the Grand Hotel, and unobtrusively made my way into the Avenue de Keyser. As you imagine, my idea was to get into one of the smaller streets as speedily as possible.

After turning two or three times I came into the Rue de l'Offrande, close by the Zoological Gardens. From here, I knew, from the directions that Rawlinson had given to me, that I had but to strike in a northern direction and I must come out somewhere near de Verviac's cabaret place—this abode marked outside by the red flare. Which meant, too, that I should be close to Philippa Castleton's lodging-house in the Rue du Sacré Coeur—the house of this Mère Rasmussen, on whose domestic staff—please understand—I had been so recently appointed.

It took me, I suppose, about twenty-five minutes to reach my first objective. I passed the cabaret, discovered the Road of the Sacred Heart, and eventually found myself staring at what I felt certain was the Rasmussen dwelling-place. The walls of it were white, and it was a high, forbidding place—which is being complimentary and saying almost the best that one can say about it. Its windows were shuttered, after the habit of the French towards their houses, and I can't truthfully say that I looked forward to entering it with any sense of passionate zest. The door had iron studs on it and looked a pretty ponderous proposition.

Anyhow, there was nothing to be gained by dithering about outside it, so I plucked up skirts and courage, stepped forward, and gave it what seemed to my ears a querulous rat-tat. The echoes of this shock resounded, so that, for some unearthly reason, I moved back a pace or two from the door and folded my haggish arms across my bosom after the approved manner of the feminine antique.

Although I was prepared for almost anything (my career as an investigator of crime has tutored me to this), I received something in the nature of a surprise when the door opened in front of me. A blear-eyed hag, compared with whom I was as G. Cooper herself, stood there and blinked at me in a complete epitome of unintelligence—which suddenly and miraculously changed. Her inflamed lids then regarded me as a man-eating tiger—deprived of bodily sustenance for forty days and forty nights—might regard a morsel of succulent humanity that was all of a sudden dangled in front of him.

In my best Flemish, pretty rotten at that, I admit, I intro-duced myself to my charming hostess. "Mère Houten" I called myself. The name had come from Rawlinson.

Mother Rasmussen, for this vision of beauty was she, made a guttural noise which I took to be an invitation to enter, and I stepped into the house, giving my wisps of hair an affectionate pat, which I thought would be in keeping with my part. Much to my relief, the feminine head of the family of Rasmussen gave me the bird very effectively, from the moment that I entered her dwelling-house. No doubt my antecedents found little favour in her eyes. "I was of the police—policy"—which was a condition that she couldn't forgive—it put me completely beyond the pale as far as she was concerned.

Goodness knows what Rawlinson had told the Belgian Police about me and what those gentlemen in turn had passed on to Mother Rasmussen. It must have been pretty foul. But whatever it was, it had put me completely off the map. The lady (ahem!) desired neither my conversation nor my company. However, Mère Rasmussen's frozen mitten didn't disturb me in the least. On the contrary, indeed, it appealed to me. It left me on my own and gave me a freedom of movement that I found most welcome. So I slunk off to the kitchen, and the quarters that adjoined the kitchen, and did as much nosing round and ferreting about as I could manage without running myself into any spots of bother.

So the day dragged on. A day that seemed of length interminable. Mother Rasmussen, with a fine sense of altruism, kept herself to herself and religiously away from me. The passing hours brought no change in our relationship. After a time I felt myself getting peckish, so I scouted round, found a larder of sorts, and helped myself to a substantial hunk of bread and cheese.

Of the girl supposed to be Philippa Castleton, I saw and heard nothing.

Once or twice I made my way into the more central portion of the house, but on these few occasions the Rasmussen woman always appeared with the most amazing alacrity and I judged it better policy to avoid, for the time being, anything that might tend to friction or lead to an open rupture.

Rawlinson had made it plain that I was to hold a mere watching brief until he was able to communicate with me again, which he hoped would be by that same evening.

When it had begun to grow dark I went into the yard at the back of the house and took a good look at this building in which I had placed myself. I estimated that it was a building of seven storeys. Of lights, that showed the present occupation of rooms, there showed but one. Here then was a problem! Was that one light burning in the room occupied by the English girl whom her friends had sought for some weeks now?

If Rawlinson were right in his theory—and the fact that he had asked me to come here proved to me that the theory which he had outlined previously had been at least *strengthened* by something—the probability was that Miss Castleton was sitting somewhere near that light at which I found myself looking. After turning the matter over in my mind, I decided to go indoors again and to wait to see if she should come downstairs. But I was destined to be unlucky. I never heard the closing even of the front door. Philippa Castleton left the house that evening for the cabaret of the scarlet flare without my hearing the slightest sound of her going.

About ten o'clock that night, when I was regaling myself with a second supply of bread and cheese, my charming hostess, *La Belle* Rasmussen, brought me a letter, which she thrust into my hand to the accompaniment of a leer and a grunt, neither of which I have seen nor heard equalled.

The note was from Rawlinson, of course, and I opened it with mixed feelings. I didn't like the situation a little bit, and that priceless specimen of a king leer that I had just seen on the Rasmussen face hadn't made me any more in love with things generally. But Rawlinson had definite news for me this time, and definite news, too, that held both the hint and the promise of action.

I am in the cabaret of the red flare (he wrote). *There are three young men here—they've just come in. I haven't seen them before in this place and I can't size them up. But they're English, I'm certain, and with the Maturin affair on my mind all the time, you can bet that I'm watching points like a terrier watching a rat-hole. One of them seems exceedingly interested in my friend de Verviac, who is dancing with the girl that I think is Philippa Castleton, as I write this note to you. I will get it brought to you by an auxiliary who is absolutely trust-worthy. If you want anything, tell him, and he will see to it.*

Then there came a postscript. Several words of it were under-lined—to do which was totally unlike the everyday Rawlinson.

I am as certain as I ever was of anything in my life that things will move to-night. Keep both eyes open.

I told Mother Rasmussen that the messenger need not wait, and the Fair Maid of Perth shuffled away. Then I put a match to Rawlinson's note and burnt it. Slowly the time dragged by and I grew unutterably weary. I found myself wishing most sincerely that the relative positions could be reversed . . . that Inspector Rawlinson could be in the house of Mère Rasmussen . . . and that I could be in a low haunt that sold beer—and more beer.

I pushed up my dirty red sleeve and looked at the watch which I still carried on my wrist. The time it showed me was twelve minutes past eleven. As I looked at it, I heard a noise at the front door. It was the sound of a key being turned in the lock. Without the slightest hesitation I slipped into the passage that led from my kitchen to the front door. It was pitch dark—Mother Rasmussen was evidently no believer in superfluous illumination.

Quick as I had been, however, the old woman was already in the passage, a yard or two in front of me. I heard the front door open and then shut again. But I could see nothing of what was going on from where I was standing. Mère Rasmussen, however, burst into copious words and made much argument. Her fluency astounded me. For sheer unadulterated force it would not have disgraced an ancient Greek school of rhetoric. Demosthenes, in his early days of speech impediment, would have instantaneously saluted her as his superior. Whoever it was that she addressed replied to her in Flemish—which, naturally, I was unable to follow. I have a little of that ancient language but by no means an embarrassment.

I could hear that it was a girl's voice that replied, and I felt pretty certain in my own mind that it was Rawlinson's missing girl who was standing a few yards away from me. I crept a pace or so up the passage, in the lee of the stairway, in an attempt to get nearer to them so that I might get a glimpse of her. But again my luck was out, for, as I moved towards her, she moved towards the stairs and away from me. All I could see was a young girl . . . and just behind her, the form of a man. Within a second, they were on the staircase and had commenced to ascend the stairs . . . in another second, they had moved from the range of my sight. At that moment, I heard a clock . . . a church clock I think it was . . . chime the quarter past eleven. That glimpse was the last that I was destined to see of Miss Castleton and her cavalier for some days.

Midnight came and went. Nothing of any importance transpired to brighten my task of vigilance. Once or twice it seemed to me that I heard steps in the passage, but, from my position in the kitchen, it was too dark to see anybody, and I was left uncertain. I had just begun to curse Rawlinson with a mathematical and scientific exactness, when the fun started. I heard the sound of the front door again.

I heard it open. I heard a light furtive step ascending the stairs of this dark, sombre, and sinister house. Whilst I was debating what to do, a dark form slid from the shadows and a hand caught me by the arm. I turned like lightning to ask what the hell, when a low voice said "S'sh"—and I knew that my companion was none other than Rawlinson himself. As he had prophesied an hour or so previously, things had begun to move. The pack was in full cry!

CHAPTER X
DEATH ON THE STAIRS
(Told by Anthony L. Bathurst)

"THAT was de Verviac whom you heard come in just then," he whispered cautiously. "He trailed Miss Castleton here earlier on. I was behind the gentleman on each occasion, but he didn't know it." Rawlinson chuckled at the reminiscence.

"Come into the kitchen," I said with an air. "Amongst other modern conveniences there's a light there. I've got a gas-jet going."

He followed me, and when I had got him inside I turned to him for information. "What's the game?" I asked. "What have you picked up? Anything vital?"

Rawlinson replied to my questions with a question to me. "Did you hear the girl come in, Mr. Bathurst? Some time ago?"

I nodded sagaciously. "Yes. She came in at twelve minutes past eleven. I happen to know that because I looked at my watch just beforehand."

He smiled at my exactitude. "You love to be precise, don't you, Mr. Bathurst?"

I shook my head at him and grinned back! "It isn't love, Rawlinson," I said, "it's worship—pure and simple."

"Was she alone?"

"No. She had a man with her. I caught just a bare glimpse of him."

He nodded—as though the news pleased him. "I thought as much. This man—what was he like, would you say?"

"There, my dear Rawlinson," I said, "you have me on the hip of hips. It was much too dark in that passage there for me to see anything of detail. To tell the truth, I was lucky to get as close to them as I did. It was a man. There, my information summarily ceases."

He rubbed the line of his jaw as though in consideration of a point of immense importance. Then he turned to me eagerly. "Wouldn't it be an ace of aces if I turned the three tricks in one. If that young fellow who is upstairs now with Philippa Castleton were the missing Maturin himself? Something keeps hammering away inside my brain—"

At that moment, somewhere in that house above us, there rang out the noise of two revolver shots. Rawlinson uttered a sharp exclamation and looked at me fearfully.

"That spells trouble," I remarked unintelligently.

The words had scarcely left my lips when there came a third report. To my ear, and although I was all that distance away, this third shot had a different sound from the sounds of the two that had preceded it. Then we heard the noise of flying feet. Above us . . . and then, as it were . . . nearer to us.

"Somebody running down the stairs," said Rawlinson to me.

"A man," I returned. "The steps are too heavy for a woman. Hark . . . they're coming nearer."

"He must come this way," said Rawlinson with a chuckle. "There's no escape from the back of the place. I have had a good look round and made sure of that. So, taking everything into consideration, I'll have a word with the gentleman before he leaves. I shouldn't like him to go without saying good-bye. Let's have a look at him."

Rawlinson ran from the kitchen into the passage and I followed him, leaving the door of the kitchen open behind me. Those escaping feet were now desperately near to us . . . although of course still above our heads . . . and, as I looked, there came into the area of my sight the figure of a man . . . running down the staircase just above me and to my left. He was taking two stairs at a time, running as though he were pursued by the devil himself or by the wolf-brethren of Galazi—Blood, Blackfang, Greysnout, and Deathgrip. When he reached the passage itself, *en route* for the front door, Rawlinson, who was a few paces in advance of me, called upon him peremptorily to stop. I heard the name "de Verviac", but he paid no attention to the order as far as I was able to see, and ran straight towards the door that would yield him exit.

At the door he raised his hand menacingly, and I saw the gleam of a weapon. Rawlinson ran towards him. There was a shot . . . a second shot . . . the agonised scream of a woman . . . the bang of the door . . . they all seemed to synchronise most marvellously . . . and then to my horror and utter dismay I saw Rawlinson sink slowly down on the bottom stair of the staircase. From the way in which his body drooped and sagged, I knew that he had been hit seriously, and I ran at once to where he lay.

Mother Rasmussen, for it was she who had screamed, ran into the kitchen uttering weird noises that I classified as imprecations and curses. But beyond that, I paid no attention to her, and tried to prop Rawlinson up against my knee. I soon saw that it was useless. All my efforts were futile and, with a sickening sense of helplessness and hopelessness, I realised that Rawlinson was dead. His grand promotion had come to him at last.

I don't think that a man's death has ever affected me so much before. It was the circumstances of his passing, I suppose: a minute before, warm, vivid flesh and blood, talking to me, keen and alert in the performance of his duty; now, but the shell of a man from which the vital spark had fled. There was also a ticklish problem for me to solve. A problem, too, that had descended upon me like a bolt from the blue.

For a moment or two I was uncertain as to my best course. De Verviac had gone from the house . . . assuming that Rawlinson had been right and that it had been he. There was little point or utility that I could see to be gained in going after him. He was, at least, identifiable. Both now, and in the future.

At that moment, for some reason that I can't explain, I was prompted to look up . . . to that part of the staircase above me, and to my surprise I saw a face bob back from the banisters of a landing high up above me. "That's the man," I said to myself, "whom Miss Castleton brought here. A hundred to one on it. And according to Rawlinson he must come this way to escape. Good."

I turned and went into the kitchen, where I held conversation with the old hag whom I knew as Rasmussen. "You understand," I said to her in my best halting Flemish—I guessed that she had little French—"I want the police and a doctor. As quickly as you can get them here. The Inspector is badly wounded. Now then, stir yourself, or it will be the worse for you. If you don't want to spend the remainder of your days in prison, get busy at once. Do you hear?"

She proved more amenable than I had anticipated from my first impressions of her, and shuffled out with very little delay. The old baggage had the fear of God in her by now, and the recent happenings in her house, coming as they had on top of whatever Rawlinson had previously told her, had completely revolutionised her outlook. "Conscience doth make cowards of us all."

After she had departed to do my bidding, I went back to the body of Rawlinson and waited there for the arrival of uniformed authority. I considered that this was the best course for me to adopt. The birds above me were trapped, so I imagined, and I could rest, from that particular standpoint, serenely content where I was.

I looked at poor old Rawlinson . . . as he lay there . . . remembered his burning enthusiasm and the bitter pity of it . . . sorrowed for him . . . and then, something that I observed strung me into throbbing mental excitement, and I thought of the man upstairs whose face I had just seen. For there was a tiny hole *in the back* of the dead Inspector's head. Whoever had shot Rawlinson, it couldn't have been de Verviac! *For Rawlinson had been shot from behind!*

Chapter XI
THE FRAGMENTS THAT REMAINED
(Anthony L. Bathurst's narrative continued)

When the official representatives arrived, volubly escorted by Mère Rasmussen, I introduced myself to the man who appeared to be their leader. I was fully conscious of the bizarre figure that I must have presented to them, but as it happened I had no cause for misgiving. Everything was satisfactory and all that I told them was accepted. For this, I had to thank Rawlinson. I soon learned that he had given them many details of the work that he and I had been doing together. Little explanation of my presence, therefore, was really necessary. I was implicitly accepted and the way was clear. The medical bloke got busy in a brace of shakes and quickly corroborated my own opinion of Rawlinson's death. It had been almost instantaneous, he told me, in perfectly good English. I described the events that had taken place exactly as I had witnessed them.

The sergeant in charge of the police party listened to my story and nodded gravely. "There is a man upstairs now, you say?" His English was by no means equal to the doctor's.

I nodded.

"How do you know, for certain?"

"Because I've seen him. When I first went to look at Inspector Rawlinson after he'd been shot down, I looked up for a moment, and there was this chap I mentioned to you, watching me."

He nodded, as though in approval, almost, of the action that I had just described.

"Do you know him? Who he is?"

I shook my head. "Haven't the foggiest. I couldn't describe a single feature of him. I merely caught a fleeting glimpse of a white face that bobbed back over the banisters just as he in turn caught sight of me looking up at him."

As I spoke, I was again acutely conscious of the absurd figure that I must have presented.

"Could he have shot the Inspector from where he was, do you think, Mr. Bathurst?"

I looked up the staircase and then at the wound at the back of the dead man's head. "Before I answer that, Sergeant, I'd like to ask a question myself. What does Doctor Hendriks think?"

The doctor cocked his head to one side and assessed possibilities. "To have done what you suggest, he would have had to be, I think, almost on a level with the dead man. Yes . . . undoubtedly that. This bullet has not entered the skull in a downward direction. To me, as I see it, it seems to have travelled from the right, if anything."

He looked across the passage as he spoke . . . measuring, so it seemed to me, distances and directions. There were two rooms to the right of this passage as one faced the front door. Dark, cheerless, empty rooms, to every appearance. Mother Rasmussen appreciated the drift of the doctor's remarks and entered the breach. His look had told her the way his thoughts ran.

"There was nobody in there, if that is what you are thinking. There was nobody in either of the rooms. To the truth of that I will swear by the Holy Virgin."

That was as near as I could get in my interpretation of her Flemish.

The sergeant ignored her. For all the attention that he paid—either to her, as a person, or to what she had said—she might have been non-existent. The sergeant gave orders. Precisely, two sets of orders. I listened to them carefully. Two of his men were detailed to make their way upstairs to bring down the man whom I had seen, for examination; the other man, a portly, cheerful-visaged fellow, was directed to search the two empty rooms leading off the passage about which the woman Rasmussen had just made her statement. What happened to these two search parties proved to be so important that I must set down the two catalogues of facts in detail.

I will deal first with the adventures of the two men who had been sent upstairs. They emulated the historic example of that ancient Duke of York of ours . . . they marched up the staircases . . . and they marched down again! The senior of the two, as I judged him, reported to the sergeant. I tried hard to gather what he was saying. I heard something about a bedroom that was lighted up, and more things about a door that held fast, but he spoke quickly and I was unable to gleam the precise details.

The sergeant harangued them for a time and there ensued much argument. The discussion developed so much, in fact, that the cheerful-faced policeman was switched off the job that he had given him to do downstairs, and found himself attached to the two men who had been sent upstairs . . . and had become Yorkists. The sergeant, also, decided to accompany the party, and I, following his example, fell in behind.

We ascended three flights of stairs before we reached the door of the room that we sought. I listened carefully for any audible evidences of its occupation, and to my astonishment and dismay I could hear none. But I still banked on poor old Rawlinson's information about the back of the house being impossible for a "getaway," and fervently hoped for the best. I was still superbly confident that our man, and Miss Castleton too, must be somewhere upstairs, and that it could be a question of time only before we put our hands on them.

The leader of our contingent decided upon action. "Break down the door," he said quietly.

Dr. Hendriks and I stood aside and the three subordinates set about their task immediately. It took them a considerably longer time than they had probably anticipated. The house was old, it is true, but that condition may be said to have cut both ways. The door was stout and solid, the wood was rough wood and tough wood, and sturdily honest in its unyielding. But eventually, of course, the inevitable happened. The combined strength of three resolute men triumphed and we entered.

I shall never forget the sight that met our eyes as we crossed the threshold. The birds had flown. More than that—the nest had been pulled to pieces. A chair lay on the floor by the door. The window was wide open, the bedstead had been pushed hard against the wall just below it, and bedclothes—chiefly blankets, I noticed—lay on the floor in a chaos of clustered confusion. There was blood, too, in many places. On the bed there had been tossed a pearl-butted revolver, and round one of the legs of the bedstead a rope of sheets was tied . . . sheets that had been torn into strips and cleverly knotted together and which now, in rope form, hung over the window-sill and fluttered lazily into the abyss below.

My friend the sergeant muttered a malediction, ran round the side of the bed to the window, and leaned out over the sill. I walked towards him, pushed the bedstead out of my way a little, and stood at his side. He was annoyed.

"Inspector Rawlinson was wrong," he cried, "they *have* escaped this way. Why did I take what he said for granted? Why did I not—"

"Don't reproach yourself," I returned curtly, "you and I are in the same boat, Sergeant. If Rawlinson were wrong, he has paid for his mistake with his life. I suggest that we will let it rest at that."

The sergeant leant farther out over the window-ledge. "Look," he cried excitedly, "down there, Mr. Bathurst. One of the birds has shed some of its feathers. When it flew away, no doubt. Rombouts."

The stolid-faced man to whom he had called came forward briskly. "Yes, my Sergeant, what is it that you require of me?"

The sergeant beckoned. "Come here, Rombouts, to my side here. Look down there."

The sergeant pointed dramatically to the narrow street below. "Can you see something lying there on the cobble-stones . . . near the kerb?"

The man craned over the sill and looked into the darkness below. "Yes, Sergeant. I see what you see. It is, I think, a coloured cloth of some sort."

It occurred to me that Rombouts must have possessed an exceptionally keen sight or a powerful imagination, for all that I could pick out in the darkness there was a blob of white. Sergeant Pauwels—this was his name as I discovered subsequently—nodded.

"Clothing of some kind, I imagine. Dropped by one of them when they swung out on to the old wall over there. That's how they went, no doubt." He turned and looked round the apartment in which we stood. "Everything here points to it. Rombouts, get down into that street and bring me back whatever it is that lies there. Quick, man!"

Rombouts turned sharply and dashed out of the room.

"May I make a suggestion, Sergeant?" I interposed.

"What is it, Mr. Bathurst?"

Pauwels' change from the quicker French and occasional Flemish that he had been using to his men to the slower halting English that he used to me, was rather startling. Each time that it occurred, it seemed that he took on the mantle of another personality. There was a complete metamorphosis. When his form of language altered, so also did *he* alter, and his methods change. I answered him.

"One of the people who escaped is wounded . . . the chances are that the blood here belonged to one of them. I saw no wound on the man who ran downstairs. And the broken glass, I should say, is the result of a bullet having gone through it. You remember that I told you that Rawlinson and I heard three shots. Which brings me to my point—that wounded person should be all the easier to trace. At the most generous estimate he can't have got very far away by this time even. How about . . . ?"

Directly I said that, I could have bitten my tongue. For I was certain that Rawlinson hadn't been killed by the man who had been upstairs, and that Philippa Castleton, as I had come to call her, was outside the real marrow of the affair. Sergeant Pauwels broke into my thoughts and finished my sentence for me.

"Capturing him?" he queried. Then he laughed boisterously. "Don't worry about that, Mr. Bathurst. We will have him all right . . . that will be as they say . . . O.K. He cannot get far away. When I see what Rombouts brings me out of that street down there, I will act, and when I act I will close all his avenues of escape. Don't you see that by waiting for definite information I may not be *losing* time, but in the long running, as you English say, I may *gain* time?"

"You're an optimist, Sergeant," I thought to myself, but as delay rather suited my book, at the moment, I didn't stop to argue the point with him. For the time being, at least, I resolved to keep in the background and let Pauwels make most of the running. On the other hand, my mind gave birth to a new resolve. I was determined to carry on from the point where *Rawlinson* had been destined to leave off. I had the fancy that Rawlinson had handed me the torch, as my heritage of service, and I resolved to do my utmost to see the whole thing through . . . if only for him who had died on his job . . . in all its phases . . . Miss Castleton . . . Maturin . . . the "League of Matthias," and now the murder of Rawlinson himself.

Let me put the matter in a nutshell. I didn't feel at all sure that Pauwels was moving in the same and right direction.

The second subordinate stepped back from the door as Rombouts came through. The latter was carrying something. Pauwels went to meet him. Rombouts handed over the object of his salvage.

"A man's pyjama-jacket," he announced with an air of triumph. "You were right, Sergeant Pauwels. And you were right too, Sir," he announced, turning to me—"the man who wore this was wounded in the shoulder. Look at this. There is the stain of blood, here—look!"

Pauwels took the jacket and examined it. I bent over him as he did so. He gave me the benefit of his impressions. "English made, I think, Mr. Bathurst. The silk and the stripes give me that impression. I always think that the French or even the Belgian—"

I interrupted him before he could complete his statement. "There, Sergeant, is the *definite* information, for which you have been waiting."

For I had seen something tucked away in the nape of the neck, that had so far eluded my companion's observation. It was an identification tab. On it was a name in black marking-ink. Sergeant Pauwels' eager eyes followed my demonstrating finger.

"You English, Mr. Bathurst, have a saying, 'wheels within wheels.' It applies to this case. Here we have hit upon mystery within mystery. For I remember the lines upon which Inspector Rawlinson was working. He had partly taken me into his confidence. This name is a certain confirmation of his theory. If he were alive he would rejoice at the discovery."

I knew what Pauwels meant very well. For the name on the tab at which we were looking was Lancelot Maturin. How near had Rawlinson been to the truth? I wondered!

CHAPTER XII
MALFROY THE POISONER?
(Anthony L. Bathurst's narrative continued)

PAUWELS gave rapid instructions to Rombouts and the others. The hunt was up with a vengeance! He had his definite trail and plan in front of him now. That latter effected, as far as was then possible, he turned to me—brimming over with ideas.

"Those other rooms downstairs, Mr. Bathurst? Those two in which the doctor was interested? I'm determined to have a look at them before I leave here. Somehow or other, I do not feel satisfied. Also, there is the matter of this revolver. Doctor Hendriks," he said, "would you say that the wound in Inspector Rawlinson's head could have been caused by a bullet from this revolver?"

Pauwels handed it to Hendriks. The doctor looked over the weapon with curious care.

"You understand," he said at length, "that I shall have to probe before I am able to extract the bullet that killed Inspector Rawlinson. So that what I say now is but the expression of an opinion, and by no means a fact. But, judging from the size of the circumference of the wound at the back of the head, this revolver is of just the kind that I should have expected the bullet to have been fired from. Yes . . . I can truthfully say that. Have I made myself clear, gentlemen?"

Pauwels and I nodded.

He turned the revolver round in his hand. "There are letters here," he said, "in the form of initials, I think. A monogram."

Sergeant Pauwels and I went to him, and the sergeant took hold of the revolver. I saw at once what the initials were, and Pauwels translated them into an exclamation.

"L.M.," he cried. "The case is becoming plainer every minute. It is obvious that this revolver belonged to the same man as did the pyjama-jacket—Lancelot Maturin. For here are the initials that we should expect to find." He nodded to himself in his extreme satisfaction, and I saw that he was a man who liked his cases to be clear and plain.

"This is good," he said. "It will not be long before we lay our hands on this Maturin. Rombouts is already hot on his track. Maturin won't be able to travel very far."

I was unable, at this juncture, to resist the temptation of interruption.

"If that be so, Sergeant Pauwels, you will certainly have achieved something."

He smiled at me—a slow, heavy smile. "You have a hidden meaning, Mr. Bathurst. I can see that well enough. What is it? Explain, please."

"As you wish. What I meant was this. You will have achieved something that the British Secret Service has been endeavouring to achieve over a period of some weeks, I believe. As you yourself pointed out to me, the particular problem was engaging the attention of even Inspector Rawlinson. Perhaps, though, I should have been closer to the truth if I had said the 'part' attention."

Pauwels' smile faded from his face. "Maturin," he muttered—"yes, you are right! My mind has been slow to grasp all the truth. But that work had been very secret. Negotiations of that kind always are. It is the diplomacy . . . but I did once happen to hear the missing man's name. Yes—I remember it just now. The name *was* Maturin. When Inspector Rawlinson mentioned it to me yesterday morning in relation to his own case, I did not connect it with the other affair."

Sergeant Pauwels rubbed the ridge of his jaw as he considered this new aspect (to him) of the problem. Purposely, I remained silent. I determined to allow him to think the thing out in his own way. After a time, he came to a decision.

"We will make our way downstairs, Mr. Bathurst," he announced, "and see if either of those two rooms on the right of the staircase can tell us anything. Lead the way, will you? Dr. Hendriks and I will follow you."

Now here comes the second remarkable feature of Sergeant Pauwels' investigation as I saw it then and as I still see it now. Remarkable, that is, in this way. All investigations of this nature, as I have said on innumerable occasions before, should be built up on foundation stones that are laid as an outcome of the functioning of the *science of deduction*. That science of which the immortal Holmes must ever remain the incomparable master! The science that deduces from a fact, from a glance, or from an observation, that a second fact must be the natural sequence or the inevitable corollary of the first factor. Pauwels, to my mind, had taken, in his investigation of this affair, two chance shots. The first, when he had anticipated a definite personal identification from a pyjama-jacket that he saw lying in the street—and *got it*—and the second, in the matter of these two rooms. Rooms which, as far as anybody knew, had been unoccupied at the time of the murder and—more than that—which Mère Rasmussen had sworn to have been empty! All through the piece, however, Pauwels seemed serenely positive that he would glean something from an examination of them which would ultimately turn out to be important.

I will attempt to describe the position of these two rooms in relationship to the staircase down which de Verviac had run. This house in which we were was what is generally know as a left-hand house. As one entered by the front door there was a first room immediately on one's left. The second room was situated just beyond the staircase, its door, I should say, being opposite—in direct relation to that staircase—to what would be about the fourth banister.

As I descended the staircase, with Dr. Hendriks and Pauwels behind me, it was natural, then, that we should turn into this second room first. It was pitch dark in there, and I groped for my matches to light the gas from the jet that I knew must be there somewhere. When I was successful in my enterprise, Pauwels, the Doctor, and I looked round the room and then at each other. It contained but few of the normal signs of habitation. There was a rickety table in the middle that gave a hint of imminent collapse, an empty bookcase against one of the walls, and two decrepit-looking chairs. The wallpaper was faded and peeling from the walls in many places, and the floor was utterly bare of covering. On the shelf of the mantel, however, there was something which, directly I saw it, and my brain took in the message that my eyes delivered, set my heart beating rapidly in wild excitement.

The significance of the object, in these surroundings, was too tremendous to be either accidental or ignored. For what I looked at was an "Apostle" spoon! Of wood! Similar, perhaps, to that wood of the bigger spoons which are habitually used for mustard. How near had Rawlinson been, I thought, and now how far was he away? The burning and sacred pity of it!

I glanced quickly at Pauwels, to see if his mind had registered the significance that mine had, but if it were so, he gave no sign of such a happening that I was able to detect. On the other hand, the sergeant was pointing dramatically to the floor. Certainly, he had scored too. There, on the nude wood where none of us had yet trodden, were the marks of a human footstep. The footstep of a man wearing a shoe or boot. There were four of these footmarks—one in the middle of the room, one right over by the mantelpiece (near the Apostle spoon, be it noted), and two against the door. Pauwels openly exulted in the moment of discovery.

"There, Mr. Bathurst," he exclaimed triumphantly, indicating each mark in turn, "and there, and there, and there! Was I not right in my assumption after all? In spite of what old woman Rasmussen insisted when I tackled her? There *has* been somebody in this room. Recently, too. That is absolutely certain."

I lounged over from the mantel where lay the spoon, and looked at the marks on the bare boards. I nodded to him. "Yes, Sergeant," I said to him. "I'm not arguing with you, because you're right. A man has been in here. And, as you say, quite recently—for the marks are undeniably fresh."

I had scarcely made the statement when an idea came to me and I turned to Dr. Hendriks to test it at its very foundation.

"Dr. Hendriks, if my memory be accurate, you expressed the opinion, just now, that the bullet which killed Inspector Rawlinson had travelled in a left-hand direction . . . that is to say, had been fired from the dead man's right. Am I correct, Doctor?"

Hendriks gave voluble agreement. "But that is so, Mr. Bathurst. I am sure of it. The edges of the wound in the Inspector's head tell me that unmistakably." His excitement increased. "And I know what you are thinking, for I find myself thinking the same thought. That the shot that killed Rawlinson was fired from the doorway of this room. Yes?"

I smiled at his eagerness. "I certainly find the idea attractive, Doctor. Much more so now that you have given it your blessing."

Pauwels attached himself to us. "And I, too, think that we have hit upon the truth between us. Let me reconstruct the crime. The murderer of Rawlinson hid in this room. He crouched in this doorway here, in the comparative darkness. De Verviac ran down the staircase, and, when the Inspector ran towards him, towards the front door, Rawlinson was an easy mark. Nothing was more simple than for the assassin to shoot him down. All that we have to do is to—"

"Find our man," I said quietly, "which, when you come to look at it dispassionately, is an investigator's normal problem—neither more nor less."

I bent down and made a rough measurement of the four footmarks on the flooring of the room. Then I placed my own foot against one of them—and held my breath. For, by a curious trick of Fate, the footmark at which I gazed was almost an exact reproduction of the shape of my own foot. I wasn't altogether sorry, when I realised this, that Rawlinson himself had vouched for my integrity some days before the murder. Look at it how you will, my story of how Rawlinson had come to his death was entirely uncorroborated, and if this Sergeant Pauwels had taken it into his head to be nasty . . .

"Here are some facts for you about him, Sergeant," I said, "the man who was in this room stands over six feet in height and . . ."

I hesitated.

"And what, Mr. Bathurst?"

I burnt my boats. "Wore dark clothes. A dark suit, I mean. Morning dress."

Pauwels opened his eyes and then shook his head in an expression of mystification. "I am afraid that I am not able to follow you there, Mr. Bathurst." He looked round the room rather stupidly, as though seeking to discover there the solution of the statement that I had made. He was a decent sort of bloke, though, so I essayed explanation.

"I may be wrong, Sergeant, of course, but I'd bet confidently that I'm not. Consider these points, for that is how I see the matter. If this man, crouching or standing on the threshold of this room, had been wearing light clothes or evening dress, with its accompaniment of white shirt front, Rawlinson would have noticed him when he ran by. He must have passed the room in his run because the bullet is in the back of the head. That is why I bank on dark clothes. It's a longish shot, perhaps, but it's pretty sound, I think, all the same."

"Taking into consideration all that we know, I think that I agree with you, Mr. Bathurst," contributed Dr. Hendriks; "the eye catches the glimmer of white . . . or of light colours and shades, very quickly . . . I have heard you English talking of seeing with the tail of your eye . . . I know what that means because I have done it myself. It is almost an instinctive action. Had this man Rawlinson good sight—would you say?"

"As far as I know, Doctor. He didn't wear glasses or anything of that kind—that I have ever seen."

"I am something of an optician myself," declared Hendriks fussily, "and have studied the general conditions of ophthalmia. When that is present, the eyes may not only be myopic—" He broke off suddenly.

"Let me have a good look at the dead man's eyes. It isn't over important, perhaps, but, if nothing else be gained, it may serve to test your theory, Mr. Bathurst."

Dr. Hendriks walked back to the staircase . . . to the body of Inspector Rawlinson. I wasn't terribly interested in the examination, and watched Hendriks look at the pupils of the dead man's eyes, with more or less unconcern. It seemed to me that he had left the main thread and darted off at a tangent to make a mountain of material out of my molehill of theory. Material, too, that was irrelevant. Another thing—the light in the wretched place wasn't anything like good enough for the job of work that he had apportioned himself—and as a professional man, he ought to have realised the fact. I saw him hunch Rawlinson's body up to a higher stair, so that he might be able to see better, no doubt. He propped the head against one of the banisters. To do this, he was forced to shift the dead man's legs. As he did so, I saw him stare in surprise at something that had evidently been lying on the stair under the Inspector's body. Dr. Hendriks bent over and picked it up. I was in front of Pauwels and, from where I stood, I was able to see that it was a piece of paper of some kind. Pauwels pushed forward.

"What is it, Doctor?"

Hendriks made no reply.

"You have found something important—eh?"

This time Dr. Hendriks nodded and came towards us with the paper in his hand. When he came near enough, he held it out to us. It was comprised of a rather unusual combination. A visiting-card, pinned to a photograph of a man that had been cut, obviously, from the columns of an English newspaper. Pauwels and I looked over Dr. Hendriks's shoulder. Although the card and the newspaper-cutting were pinned together, I think that both the sergeant and I looked at the visiting-card first. Anyhow, I know that I did, and I'm moderately certain that Pauwels followed suit. This is what I read on the card:

LISLE MALFROY,
Barrister-at-law,
19, Remenham Court, S.W.

The photograph had the same name below it, with this addition of description in brackets—"the young barrister who was tried yesterday, for the second time, in respect of the murders of William Waller and Lucy Waller, his uncle and aunt, in the case that has come to be popularly known as the 'Purley Poisoning Mystery.' As on the previous occasion, the jury failed to agree upon a verdict and, in consequence of this second failure, it is understood that the Crown has decided to enter a *nolle prosequi*. Lisle Malfroy was defended at each trial by Sir Gervaise Ackland, K.C."

I remembered the case instantly and told the others so. I suppose that I should be uncontradicted if I said that ninety per cent, of the population of England considered Lisle Malfroy to be an exceptionally lucky man to have escaped the gallows. But the prosecution had been unable to shake the evidence of Isabel Waller, the younger daughter of the two people believed to have been poisoned, and cousin of the accused. Her statement, unshaken after a relentless cross-examination by Sir Hubert Kortright of nearly two hours in length, that she herself had partaken of the contents of a certain bottle of sherry, turned the scale in favour of Malfroy, and the jury, in consequence, had failed to agree. The second trial, as the paragraph stated, concluded with a similar result, and Lisle Malfroy now walked the streets a free man. Though what on earth this English poisoning case had to do with the house of Mother Rasmussen in Antwerp, and the murder of Rawlinson . . . At that moment I jerked my wayward thoughts to a standstill and tried desperately hard to achieve intelligence. I suppose that it was the name "Rawlinson" that brought about this condition. I remembered Rawlinson's theory of the Matthias League, his general ideas about de Verviac, and, somehow or other, when those reminiscences came to me, the presence of Malfroy *dans cette galère* seemed to be by no means so fantastic after all! On the other hand, it dovetailed into the pattern, I thought, exceedingly well.

CHAPTER XIII

IN THE NEXT ROOM

(Anthony L. Bathurst's narrative continued)

THERE was one thing, however, that I still noticed. Sergeant Pauwels appeared to have paid no attention to the spoon on the mantelpiece. He gave a further quick glance round the room, thrust the Malfroy paper, with card attached, into his pocket, and addressed himself to Dr. Hendriks.

"There is just one more thing I want to do, Doctor, before I leave here—and that's to have a look in the other room, the front one. For I tell you, Dr. Hendriks, and you too, Mr. Bathurst, that I am far from satisfied about these rooms. So far, I can claim that my suspicions have been more than justified. There is nothing clear about the case at all, as I see it. This is no ordinary murder. I am sure of that. We are in conflict with dark forces."

"Exactly, Sergeant," I returned. "I appreciate all that you say, believe me. None better, Now, what about this other room? I'm with you to this extent—there's nothing to be gained by wasting time."

With a magnificently dramatic gesture, intended doubtless to mean that the doctor and I should follow him, Sergeant Pauwels led the way into the front room—the room, that is to say, that looked on to the Rue du Sacré Coeur. This time, the sergeant assumed my mantle, groped for the matches and lit the gas-jet. Immediately he had done so, a cry of amazement burst from his lips. Sergeant Pauwels had scored again! From the doorway, Dr. Hendriks and I rushed towards him. As in the other room, the sergeant pointed to the floor. The plain wooden table, positioned originally, no doubt, in the middle of the room, was overturned and the drab red cloth that had formerly been its humble decoration had fallen in a dragged sort of heap on something that lay huddled and helpless under the table itself. Pauwels moved quickly towards the scene and pulled away the faded red covering from the top of this grotesque heap.

There, revealed now in its entirety, lay the body of a man . . . face downwards . . . his two arms flung out in front of him. Dr. Hendriks turned the body over, lifted the head, put a hand on the forehead and turned to speak quickly to Pauwels and me.

"Thank God," he said, "he's not dead. Only unconscious. I was afraid! I didn't like the look of him as he lay there. He's been stunned, I think, by a blow from something. Yes—he's been hit on the head."

The doctor felt the man's head again. "Yes—yes. Here is the blow—as I thought. A nasty swelling—that's caused the trouble. Get hold of that old woman again, Pauwels. She may have something in the house here that I can give him to bring him—"

I interrupted the worthy doctor. I had spotted the first signs of returning consciousness already flickering on the man's face.

"He's coming to, I think, Doctor. Your moving him from underneath that heap has probably done the trick."

Hendriks nodded his acquiescence excitedly. He was chafing the man's hands now, although I don't believe that he was properly aware of what he was doing.

"Yes, Mr. Bathurst. He's pulling round. Perhaps he'll be able to tell us the truth of to-night's work . . . maybe he saw more than you did."

I found myself looking curiously at this man upon whom we had come in such an extraordinary fashion. That he was English, I felt moderately certain, and, although I couldn't reconcile it with my intelligence and with the facts as I knew them, the thought flashed through my mind that he might even be the missing man Maturin. He was certainly of the type and about the age, I should have said . . . still, conjectures of this kind were absurd when, with any luck, definite facts should be obtainable within a comparatively brief space. I will describe this man as I saw him when I looked upon him for the first time. He was tall, slim, and dark . . . "good school" written all over him. As I was forming these opinions, the man whom I was mentally dissecting, gave a little start and looked wonderingly up at us as we grouped ourselves round him. The first remark came from him.

"Where am I?" he asked in English . . . "and who are you . . . what's the big idea?"

"I'm a doctor," replied Hendriks. "You are in a house in the Rue du Sacré Coeur, in Antwerp. You have been hurt in some way. Your head has been struck and you have been unconscious for some time. Don't worry—you are better now. Try to think clearly so that you may be able to tell us what happened to you."

The man grinned at us in a feeble attempt to put some humour into the situation. Then he held his hand to his head—rather ruefully.

"D'ye know—I feel like the morning after the night before. There's a horrible dark brown taste in my mouth—reminds me of the bottom of the parrot's cage."

Sergeant Pauwels and I restored the table and table-cloth to their normal places in the schemes of utility and ornamentation. Dr. Hendriks assisted the man to rise and seated him in the one chair of which the room boasted.

"It's the blow that you've had, that makes you feel like that. Try to think, now, so that you can tell us what happened to you," he said again.

"Ask me something easier and I'll answer you as sweetly as Mary's little lamb," came the reply. There was no mistaking the accent. I had been accurate in my judgment of him.

"D'ye know," he continued, "I wish I could tell you. Seems pretty daft of me, I know, but there you are."

He rubbed his head again and shrugged his shoulders. A note in his tone caught and held my ear. Apart from the academic qualities that go to make up speech technique, such as clear enunciation, careful articulation, and pleasantly controlled modulation, there are, too, I always think, qualities which the voice should have that may be described as non-academic. Clarity of voice, resonance of vowel tone, strength, and sincerity or earnestness. These four qualities that I have just enumerated are fair examples of what I mean . . . and as I listened to this rather charming young man seated on the chair where Hendriks had placed him, my ear detected a distinct trace of insincerity. I formed the opinion, there and then, that he was finessing, playing for time, as it were, with one eye on the ball and the other on the hands of the pavilion clock crawling towards the luncheon interval. Finessing for what, I asked myself? Where did he fit into the scheme of things? Was he preparing a story for us, hanging out the time, or waiting for something to happen or somebody to appear? I was inclined to pin my faith to the first idea—especially when he went on to tell us something else. Pauwels had entered the breach with a question.

"Perhaps you will first tell us who you are and how you come to be in this house—eh? After that, you can tell us the rest."

The reply to the sergeant came in clipped English.

"Oh—that part's too easy. If it's sufficiently important—my name's Fawcett—Adrian Fawcett. I'm on holiday—two friends and I have been touring Belgium. We came into Antwerp three days ago—we're at the Hôtel de Lutèce. Not a bad show—taking it all round—if any of you are looking out for a decent place. They don't do you at all badly there—believe me! Grub damn' good— plenty of it and quite good variety." He paused, and, because he paused, I pressed him instantly. I didn't wish him to have too much time for either thought-transition or concentration.

"Well, Mr. Fawcett, go on."

He regarded me with surprise in his eyes: "I say—are you English? Good Lord! Well, I'm—fancy that now."

I nodded—but declined to spare him beyond that.

"Well?" I repeated. "I could bear to hear a considerable amount more."

"More? Oh—yes. Now where was I? Oh—I remember—I was telling you people where we were staying."

I was absolutely positive now that friend Fawcett was play- ing for time . . . "gagging," almost, if I may use the Thespian term legitimately in this connection. Giving us "blah."

"Well?" said Pauwels rather impatiently—"how do you come to be here? That's what we want you to tell us."

"Don't rush me—I was coming to that," returned Fawcett nervously. "I had spent part of the evening in a sort of caba- ret affair. Don't know its name or the exact whereabouts of the show . . . but there's a brilliant red light outside just where you go in . . . enough to show the holes in your socks or the overdraft on your current account . . . but I expect you people know the place I mean all right. Well, after the show had finished—it was a septic business all through—I had three or four beers and then made my way back to my hotel. I didn't feel very much inclined to turn in, so I hung about in the lounge . . . until it was latish

. . . until past twelve I suppose it must have been. Then something happened. Damned extraordinary it was, too, when you come to think of it."

Yet again he paused.

"What was this that happened?" Pauwels was in this time.

"Well, a fellow rolled into the smoke-room—a tall rough-looking chap—complete stranger to me—and pushed a note into my hand. When I read it, you could have waved me to rest with a feather! 'Pon my honour, I nearly took the K.O. over it. Cutting a long story short, the note asked me to come here at once . . . to help somebody 'very dear to me.' It was signed—er—'One who wishes you well.'"

Fawcett looked at us. From one to the other of us . . . individually almost, with deliberation and intention aforethought. I was certain that he was weighing us up to see how we were accepting this story.

"This note of which you speak—was it written in English?" I asked.

"Of course," he replied, eyes wide open and brimming with innocence and guilelessness.

"Please show me the note," I said to him.

Pauwels nodded vigorous approval of my request.

"Yes. Where is the note?"

"I burnt it," Fawcett answered.

"Why?"

"It told me to. Made a frightfully strong point of it. Said it would be dangerous for me to keep it."

His replies were ready and rapid.

"Did the note give the full address of this house?" I asked him this question quite nonchalantly. Reply not so spontaneous this time.

"Er—no. It said the house with the white walls in the—er—Rue du Sacré Coeur."

"I see. You were able to find it from the description—eh?"

"Yes. It wasn't too difficult. Amongst my other bumps"—Fawcett rubbed his head whimsically—"I happen to have the bump of locality. Ever gone in for phrenology? Damned interesting stuff. I remember once when I was—"

"Never mind that now. Tell us what happened when you got here. It's obvious that you decided to come. First of all—how did you manage to get in?"

"Rapped on the door. An old woman let me in. Then she got huffy, walked away from me and left me more or less at a loose end. Can't remember when a lady treated me like it before. I was alone! High and dry in the passage. More dry than high, though. So, without thinking very much about it, I crawled in here. Into this room."

He glanced round. Not apprehensively, I thought, but *warily*. As though he were sizing up the general situation. Taking stock. Assessing possibilities . . . probabilities perhaps. Generally putting himself, on his guard.

"It was hellishly dark in here," he proceeded, "so I thought I would see about getting a light. It all seemed so damned strange . . . the place so utterly deserted, save for the old girl who had let me in. I began to ask myself questions. Perhaps I ought to have asked them of myself before. Where was this person, so 'dear to me,' who needed help? Had I been enticed into something uncommonly like a trap? I began to feel horribly uncomfortable, and, after a few moments of self-communion, I wondered if it would be a sound policy on my part after all to get the jolly old lights going. There might be a certain safety, I argued, in darkness."

Yet again, he paused in his narrative. We waited for him— each one of us silent. There was a curious expression on the face of Hendriks.

"This is the part of my yarn where I begin to get a bit muzzy. Let me see what I can remember—*definitely* remember. I was there, I think. Standing just where the table is."

He pointed to the middle of the room. "And I was walking towards the door. Yes—I can remember doing that. But that's almost the lot, gentlemen. The sum total of my active reminiscence. As I was proceeding, gracefully, and with my usual distinction, towards the door, something fell on me, shall we say Huge, heavy, horrible. I had an idea at the time that it was the leaning Tower of Pisa—that it had leaned over a trifle too far. The next thing that I can remember is coming to and the great big bunch of you standing in front of me. Suppose I must consider myself lucky—eh?"

He grinned again.

"Certainly not unlucky, Mr. Fawcett," contributed Hendriks. "All you got was a bang on the head."

"Bringing your story down to plain facts," I supplemented, "you were assaulted by somebody—that's your meaning, isn't it, Mr. Fawcett?"

He nodded. "You're certainly the bright-eyed boy of this outfit. You're arrived."

"By a man—I take it?"

"Call it a 'man-mountain' and you'll be a trifle nearer to the truth. Carnera—if you like."

Pauwels began to show signs of annoyance at the fellow's flippancy. "You are not aware, then, Mr. Fawcett—I'm judging chiefly by your manner—that a murder has been committed in this house this evening?"

Fawcett's jaw dropped. It struck me at once that his consternation was absolutely sincere.

"Good Lord, no! You don't say so—what? Who's been bumped off?"

The sergeant supplied the details. "Inspector Rawlinson, an English detective from New Scotland Yard, has been shot through the head. What do you know about that, Mr. Fawcett? Anything?"

"I? Nothing whatever. How should I?" He looked round at us. "Believe me—it's the truth. I've told you all that I know."

One has to come to quick decisions sometimes, and that was the case with me now. I had to make up my mind whether this man Fawcett's story was true, false, or even true in parts. I came to the conclusion that most of it was untrue; that if I challenged it strongly enough at its weakest links, I might be enabled to break the chain and come upon something tremendously valuable. So I set about the task immediately.

"There's something about which I am not quite clear," I said. "When you received this romantic message, Mr. Fawcett, calling you to the assistance of somebody who was very dear to you, whom did you imagine you were about to help?"

Fawcett shook his head. "Hadn't the foggiest—and that's a fact. Not an earthly! It's no good saying I had."

I didn't let him get away with that, however. "But surely you considered that matter? I'm certain that I should have done had I been in your position."

Fawcett wriggled. "I tell you that I couldn't think of anybody in particular. It's no good saying that I could. That's the only answer that I can give you."

"I see. You could think of nobody. Then I'll ask you another question. Did you stop to consider who could have sent you the appeal? Who was this altruistic person who wished you well?"

"No. What was the good? *I* had no idea—and, as it was no good scratching my brains in what must almost certainly be a futile business, I accepted the situation. Put it like that. I had no option. There it was. I've been duped, no doubt, but it's easy to be wise after the event. It's like finding winners after you know the result."

He gave me a sidelong glance.

"The writing of the note was unfamiliar, of course?"

"Oh—absolutely."

Then I bethought myself of another line of attack. "Did you mention it to either of your companions?"

"Mention what?"

"The fact that you had received this strange message?"

There was undoubted hesitation now. Several seconds elapsed before Fawcett replied.

"No," he said shortly. "I didn't."

"Why not?"

"Why should I? We aren't children in uniform. We don't crawl about holding each other's hands. Why should I bother men with my private moans just because I happen to be spending a holiday with them? Good Lord man, have a heart."

It didn't sound convincing to me, but for the time being I accepted it. I judged that to do so would be the best policy.

"Did either of them see this man, of whom you speak, hand you the note?"

Fawcett shook his head. "No."

"Are you certain of that?"

"Of course. But what's the odds, anyway? Is it frightfully important?"

I thought the time was mature for a change of front on my part. "There is just this point of view, Mr. Fawcett, which we can't possibly overlook. Everybody's evidence, and that obviously includes your own, will of a necessity have to be sifted pretty thoroughly. After all, the main facts stand out clearly. A man has been murdered in this house. An English detective, in the execution of his duty. No stone will be left unturned to trace his murderer and bring him to justice. You know that as well as I do! The law does not forgive the murderer. Any corroboration of your statements that might have been forthcoming would have had a tremendous value."

Fawcett's face twitched. My words had affected him. I had hit home.

But he replied stubbornly. "Neither of my friends saw me receive the letter. I am certain of that. They had gone to bed."

He sounded irritated and sullen.

"They had gone to bed—but you elected to stay up?"

"Yes."

"That settles the matter, then, Mr. Fawcett. You are prepared to assert that they had gone to bed and you had stayed up."

"That's pretty obvious. You aren't a super Sherlock to think of that."

"No," I said reflectively. "I am aware of that. The only thing is that your statement set me thinking. That chance messenger was rather lucky to find the one man he was seeking—the time was after midnight, remember. You didn't by any chance stay up purposely, did you?"

"I told you that I didn't. It was just a stroke of luck—that's all."

"You will, of course, let us have the names of the two gentlemen who are staying with you at the Hôtel de Lutèce?"

"Certainly—though I fail to see what good that will do you. I've told you that they know nothing about the affair. Their names are Dennis Hilleary and Lance Maturin."

He appeared to become impatient. "Seems to me that I'm being handed the dirty end."

But my senses had tautened at the latter name, and Sergeant Pauwels, too, was unable to restrain a gasp of satisfaction—or astonishment—I'm not sure which.

I looked Adrian Fawcett straight between the eyes.

I resolved to test him.

"That's rather extraordinary. That second name! Because Lance Maturin is the name of the diplomatist who has been missing for some little time. The affair has been kept secret—officially—but I can assure you that it is so."

To my amazement Fawcett shook his head vaguely. "That's a new one on me," he replied. "But you seem to know a hell of a lot about most things, so I'll take your word on it, big boy. Don't look in my direction for contradiction. But if Lance Maturin's a diplomatist, you can put me down as next year's Queen of the May. Mother will be pleased! I never could get up in the morning. I simply love to read in bed."

CHAPTER XIV
WE LEARN OF RAWLINSON
(From the MSS. of Lance Maturin)

WHEN Philippa fainted, I was at a complete loss, for the moment, as to what to do. Luckily, the newspaper chap, who had unwittingly caused the trouble, had his back to us when she slid from the seat, and there was no other person near. As I looked at her prostrate form, for the life of me I didn't know what would be the best for me to do. There might be people coming along at any moment, and the last thing that I desired to do was to attract attention. Especially in the further light of what we knew now.

I had no water to give her; to obtain any meant that I must leave her there on the grass. I thought hard, and out of my quandary I achieved this determination. I would trust to luck and wait for her to return to consciousness. She was in the open air. She was young, and, I should say, judging from all external appearances and signs, healthy in her youth. So I did nothing active. I just waited for her to come round. I was soon rewarded by the signs of animation coming back to that still form that lay in front of me. Gradually the deathly whiteness passed and the normal colour began to return.

When she was fit enough, I helped her to the seat again, at my side. And as I put my arm round her to support her I knew beyond any doubting that I loved her. For I felt that she *wanted* me . . . that she had called to me because she wanted me . . . that she still wanted me . . . that there was yet urgent need for me to serve her. Since I had been turned down by Dorothy and another had reigned in my stead, I had not known what it was to be wanted. . . . which is worse, I think, than death. Because, from a vital vivid creature, you are turned into a living corpse. Love is often termed reflex self-love, I know, or even a convenient peg upon which to hang human idolatry, but is it vanity alone that makes a decent man or woman eager to be loved? Anyone who hasn't felt the stark terror of the realisation that he or she is unloved, where once love has been, may be counted as thrice blessed. It has always seemed to me, and I shall think so until the end of the chapter, that unless one is *wanted*, Life's a blank. One can't keep one's head up . . . or it's damned hard to, at any rate, and the inferiority complex is soon scratching and whining at the door of one's manhood. I stroked the silky hair of my companion and my action seemed to steady her. She turned to me with a little smile.

"Forgive me for being so foolish. It was utterly stupid of me to go through all that we've been through and then to give way over a tiny thing like that."

I nodded. "It's easily explained. You were over-wrought. You had just reached the limit of your endurance. That's the reason why so many people break down . . . something suddenly gives way . . . snaps in the brain. After all, the main fact couldn't have come to you as such a tremendous surprise . . . you knew that somebody had been killed . . . even though you didn't know that it was an English detective. I don't see that makes much difference, myself."

She looked at me with curious interest as though she were trying to probe me for something.

"It was silly of me, Mr. Maturin, I know . . . I promise that I won't offend again."

Her first use of my name, with the formality of its address, jarred me. After our night of common peril it occurred to me that she was establishing a barrier between us, while every part of me was fiercely demanding the intimacies.

"For Heaven's sake, don't call me that," I said impatiently. "It sounds so reserved and—er—stand-offish—so frightfully English. We're comrades. You asked me to call you Philippa. Please return the compliment. Call me Lance."

She made no answer. I continued therefore.

"Extraordinary though it may seem—all my friends do."

She put her hand on my arm and looked me straight in the eyes. "Forgive me—but I can't do that. Please don't ask me to explain. I *can't* explain—and you wouldn't understand."

As she spoke, tear-wet eyes fluttered at me and, although I felt a sense of hurt, I could see gratitude shining at the back of them.

"You're rather a dear, you know," she whispered.

The Syro-Phoenician woman spoke of the crumbs that were the heritage of the dogs, after they had fallen from the children's table . . . it seemed to me that a crumb from an alien store had been flung to me. I was nettled and I was humiliated. So, as usual with me, when seeking to evade a direct conflict of conversation, I sought more practical issues.

"We won't discuss those things now. There are other matters that you and I must settle before we waste any more time. Plans and so on. That newspaper chap's coming back. Along this path, too. I'm going to buy a paper off him. It won't hurt us to know what they think they know at the other end. That knowledge,

Philippa, looks like being infinitely precious to us before the day's out."

The newspaper seller reached us again. I beckoned to him, as casually as I could, and bought a copy of his paper. Until the fellow had got well away from us, I showed no haste to examine the columns of the paper. When the coast looked clear, however, Philippa and I sought eagerly for the information that we desired. We didn't have very far to look. The column of our search hit our intelligence sharply, directly we opened the paper. Here follows what we read:

MURDER IN ANTWERP LODGING-HOUSE
STRANGE AFFAIR TAKES PLACE AFTER MIDNIGHT

Chief-Inspector Henry Rawlinson of the C.I.D. New Scotland Yard, London, who has been carrying out special investigations in Belgium, was shot dead in the early hours of this morning at an Antwerp lodging-house situated in the Rue du Sacré Coeur. The place in question is kept by a woman known as Victorine Rasmussen. So far, there is little clue to the identity of the assassin, but the police authorities are desirous of getting into touch with the young *danseuse* known under the sobriquet of "Philippa," who, it is believed, lodged with the woman Rasmussen and left the house in rather unusual circumstances shortly after the murder is known to have been committed.

Appended was a short, and, to my mind, utterly unworthy, personal description of Philippa Castleton. Of any man, supposed to be in her company, there wasn't the slightest mention or suggestion. After secretly congratulating myself on the fact, I began to wonder why this thing should be. I concluded at length that Mère Rasmussen had realised the value of the tongue that is still, and for that reason the police authorities, as yet, knew nothing of my personal contact with the affair. I used special arguments to convince myself of this. I argued that Mother Rasmussen (with the exception of de Verviac, of course) was the only living person who knew of my entry into the house and that she, lacking nothing on the score of cunning, had remained tight-lipped with regard to it.

Subsequent events, however, were destined to prove how hopelessly unsound my conjectures were.

I glanced at the girl at my side.

"They're looking for you, Philippa," I said to her quietly, "but apparently not for me. So, in a way, we're 'one up' on them. And that's one better off than I thought we were."

"I'm not so sure," she said with a wistful seriousness; "it may be a trap. They may be withholding certain facts deliberately—in the hope of catching us. The police often publish wrong things in newspapers in order to put criminals off their guard."

"We're not criminals," I replied.

"No—but the police may think that we are. Probably do, I expect, if the truth be known."

I realised that there was sound sense in what she said, and once again began to consider our personal problem.

"Look here, Philippa," I eventually said to her. "It's no good swopping horses while we're crossing the stream. I'm going through with the plan that I proposed first of all. I'm going back to Antwerp somehow, and I'm going to get away by this evening's boat. It's very much like putting our joint heads into the lion's mouth, I know, but in my opinion it's the very last thing that will be expected of us, which is always pretty sound policy. *Toujours l'audace!*"

She became critical. "I'll tell you what I don't like about it," she said—"it means us going to the stations again. Both here and at Antwerp. Have you thought of that? They're certain to be watching for me at all the railway stations."

There was no gainsaying the truth of this last statement, and I fell again to pondering. Suddenly I had a brain wave. Perhaps that's saying too much—but you know what I mean—I had the next best thing to one.

"Half a jiffy," I said, "I believe I've thought of something that might turn out in the end to be a sound stunt. Look here. I remember seeing something advertised about it in Antwerp

On the hoardings. Now what the blazes was the name of the beastly place?"

I closed my eyes and thought hard. Understanding came to me and the reminiscence tor which I had groped came floating back to me.

"I know," I cried—"the name of the place is Laeken. There are the steamers that ply between Laeken and Antwerp. On the Canal Maritime. They go through—or rather past—Vilvorde. See what I'm getting at? That wouldn't be the worst of ideas, would it, if we could bring it off?"

Philippa was smiling at me—there was an indulgence about that smile—and by a seemingly irresistible impulse we looked into each other's eyes. It seemed, too, to me, hungry as I was for signs and portents, that the look lingered and was loth to end. Then she dropped her lids and began to speak to me—very quietly—but with a definite suggestion and determination. She looked pale and harassed, but there was still tons of pluck in her, and I rejoiced thereat. As she spoke, she caught at my hand.

"Oh—but you are right. I know that steamer. I have seen it many a time on its way along the canal. Let me think now! Laeken would be about three miles from here. We can get there easily by tram. I know where to go for the tram, too. It starts from the Place Charles-Rogier."

"Laeken it is, then," I returned with bold assurance, "and I don't see why we shouldn't board that friendly tram as soon as ever we can get to it. Our motto shall be 'Do it now.' Come on, you vile miscreant that flies from justice—to the tram!"

I held out my other hand to her.

"There's one thing," I continued—"if they take you, they'll take me too. We're travelling in double harness you know . . . even though that harness is destined to be used but once."

I glanced at her face, crowned with that clustering hair, to see how she would react to the phrase. Her lips were quivering and her eye lashes were fringed with tears. She put her hand to her breast . . . held it there and brought it away again. Then she gave me a tiny-linked gold chain; pendent to the chain was a dainty Crucifix.

"You have already risked your life for me," she whispered, "and you are still in danger because of me. I can never forget that. Will you take this?"

My fingers closed over the gift.

"Keep it until you find a girl to love and who loves you. She will give you something, doubtless, in token of that love. Then you won't need this any longer. Till then, keep it in memory of my thanks and gratitude to you. Afterwards—do with it as you will."

I shook my head. It was on the tip of my tongue to ask her more of the man for whom she had waited. Of the man who had failed to come. But the look in her eyes dissuaded me.

"I shall find no other girl," I said.

She moved her head in disagreement.

"You don't know that. Wait until your bitterness has passed and you are your real self again. You will think differently."

Again I shook my head.

For she had failed to understand. My bitterness *had* passed. I *was* my true self again if only for the fact that the glory of Philippa herself had come to me!

Chapter XV
RUN TO EARTH
(Lance Maturin's story continued)

AFTER that, we wasted no more time and took no more chances where we were. We caught the tram from the Place Charles-Rogier, as Philippa had suggested, and rode through to Laeken, passing the docks and the famous ship canal on our way. At Laeken we boarded the steamer that took us back, on the canal through Vilvorde, as I had said, to Antwerp.

On the steamer we encountered nothing in the way of untoward incident, and gradually, as we came near to our starting point again, I found my spirits rising. Candidly, I considered now that we had more chance of breaking through the cordon than I had in the first place anticipated. For these reasons: the newspaper that we had seen contained no description of the *clothes* that Philippa was wearing. This was important, for the points of merely personal descriptions are extraordinarily difficult for the casual observer to pick out when he gazes on humanity more or less *en masse*. "Fair hair," "blue eyes," "fresh complexion," and all the other stock-in-trade terms are so vaguely general that when the mind receives them it very often fails to record anything at all tangible or definite.

It was on these vague, nebulous impressions of other people that I banked for safety; had the paper contained a detailed description of what Philippa was wearing, I should have thought very differently. We had some grub on board our steamer towards midday, had a wash and brush-up—badly wanted, this, by each of us—tea in the afternoon—and floated into Antwerp—alongside the quay—with ample time in which to catch our Harwich boat. I remembered that it left for England some time early in the evening, and inquiries elicited the fact that the actual time of departure was ten minutes past seven. A "British India" boat was leaving for Hull an hour later, but I decided to get away at the earliest possible moment. Added to which, Harwich was far more convenient for me than Hull. I had arranged with Philippa that neither of us should leave the quay-side during this period of waiting, and the plan worked satisfactorily.

To my relief, Philippa accepted, without the slightest demur, the situation as I outlined it to her. She was prepared to come to England with me if we could get there; when we got there, other matters could be discussed, and perhaps settled, between us. Also, unduly optimistic though it may appear to have been, I drew sweet comfort into my soul from the fact of her acquiescence. I deduced from it that she had determined to wait no longer for the lover who had failed to keep his tryst with her. The lover whom I knew not, whom I had never seen, but whom I had begun to hate with that bitter jealousy that is the wedge that a woman drives between man and man. But who amongst us can tell the workings of a woman's mind . . . was not Irene Adler too clever for Sherlock Holmes, the master of deduction? My lady's face may appear hard and unyielding and her eyes unrelenting, when her heart—if we but knew—is tenderest; and, contrariwise, she may whisper tenderness to us when treachery should be the truest translation of her trickster tongue.

For these reasons, therefore, conjectures and deductions from the ways and the demeanour of a maid which the cleverest of men may make are builded on shifting sand, and, on that account, of nothing worth. I thought over these things an hour or so afterwards, as I paced the deck of the *Antwerp*—Philippa, in true discretion, having sought the seclusion that the cabin granted.

The weather was set fair, and our eleven hours' crossing, I felt certain, was going to be as placid as it ever had been. After we had been going for a couple of hours, the passengers on deck thinned in numbers considerably, and my attention began to be drawn to a tall, clean-shaven man—obviously English— who paced the deck in front of me and whom I found looking over the side, near to me, on more than one occasion. He was a man of such distinction of bearing and undoubted personality that I found myself watching him and wondering who he was—against my inclination almost, at times. Like the fatuous, complacently self-satisfied ass that I was, however, I entirely failed to assess him at his rightful standard. Even when I moved away to go below, to turn in for the night, the fact that his eyes seemed to be on me with more than ordinary interest made no serious impression on me. This may sound to be an extraordinary confession for a man who was seeking to evade the hand of authority—but there it is—it's the truth—beyond which I, or any other man who travels the path of sincerity, am unable to go. I did not *connect* this man with the police or anything like that— and that's all there is to it.

We were a matter of eighteen minutes late on our one hundred and thirty-five miles' journey, making Parkeston Quay in a slight mist, but eventually set our escaping feet on the landing-stage at twelve minutes to seven. My first job on landing was to send a telegram to my people. As I put Philippa into a taxi, I was but mildly interested to see that my tall stranger of the night before walked towards a big car just behind.

My father's place is at Trueloves, a few miles the London side of Colchester, and I told the taxi chap to get a move on and dump me there as soon as he knew how. For one thing I wanted the wound in my shoulder dressed properly, and, for another, I wanted a place that, at any rate, would *seem* like sanctuary. He was a cool and efficient customer—the driver chap—and we slid away from Parkeston Quay under his most able pilotage, like a well-greased arrow. When we reached Trueloves, I knew that the mater would behave like the angel that she always is and always has been. I made but one arrangement with Philippa. I was determined, for the time being at least, to preserve the secret of her real identity. It seemed to me that this was vital. To disclose who she was, at once, would mean inevitable sensation and all the consequences of publicity that would attach themselves thereto. When I told her of my view she cordially agreed with me.

"What shall I call you?" I asked her playfully. "Is there any name you particularly fancy?"

She smiled and her upper lip curled in the way that was always so delightfully her own. Perhaps "crinkled" would be a truer word than "curled." Although she didn't lisp, that lip, after speech, always gave you the impression that she very easily might have done.

She pointed out of the window. "There," she said. "Look over there. There's a windmill. We might be in Holland. I've always loved them. Introduce me to your people as—Philippa Windmill."

I laughed at the quaint conceit. "Rather a compliment to me, that, isn't it?"

She nodded. "You're quick, aren't you? I thought of that directly I said it. But it's true. Because you've been quixotically kind to me. I don't think anybody could possibly have been kinder."

I glanced at her sideways. "Or as kind, even?" I said the words purposely. I was all eagerness for truth.

She shook her head. "I said 'kinder.'" She caught my fingers and gave them a little squeeze. "We've only discussed what you're going to call me. I'm wondering how you're going to *explain* me. That's a much bigger problem. Have you thought about that?"

I had been expecting this question for some little time, but I affected to evince a tremendous interest in the scenery through which our car was passing. At length I answered her.

"There is one suggestion that I might make. I don't know, though, that it will commend itself to you. As a matter of fact I'm rather afraid that it won't. But it's a good one—and the best, I think, that anybody could make in the circumstances."

"Tell me what you mean. Then I'll let you know what I think about it."

Her eyes—curious and wondering—fascinated me. I chose the words of my answer carefully and deliberately.

"In Antwerp—when our little show started—I was featured as your husband."

I paused.

"Well?" she questioned me.

"Here, in England, let me feature you, just for the time being, of course, as my future wife. Then my people will understand why you have come home with me and very few questions will be asked. Those that are asked won't matter two hoots. Your luggage, for instance, is on the way."

I looked at her, in an attempt to measure the success of my suggestion.

"Well—do you approve of the idea—or otherwise? Put me out of my pain quickly."

She made no answer. Sensing a struggle, I endeavoured to fortify my position.

"The engagement—or, er—understanding—will be a merely superficial one. You can trust me to play the game. Don't forget that I can supply testimonials to that effect. Are you on?"

Her eyes were wide open.

"Testimonials?"

"That's what I said. Testimonials."

"From whom, may I ask?"

I affected surprise. "From you yourself—surely? Have you forgotten, Philippa, so soon? That night, that wondrous night in June?"

She laid a hand on my arm. "I'm sorry. Please don't say any more. But I didn't understand you for the moment. Please forgive me."

I brought her back to realities. "You haven't answered my question yet."

Again she was silent for a time. Then suddenly she seemed to come to a decision.

"Very well, then, I agree. I'll call you Rudolf, though—not by your own name. There are particular reasons why I don't care to do that. Do you mind?"

I knitted my brows. I was puzzled. The source of the allusion eluded me.

"Rudolf?" I queried. "Why Rudolf?"

"Rudolf Rassendyll, who once reigned in Strelsau; he was a very gallant gentlemen, too, if you remember."

She blushed deliciously and I coloured too, I'm afraid, in my embarrassment.

"Thank you, Philippa. That's a bet, then," I answered.

She had an air of trouble.

"What is it now?" I asked.

"Will there have to be—er—public performances?" She was definitely anxious.

The question showed in my eyes. "Public performances?" I echoed.

"Of our affection?"

I understood. "Don't distress yourself on that account," I said rather coldly. "I shall make no demands that by any stretch of imagination could be termed exacting. Even if I did—"

I stopped abruptly.

"Go on," she counted rather imperiously.

"I played up to *you*, when *you* wanted it. I was far from a success, I admit. Still . . ."

She set her lips. "I know. But that was different. Very different. In this case . . ."

"How do you mean?"

She reddened again—exquisitely. "The occasion to which you referred was dreadfully urgent. What you did for me was to save my life. To save something perhaps dearer to me than life. That makes a difference, doesn't it?"

"This is all a piece of the same pattern," I returned, with a kind of sturdy persistence. "I don't know that I'm exactly joy-riding."

Her mood changed suddenly. "Very well, then—partner. Count on me until I withdraw the promise. When things quieten down a bit, I'm going back to Daddy. And I don't know that there'll be any terrific mortality amongst the well-covered veal when *that* happens. Daddy's a dear in his way—but terribly old-fashioned. He's a Bishop, you know. He frowns uncompromisingly on all breaches of the conventions, and I always think that he's getting ready to say, 'Defend, O Lord, this Thy child,' even when I go to a dance."

I looked out of the window again.

"We're getting close to Trueloves," I said. "You'll like my father and you'll love my mother. So keep smiling."

Within a few minutes, the car drew up before the guv'nor's place. I helped Philippa out, paid the taxi-man, and delivered my charming burden into the care of my mother. The preliminaries of the introduction having been effected, and satisfactorily at that, I was just feeling on excellent terms with myself—better than I had felt for some considerable time in fact—when I was destined to receive a distinctly healthy shock. Which was all the more disconcerting to me because it was so entirely unexpected. My father, of all people, was the agent of transmission. He beckoned to me.

"Now you've arrived home, Lance," he said, "I've some news for you. Somebody called here about a quarter of an hour ago— to see you—he was rather surprised, I think, from his manner, not to find you here. Seemed to think that you must be here somewhere and was extremely loth to wait until I assured him to the contrary. Come into the library and have a word with him, will you, Lance?"

Hastily excusing myself to Philippa, and wondering what the hell, I followed the guv'nor into the library, to meet this mysterious stranger, whoever he might turn out to be. To my utter astonishment, the man who rose to greet me was the tall, distinguished-looking person whom I had spotted on the Antwerp boat.

"This is my son, Mr. Bathurst," I heard my father say. "He's just turned up. I told you that he wouldn't be very long. Directly he came in I informed him that you were here and would like to have a chat with him. Lance—this is Mr. Anthony Bathurst."

The tall bloke bowed to me, but, on the whole, I thought his manner was on the distinctly cool side. There seemed to be, and for no reason that I could imagine, something of an "atmosphere" between us, which most certainly didn't emanate from my side.

"I'll leave you two together," said the guv'nor, "and then you can get on with your business."

"It would be as well if you stayed, I think, Mr. Maturin," said the tall bloke quietly, "especially when you hear what my business with your son is."

He turned to me.

"As I expect you heard, my name is Anthony Bathurst." He paused—to go on again almost immediately.

"I returned from Antwerp on the same boat as you yourself."

"God"—I thought—"Antwerp—what's coming next?" But I plucked up courage to take the bull by the horns and intervene somewhat jerkily.

"Yes—I—er—remember noticing you. You kept pretty close to me best part of the time, didn't you? I wondered—rather—why that was."

He grinned, and directly I caught sight of the grin on his face I began to like him a lot better. Funny thing, isn't it, how the slightest touch will cause your heart to warm to a chap?

"That's perfectly true, Mr. Maturin," he said in clear, incisive tones—"but I'll be quite frank with you—I had a good reason." He grinned again. "I wanted to keep in close touch with you so that I might discover where you lived. I was rather keen on knowing your intended destination. You see—I'm interested on one or two matters that appear to have aroused some interest in you. In other words, Mr. Maturin, we're human radii of the same circle."

Where was he getting? I nodded awkwardly and replied—"Oh—I understand. That—er—explains it. Yes—of course."

"I wonder."

"Well, it does in a way, doesn't it? You know what I mean."

Heavens—how lame and utterly futile my words sounded!

Bathurst advanced a pace and came to grips. "I'll make myself perfectly clear, Mr. Maturin. I went to Antwerp originally, on a commission from Scotland Yard. There wasn't a clean-cut issue attached to it, and the farther we got into our little problem, my colleague and I, the more complications we ran across. Those complications were, to say the least of it, extraordinary. In the first place, there was that singular complication of the missing lady."

His eyes played with me now and I began to fear the worst—the worst from my own point of view, I mean, apart from anything to do with Miss Castleton. But hang it all, I decided, he wasn't going to get me down without a scrap, so I took the plunge.

"Oh—yes. I think I see what you mean now, Mr. Bathurst. The missing lady, as you describe her, is here at Trueloves. She is with my mother at the present moment. I—er—escorted her home."

"Miss Philippa . . ." he paused.

The pause was far too significant for me to misunderstand his intention.

"Windmill." I answered, without turning a hair. "Miss Philippa Windmill."

As I spoke, I marvelled at my own composure.

Bathurst eyed me curiously but, to my surprise, let it be said, made no comment on the lady's choice of alias. He returned, instead, to the main issue—still very incisive and definite.

"I will proceed," he said, "to explain further the mission that took me to Antwerp. In the second place, there was your own little trip, Mr. Maturin, and finally, there was an international complication that turned up and worried us a great deal. By 'us' I refer to myself and to my colleague—my late colleague rather—Detective-Inspector Henry Rawlinson of the Criminal Investigation Department, New Scotland Yard. That name, Mr. Maturin, is doubtless familiar to you?" He looked at me searchingly.

The word "Rawlinson" scourged me like the lash of a whip. And, what is more, I was moderately certain that Anthony Bathurst knew it. I felt my father's eyes on me now, beginning to probe me, just as were Bathurst's. I was between two fires with a vengeance. Consider, also, what there was for me to say. To tell the truth meant surrendering the story that so far was the secret of the girl whom I had learned to love, and I was resolved not to betray her until I was forced to the very end of my resources. At the same time, if I were to attempt to protect myself, a certain amount of caution on my part had become absolutely essential. Once again, I determined to put on a bold front and to take the bowling by the scruff of the neck.

"Rawlinson," I said, with a hint of carelessness and a touch of query, "the name *is* familiar! Why—I've got it—it's just come to me—that's the name of the English detective who was shot in an Antwerp lodging-house."

Bathurst became very serious.

"That, Mr. Maturin, is unfortunately only too true. Which brings me to the real object of my visit here. What can you tell me about the murder of Inspector Rawlinson? I ask you in the hope that you will answer me frankly. You understand that you need not answer me unless you choose, of course."

I heard my father gasp in astonishment—or incredulity—one of the two.

"I?" I queried—"I'm afraid I don't understand. How should I be able to tell you anything about it? The sum total of my knowledge in regard to the affair came from a Belgian newspaper that I purchased in Brussels yesterday morning."

In my anxiety to appear absolutely emphatic, I moved rather quickly and sharply, and the pain from the bullet wound in my shoulder hurt me like hell and must have shown in my eyes. I winced—I know—and Anthony Bathurst's glance registered his appreciation of the fact. His tone assumed more confidence than ever.

"In Brussels—did you say?"

"In Brussels," I replied, steadily and without emotion.

There came a gleam in his grey eyes.

"Mr. Maturin," he said. "I have every reason to believe that you were in that lodging-house in Antwerp where Inspector Rawlinson was shot—*when* Inspector Rawlinson was shot. Come, now."

"Absurd," I returned, like the fool that I was . . . but I couldn't for the life of me see, at that moment, how my inquisitor could possibly prove his allegation, and, because of that belief, I possessed a fortitude the quality of which only I can understand.

"Are you prepared to deny, then, Mr. Maturin, that you entered that lodging-house in the Rue du Sacré Coeur, in company with that lady we previously mentioned, Miss Philippa—er—Windmill—at about a quarter past eleven on the night that Rawlinson was murdered?"

"Yes," I said, lying bravely and blindly—"I've never been within a mile of the place. I don't know the source from which you obtained your information—but you have been misled."

"You know where the place is, then?"

"Yes." I paused. "From you own description, naturally. You mentioned the Rue du Sacré Coeur—I know where that is. There's a church at one end of it. As a matter of fact, I've been in Antwerp on a holiday."

He turned, to take up a suitcase that had been placed by the side of an arm-chair. Unfastening the catches, he took something out . . . and I looked at the pyjama-jacket that had been dropped as I had swung out over the abyss when I had escaped with Philippa from Mother Rasmussen's. Even now, faced as I was with this vital piece of evidence, I was unabashed and unafraid. To whomever it had belonged, it had certainly never been mine!

"This doesn't belong to you by any chance, Mr. Maturin?"

"Decidedly not," I answered—"what on earth gave you that ridiculous idea?" I was lofty and disdainful, but, as ever, pride preceded the fall.

"In that case, then," returned Anthony Bathurst gravely, "how do you explain the fact that this jacket bears your name on it?"

He turned down the neck part, with a gesture of exposure, and I fairly goggled in amazement at the tab which I saw sewn in there. For the name on that tab—in the plainest of plain lettering—was "Lancelot Maturin"! I drew a deep breath and foolishly, I supposed, clenched my fists. Into what damnable trap had I been so cunningly lured? Why? And by whom? Then my father came across the room and stood between Bathurst and me.

There was a long period of silence. Not one of us three men moved or spoke a word. The only sound of which I was fully conscious was the ticking of the clock on the mantelpiece.

CHAPTER XVI
FROM THE WATERS OF THE SCHELDT
(Story continued by Lance Maturin)

BUT my blood was up now and my brain hard at work, and eventually there came rejoicing in my heart. For an excellent reason too. For, if Anthony Bathurst had scored over me in the matter of the pyjama-jacket and had definitely put me on the wrong side of the fence, as it were, it was now my turn. The time had arrived for me to score over him, and who is there amongst us big enough to scorn the sweet delight of the equalising goal or of the try that levels matters?

Consider the position as it appeared to me at that identical moment. I had worn the jacket—it is true—but who could prove that fact beyond Philippa Castleton and—very improbably—the dancer, de Verviac? But, against this, the jacket was not mine and never had been, and that is where Mr. Anthony Bathurst had hit a snag. Moreover, the truth had come home to me that the jacket must be my cousin's—most of us Maturins are christened Lancelot, after our ancestor, the famous cavalier of that name who rode single-handed through a detachment of Iron-sides at Marston Moor in 1644.

Although the direct and damning significance of the jacket in relation to Miss Castleton stung me beyond the telling, I realised that I might benefit from it because it afforded me a loophole of escape. So I drew the guv'nor away by the arm, and turned to Bathurst with a smile on my lips.

"I can't explain," I said to him curtly.

"You can't? Or you won't?"

Even then, although the beggar was questioning me and putting me through the mill, as you might say, I never felt that he was the slightest bit inimical or hostile towards me.

"No," I said lightly. "It's not that. I can't explain—because I don't know that that jacket actually *has* my name on it."

Bathurst raised his eyebrows—critical and interrogative.

"I'm sorry, but I'm unable to follow you there, Mr. Maturin. Let me tell you that this pyjama-jacket was found in the street that runs along the back of that Antwerp lodging-house in which Inspector Rawlinson was shot. On the tab in the neck is a name—you've just seen it yourself—that name is Lancelot Maturin. Now you have just returned from Antwerp and your name is Lance-lot Maturin. Also, you have escorted a lady home—to use your own words of a few moments ago—who is known to have lodged for some time in that particular house. And yet, despite this accumulation of evidence, if I understand you aright, you assert that you don't know that this jacket *does* bear your name. Come, Mr. Maturin, you intrigue me, as our lady novelists would write. And, besides intriguing me, you interest me profoundly. Please proceed. I am all ears. You were about to remark . . . ?"

The beggar grinned at me again but in such a matey sort of way that my desire to score off him and get him down grew considerably less frantic. I decided to cast finesse to the winds.

"My name is Lancelot Maturin," I answered him. "You're quite right with regard to that, but I'm more generally known as Lance."

"Rather unconvincing. If I rack my brains thoroughly and systematically I can even recall a 'William' who was usually called 'Bill.' Strange though it may seem. To the precisians, pedants, and purists such a thing is no doubt almost incredible." His tone changed. "What is your real point, Mr. Maturin?"

I fired my shot. I intended it to be his *coup de grâce*. But at that time I was an infant in these matters. I knew not my Bathurst.

"Has it occurred to you," I asked, "that there might be two of us?"

"Candidly, Mr. Maturin, it has. Sorry if I disappoint you, but I've been helped over that—there was a gentleman named Fawcett—you see. Tell me the answer—please. I could bear to hear the fullest of details. They must, I think bring us close to the Diplomatic Service. That must be the path to explanation and understanding. Who's your namesake? Or is it, as I think more likely, a relation?"

His mention of Fawcett's name at this juncture aroused my wildest curiosity, but I let it simmer for the time being, to answer his last question.

"My cousin, Lancelot Maturin, Diplomatic Service—Intelligence. As you so cleverly surmised."

Bathurst shook his head, smiled at the guv'nor and rubbed his hands. I went on with fine carelessness.

"He's always called 'Lancelot.' I'm always called 'Lance.' It distinguishes us a bit, you see."

And as I spoke, I knew why my girl of Antwerp had refused to call me "Lance" . . . and could hear her soft voice calling my cousin "Lancelot."

There was a light in his grey eyes now that startled me. The light of excitement and eagerness.

"What I say pleases you?" I interrogated.

"I wouldn't assert that, Mr. Maturin. Because, to an extent at least, it makes confusion worse confounded. Which is never a matter of pleasure or self-congratulation to an investigator of problems such as the one we have here. But . . ."

He paused and thrust his hands into his pockets.

"But what?"

"I think I do see just a glimmer of light. A tiny shaft, perhaps—but *light* all the same."

He turned to the guv'nor with that irresistible smile of his.

"I really think that my first duty should be to apologise, Mr. Maturin. I must have appeared to be a little high-handed when I first came in. I seem to have barked up the wrong tree—chased the wrong man. The fact that it was a namesake must be my only reason—I won't say excuse. Am I forgiven?"

It was on the tip of my tongue to tell him the truth there and then, but for Miss Castleton's sake, I determined to hold on until we reached the last ditch. There was no knowing where the truth was going to land us. I hadn't a "down" on Bathurst, and I knew in my heart that I wasn't playing the game by him—but with me, Philippa came first and the rest nowhere. When you love, that's how it should be—in all big things, that is. Lip-service is dead easy—it's only real, unselfish, self-sacrificing service that counts. At least, that's how I see love and the things to do with love.

"Oh—absolutely," I answered him, with an attempt at studied magnanimity. "You aren't to blame. You very naturally drew certain inferences from the facts as they were presented to you. I should have done the same thing had I been in your place."

"Thanks, Mr. Maturin," he said, dryly. "That's very sporting of you and it lets me out. Although I scarcely deserve it. I feel intensely relieved."

It was my turn now for a spot of inquisition, and I seized my chance.

"You said something just now, Mr. Bathurst, that surprised me a little. You said that you had been *helped*—about my cousin Lancelot, I mean. That there had been a gentleman named 'Fawcett.' That was how you put it, I think—relying on my memory?"

Bathurst nodded, and I saw the old man prick up his ears too. He knew Adrian Fawcett.

"Yes," returned Bathurst. "You're quite right. I did mention the name 'Fawcett.'"

He waited for me to come to the point.

"I know a Fawcett," I went on. "Adrian Fawcett, to give him his full name. He was with me in Antwerp. One of my personal party, in fact. We've been knocking round together for weeks. How did you manage to run across him?"

The lines round Bathurst's mouth tightened and deepened. I saw at once that I had said something that, from my point of view, had better have been left unsaid. His reply, when it came, left me in no doubt as to this, whatever.

"Your friend Adrian Fawcett was in Mother Rasmussen's lodging-house on the night that Rawlinson was murdered."

"Never!" I cried incredulously. "What on earth could have taken him there on that night of all nights?"

Bathurst shrugged his shoulders at my outburst. "That isn't all, Mr. Maturin. Your friend Fawcett was found unconscious on the floor of one of the front rooms. Somebody had bumped him one on the head."

My incredulity became superlative.

"Are you absolutely sure of all this that you say? Are you certain that you haven't been given false information? You see—I know Fawcett so well. He's a most inoffensive sort of chap—of the kind that wouldn't—"

Bathurst checked my flow of oratory with a remark that took the wind out of my sails completely and left me becalmed.

"You can take it from me, Mr. Maturin, that what I have just told you about your friend Fawcett is true. The house where Inspector Rawlinson went to his death is situated in the Rue du Sacré Coeur, and it is kept by an old woman named Rasmussen. On the left of the main staircase there are two rooms—one right in the front of the house, the other in the usual position beyond it. On the floor of that front room, beneath an overturned table, an hour or so after Rawlinson was murdered, lay your friend Fawcett—unconscious. As I told you, he had had a blow on the head that had put him out of mess for a time. And the reason why I am so absolutely sure of what I am telling you is that I happened to find Fawcett on that floor myself. Good enough?"

"You didn't?" I gasped incredulously.

He nodded. "I did. With a certain amount of assistance, that is. If you're interested to hear further details, he came back to consciousness shortly after we picked him up."

I was still at a loss, however, for this new and unexpected turn had revolutionised things, as far as I was concerned. So I sought a solution. I asked questions.

"What on earth was Adrian Fawcett doing there?" I asked.

Bathurst looked at me with a significant directness. "I don't know, Mr. Maturin. All I know is what he *said* he was doing there. I'm uncharitable enough to think that the two things were not the same. When he came to his normal senses we questioned him, as you may well imagine, as to what had transpired. His story amounted to this. Late that night he had returned to his hotel—the 'Lutèce,' I think. Yes?"

I nodded corroboration. "That's right."

Bathurst went on. "When he got into the smoke-room, a stranger handed him a note. This note requested him to go to Mother Rasmussen's house to help somebody 'who was very dear to him,' and was signed by 'one who wished him well.' So he rolled up to the Rasmussen lodging-house straightaway, got inside, groped his way into the room where we had found him, and clicked for the bump on his head. There you have Mr. Fawcett's story as he handed it to me just after I found him. Would you care to comment upon it, Mr. Maturin?"

I bit my lip. For I most certainly didn't. Anything but! Through my brain raced perilous thoughts. This was a new tangent that the case had taken. What was the true reason that had taken Adrian Fawcett into that house of Mère Rasmussen? Until I knew that, I must stand by him and say nothing. Why, too, had Anthony Bathurst himself been there? With Rawlinson, who had met murder on the way? That fact alone made me think uncomfortable things. I resolved to play for safety.

"I'm not in a position to comment on it," I stated. "How can I? Obviously, I don't know what happened if I were not there. I left the Hôtel de Lutèce when I—er—received instructions to escort Miss Windmill home and I had no idea what took place after I left. I had little time to spare, as you may guess—which fact alone should explain why I know nothing about Fawcett's movements."

"You mean that you left the hotel in a hurry? You had not been expecting those instructions with regard to Miss Windmill?"

"You've got it," I replied; "exactly as it happened."

He took something from his pocket, and, directly I realised what it was, I prayed that my face would not betray me.

"This revolver, Mr. Maturin," he said quietly—almost ominously it sounded to me—"you've never seen it before, of course?"

I lied bravely—I could almost hear applause from the shades of Ananias and spouse supporting. "Good Lord—no. Where did that come from?"

"From the house where the murder was committed. The bullet that killed Rawlinson *might* have been fired from it. Do you notice the initials on the butt?"

He held the revolver out to me. I took it and examined it.

"L.M.," I said weakly.

"Your own initials, Mr. Maturin. You won't mind my mentioning the fact, will you?"

"No," I returned; "not a bit. I can't blame you. You are in the same position as you were with regard to the pyjama-jacket." I essayed a feeble smile.

"You mean that this revolver also belongs to your cousin? Is that what I am to understand?"

I began to realise now where we were getting, but there was no intelligent retreat for me that I could perceive.

"I don't know that, so I can't say. But I suppose it must. At least, it looks as though it does, doesn't it? You found it near the jacket, I suppose—didn't you?"

He didn't answer at first but looked at me piercingly. When the inevitable question came, the nature of it surprised me.

"When did you last see your cousin, Mr. Maturin?"

This was a nasty one—for on my reply hung much. I compromised with myself. I didn't want to admit certain things that affected Philippa. I was determined not to—until the need became absolutely imperative, and I kept that resolve steadfastly in front of me.

"I last saw my cousin," I answered slowly, "some few days before I left for my Continental holiday."

I glanced at the guv'nor to see how he took my reply, but his face was impassive. He knew that what I was saying was true, and it gave me confidence and assurance to know that he knew it. What pleased me, too, about him was the fact that he didn't jump in spontaneously to corroborate my statement. Time enough for that when it became definitely necessary; until then, his son's word was unimpeachable. My soul rose to him! Jolly well played, guv'nor!

"That would be how long ago?" queried Anthony Bathurst.

"Three months—almost," I answered. Then I made a rapid mental calculation and corrected myself. "Over three months. Just a few days over to be exact. Sorry I was wrong before—but I don't suppose it's terribly important."

I saw Bathurst rub his chin. There was doubt on his face—unmistakable doubt. It was there for everybody to read and see. After glancing round the room he turned to my father with a curiously charming gesture.

"May I use your 'phone, Mr. Maturin? I should be tremendously obliged. You see—your son's story has made a great difference to me. To everything. The case that I had begun to build up has toppled over somewhat ingloriously. I shall have to reconstruct most of my ideas."

The last sentence was almost whispered.

"With pleasure, Mr. Bathurst," answered my father. "Come with me at once. I'll show you where the 'phone is."

The two of them went out together. I wasn't left alone for long. The guvnor was back almost immediately. Once again I was grateful for the fact that he asked no questions of me. I knew that he must be desperately uneasy about the whole affair, but out of sympathy for me, and with a delicate sense of the fitness of things, he conquered both his curiosity and his impatience. For the space of about five minutes, I suppose, my father and I sat in the library there at Trueloves and looked at each other . . . tight-lipped and wondering.

Suddenly the door opened, to re-admit Anthony Bathurst. Directly I looked at him, I realised that something vital had happened. By that, I mean to convey that I knew that his outlook on the case generally had changed again since he had spoken on the telephone.

"You will pardon me for a moment, gentlemen, please," he said quietly. Seating himself at the table, he took a small book from his pocket and proceeded to make some entries in it. From the position where I was sitting, the book looked to me like one of those New Year inflictions—a diary. He closed the book and replaced his fountain-pen. Then he rose from his seat at the table and walked to the fireplace. He stood there—with his back towards us—for an appreciable time. Then he turned and addressed himself to my father. His words seemed to come to me as the incidents of a dream come to me . . . from a great distance away. I listened spellbound. The operation of hearing them seemed to detach me from everything else in the room and to do with the room. I seemed to be separated from everything else in the world.

"Mr. Maturin," he said gravely, "I have bad news for you."

The guv'nor lifted his head. All his old courage showed in the movement. God knows the nature of the blow that he anticipated was coming to him, but I knew very well that he feared for me.

"Well, Mr. Bathurst," he returned quietly, "let me hear it, please. Suspense will not lighten the burden."

"When I used your 'phone, Mr. Maturin, I spoke to the 'Yard.' To Sir Austin Kemble, the Commissioner of Police. I always make a clean breast of things when I bungle a job, and I'm very much afraid that I've bungled this. At any rate, I took a lot too much for granted, and it's landed me into a spot of bother."

He paused. "And the Commissioner has just given me a remarkable piece of news. The bad news to which I made reference just now. The body of your nephew, Lancelot Maturin, who has been missing for some time, let me tell you, was taken from the Scheldt this morning. I am so sorry."

The words made me feel dizzy. My almost famous cousin Lancelot—dead! A man on whose life I would cheerfully have taken a lease. It was almost unbelievable. Then I saw Anthony Bathurst's grey eyes fixed on me, and almost unconsciously I steeled myself for what I feared was coming in the shape of clash. He spoke to me.

"And it may interest *you* to know, Mr. Maturin, that your cousin, according to the medical evidence, had been dead for some considerable time before his body was recovered from the Scheldt waters. That is to say, he couldn't have worn this pyjama-jacket . . . couldn't have used this revolver . . . couldn't have been in the house of Mère Rasmussen, and couldn't have been in the position in which we were disposed to place him."

I stared at him—temporarily inarticulate.

"But *somebody* did all those things, Mr. Maturin . . . and somebody killed my colleague, Inspector Rawlinson."

With a rapid movement he whipped a small object from his pocket and held it out to me.

"Ever seen *this* before, Mr. Maturin?"

"No," I said in some astonishment; "never."

He pressed me. "You are certain of that?"

"Certain."

"One like it, perhaps?"

I shook my head. "No. Not even one like it."

"Thank you, Mr. Maturin."

He replaced the object in his pocket. What he had held out to me was an Apostle spoon. A yellowish spoon—which, to my eye, looked as though it were of carved wood.

Chapter XVII
PHILIPPA WALKS INTO A TRAP
(Told by Lance Maturin)

EVEN though I knew that the death of my cousin tightened the net that had been flung round me, I was the prey to yet another thought. A thought, this, from which, to my utter shame, I confess, I actually drew comfort. If my cousin had been Philippa's lover, I knew of it! No longer was I an eavesdropper, as it were . . . an outsider . . . a stranger, who knew nothing of her secret heart. I could go to her with knowledge . . . I would no longer be put off with vague hints and drab generalities . . . he was no longer an unknown mystery, drawing invisible strength and occult power from his ghostly immunity . . . but flesh and blood like myself . . . and dead flesh and blood at that. Why should I feel sorry for him I argued to myself? He had failed her . . . made tryst with her and let her down. Let her make tryst with me, I swore most fiercely, and judge then the measure of my loyal and loving service. Let them bring against me as test and trial, fire and water, forest, frost, and flood . . . let her see how I would meet them! This man for whom she had waited in Antwerp in vain *must* have been my cousin, Lancelot . . . it all fitted now, I could see. The revolver with the initials and the pyjama-suit. That was why, too, she wouldn't be able to call me "Lance." Too much like his damned name . . . of course. The use of it . . . 'twould have seemed to her like a treacherous tenderness and meant the awakening of too fragrant memories . . . that burned rather than blessed.

Then I began to pull myself up a bit and see my beastliness. Lancelot was dead . . . poor devil . . . drowned. That alone meant that to Philippa must come the bread of sorrow. Again—had my cousin been murdered? Bathurst had shown me a spoon . . . What did that mean? From where had it come?

"Tell me," I said to him—the guv'nor was silent—"was my cousin drowned . . . or murdered before he was thrown into the water?"

"I haven't full details yet, Mr. Maturin," he replied rather frigidly, "so that I can't tell you, but no doubt they will be in my possession very soon. Why do you ask? Do you suspect foul play? Have you any reason behind that suspicion? Or are you just asking out of curiosity?"

His eyes held me mercilessly.

"No," I returned. "But my cousin has at times been engaged on ticklish work . . . and I can't imagine him getting himself into the Scheldt . . . by accident. He was no fool, my cousin Lancelot . . . in anything I can assure you."

"I see. But we don't know anything definite yet. Until we do, conjecture is both foolish and useless."

He sounded impatient and dissatisfied. But I had Philippa to care for and consider, so I surveyed his dissatisfaction with comparative equanimity. His next question both alarmed and surprised me.

"You spoke of a party, Mr. Maturin, just now, in connection with your holiday jaunt to the Continent. Would you mind telling me the numerical strength of that party?"

"Three," I replied laconically.

He sought details. "Adrian Fawcett, you yourself—and . . . ?"

"A man named Hilleary. An old crony of both of us. Dennis Hilleary."

"You were all three at the Hôtel de Lutèce, of course?"

"Naturally. We stayed there together. We had been together all the time."

"Forgive me this question, Mr. Maturin. My excuse must be that there are tremendous issues at stake. From whom did you obtain your unexpected instructions with regard to the escorting of Miss Windmill?"

His tone was frank and eager, but I refused to budge from the position in which I had resolved to entrench myself. I shook my head at him.

"I cannot tell you that."

"I am sorry. I had hoped that you would have seen your way to do so. It would have been of such invaluable help to me."

"I am sorry, too. But I am not a free agent in the matter. I am not at liberty to betray confidences. My hands are tied."

He was on me like a flash.

"Your hands are tied? How? By whom?"

Again I refused him. "There are other interests to be considered as well as my own. I have given my word. As I told you, I am sorry. But I can assure you . . ."

I hesitated.

"Yes," he said gently, "go on, please."

"I was going to say this. I can assure you that my escort of a certain lady had nothing whatever to do with the shooting of Inspector Rawlinson. I am absolutely positive of that."

He shook his head slowly and gravely.

"I have no wish to be hypercritical, but I don't see how you can logically come to that conclusion, Mr. Maturin. All you can assert is that it had nothing to do with Rawlinson's death *as far as you know*. Which is a very different matter. For neither you nor I have all the facts in our possession. And if all the people whom I interview help me no more than you have chosen to do . . ."

He broke off with a shrug of the shoulders. But I was adamant and raised no finger as his auxiliary. For a time, neither of us spoke.

"Will you answer me this?" He returned to the attack. "Did Fawcett know of your instructions with regard to the lady?"

I could answer this, I thought, without damaging my cause.

"He may have done. I don't really know."

"You didn't tell him?"

"No."

"H'm." He fell to consideration. "How could he have known, then?"

"There's the chance that Hilleary might have told him."

"Hilleary knew, then?"

His voice held added interest . . . and a note of critical doubt . . . as though he were assessing something . . . something that he hadn't thought of before.

"Yes."

"You told Hilleary, then?"

"Not exactly. But you can take it that Hilleary knew that I had attached myself to Miss Windmill's service. But all this conjecture is not important or even relevant, believe me."

He shook his head. "Say that you don't know, Mr. Maturin, and you'll be nearer the truth."

He began to pace the room.

"Malfroy," I heard him say to himself in a half-whisper. "Lisle Malfroy! Svenhardt, Busigny, Whitsbury—now Malfroy.

Where do they all come in? And *if* they come in, where do they fit?" Then he turned on me again.

"Of what sort of a man is this Hilleary?"

"How do you mean?"

"Character. Reputation. Either. Both. You know him well, I take it?"

"Hundred per cent sound man. All the way and then some more. But why?"

He ignored the query. "And Fawcett?"

"The same. As you say—I know them both—*well*."

"Yet one of them—or both of them—might have secrets—eh? Personal skeletons hidden in personal cupboards?"

I grinned. "Homer occasionally has been known to bend his head," I observed; "and Brutus, if I remember aright, besides being the noblest Roman of them all, was known as Caesar's angel—but . . ."

I paused significantly.

"Conjecture, Mr. Maturin, all conjecture," he said, just a wee bit testily—"and it gets us nowhere. You may be right, of course—but haven't you ever heard of double lives? Hasn't the history of the late Mr. Peace ever reached you—or the story of Wainwright, the lecturer and popular entertainer, who murdered Harriet Lane? Are there no women in the world? Women with the external lure who entice men into 'sexploits' and 'sexcursions'? Do Hilleary and Fawcett live in a world of their own creation? Really, Mr. Maturin—I ask you."

I could see him thinking hard. "Miss Windmill," he said suddenly, in a kind of afterthought. "This lady whom you escorted home—have you any objection to my having a word with her?"

I hadn't anticipated the request, so that I was forced to decide quickly. I couldn't see Philippa giving herself away, and if I were able to have a word with her as a preliminary, I considered that no great harm would be done. After all, it wouldn't be possible to keep Bathurst away from her indefinitely if he once made up his mind to get into touch with her.

"None whatever," I answered him. "I'll tell her that you would like to see her. Wait in here, will you? Shan't be half a sec."

Without further ado, I dashed out of the library to find Philippa. She was with my mother and I saw that she held a copy of *The Times* in her hand. Upon my entrance, the mater slipped out and Philippa put the paper on the table and looked at me. Her eyes seemed troubled. It occurred to me that she was distressed, but I let her go for the minute and came to the immediate point.

"Look here, Philippa," I said, "don't be alarmed, but there's a chap here from Scotland Yard. He's a very decent bloke and up to the present I think I've fended him off and kept him at arm's length. All I've admitted is that I escorted you home—as Miss Windmill, of course—*under instructions*. That's the lot. Just remember that about me and no more. I've been vague all the way through because I'm certain that he doesn't know very much. D'you feel confident that you can face him?"

I asked her the question anxiously. When her reply came, it came, I thought, a little wearily.

"My dear Rudolf," she said, "why do you shut your eyes to facts? If they have been clever enough to trace us here so soon, they must *know* something. Which means, too, that they are bound—sooner or later—to ask me questions. Tell me this, though, before I face the music again. How did you tell him that you meet me?"

"I've told him nothing of that. All I've said is that I escorted you home 'under instructions.' Let him make of that whatever he chooses to."

She nodded her acceptance. "I see. All right, then. I'm ready."

I led the way to the library.

"Miss Windmill," I said. "Mr. Anthony Bathurst."

Bathurst smiled courteously. "Good morning, Miss Windmill. It's extremely good of you to spare me a few moments. But I'm investigating the murder of the late Inspector Rawlinson who was shot in a lodging-house in the Rue du Sacré Coeur in Antwerp. The house was kept by a woman named Rasmussen." Against this array of significant facts, deliberately marshalled against her by Anthony Bathurst, Philippa turned deathly pale.

I motioned to my father to leave us, and to my intense relief the guv'nor took the hint and acted upon it immediately. In fact, all through the business—from the alpha to the omega—he turned up trumps. Then Philippa made a bold stroke and I mentally applauded her.

"I know the house well, Mr. Bathurst. I lodged there."

"I am aware of that, Miss Windmill."

She attacked again before he could. "I was in the house when Inspector Rawlinson was shot."

"I am aware of that, too."

She continued imperturbably.

"I was in my bedroom. A man named Raoul de Verviac attempted to break into my room. I defended myself . . . and he went away . . . after a time. He ran downstairs. There were shots. I heard them from my room. I was very frightened . . . and escaped from the house. And went to Mr. Maturin here . . . who befriended me. That is all I know. If I were able to tell you more, I would."

Anthony Bathurst's eyes never left her face.

"Who was the man who accompanied you home the night that Rawlinson was killed?"

Close fighting now in all conscience . . . and Philippa unprepared. There were no stepping-stones here for her unwary feet . . . and, as I knew she would, she blundered.

"De Verviac," she said in a faint whisper. "I told you that he harboured designs . . . on me. He is the incarnation of evil."

I read the sympathy in Anthony Bathurst's eyes. "I am sorry, my dear young lady, to be compelled to prosecute an inquiry that must be painful to you . . . but if you went in fear of this man, de Verviac, why did you allow him to accompany you home?"

Philippa fought hard.

"I could not rid myself of him. It is impossible to insult a man like Raoul de Verviac. He forced his attentions on me. I thought that I had made that clear."

He shook his head at her gravely. "Why don't you tell me the truth, Miss Windmill? It will help us all in the long run,"

"What do you mean?" she countered with well-simulated indignation. "Do you insinuate that I have not told you the truth?"

"You know your own business best, of course, but you are shielding somebody, Miss Windmill. That fact is transparently obvious. Who that somebody is, is unfortunately my business to find out. For instance, consider the spoils of the struggle, that fell into my lap. This, for instance. And this."

He held up in one hand the blood-stained pyjama-jacket and, in the other, the pearl-butted revolver.

"Whose livery were these? Not Raoul de Verviac's—because he came to Mère Rasmussen's some time after you arrived with your cavalier. Your time was in the region of a quarter past eleven . . . and a man came with you . . . and went to your room with you . . . de Verviac came well after midnight."

Philippa looked at him wild-eyed and began to sway ominously. Here was not opinion, but knowledge, and knowledge with which she hadn't reckoned. Anthony Bathurst continued inexorably.

"Not Lance Maturin here, because he has given me a total denial . . . neither the revolver nor the jacket belongs to him . . . his sworn story is that he was your escort to England, and no more than that."

Philippa still swayed . . . backwards and forwards, I watched her anxiously. Bathurst's voice came again.

"And not Lancelot Maturin, of the Secret Service . . . whom we might have suspected . . . very reasonably . . . because of certain facts in our possession . . . because such a contingency is absolutely impossible . . . he had been dead for days when Rawlinson was murdered . . . his body had lain in the waters of the Scheldt for days. . . ."

"You lie," cried Philippa in shrill agony. "It's not true. I can't believe it. Lancelot can't be dead. I should have known. My heart would have told me, It would be too . . ."

With a despairing sob she swayed again, looked at me helplessly and hopelessly and crumpled to the floor. For the second time within twenty-four hours she had fainted in my presence.

Anthony Bathurst spoke to me very quietly.

"I'm sorry for what has happened, Mr. Maturin," he said. "Help her ... will you ... I fancy that she is in sore need of you."

CHAPTER XVIII
"VICTORIA 9. SECTION 123"
(Told by Lance Maturin)

YOU can guess at once what I did. I went like a flash and fetched Mother to Philippa and she got her round after a moment or so, with little trouble. Mother asked no questions ... bless her loving heart ... but I felt that I must say something to her.

"She's tired," I said by way of explanation—"tired and worried and overwrought. The journey and ... When things settle down a bit, I'll tell you all about everything."

The mater nodded sympathetically and asked no questions, and Philippa fluttered her eyes at us.

"Just as I had started to hope again," she whispered.

The words puzzled me and I bent down so that I could hear her the more clearly.

"Don't worry about anything," I said to her ... "you're all right. What is it you want to say?"

But she seemed bemused and I attached little or no importance to what I heard her saying. "The best shall be," I heard her whisper ... and then ... only just audible ... "I wonder ... if only I could be certain ... but it must be. It *must* mean that ... it couldn't mean anything else."

Mother and I lifted her into the most comfortable chair. She lay there for a time without moving. Then she looked up at us and spoke to my mother.

"Would you mind, Mrs. Maturin, if I were to lie down for a little while somewhere ... upstairs, perhaps? I'd like to be alone for a little time ... quiet and undisturbed ... I feel that I need rest ... I must think something out ... nobody can help me over it. Could I?"

Mother nodded brightly, put an arm round her and assisted her to her feet.

"My dear—of course. I was going to suggest the very same thing. I think it's the best thing that you can do. Come with me at once. I'll take you to the room where we'd decided to put you."

Philippa smiled grateful thanks and mother took her away. For a matter of five minutes, I suppose, I stood on the rug in front of the fireplace. Candidly, I was mentally unstable at that moment. Consider what I had gone through since I had crossed the threshold of the place of the scarlet flare. With this terrible and desperate climax—the death—or murder, more probably, of my cousin Lancelot! And, by one of those short, sharp strokes of Fate, I, too, was almost within the meshes of the net.

In that short time of my acquaintanceship with him Anthony Bathurst had shown me convincingly and unmistakably that he knew a great deal more than I had been inclined to credit him with knowing. And I had lied to him! I couldn't get away from the thought of that—for Philippa's sake, it is true, but the lie was there—my honour rooted in dishonour stood . . . my faith unfaithful . . . and who could tell what tree of trouble would rear itself from the false seed that I had sown?

I turned—to find Bathurst at the door. He held a newspaper in his hand. A quick glance told me that it was *The Times*—and the same paper that I had seen in Philippa's hand a short time previously.

"Mr. Maturin," he said, and again his irresistible smile attracted me to him, "I am going to return good for evil and confide in you. You don't mind, do you? I feel that you and I can help each other considerably. And if we come to help each other, we shall eventually begin to understand each other a great deal better. That must be something like a *sine qua non*. Are you on?"

My answer was lame and ridiculous. "If you—er—want me . . . I suppose that what you say is . . . you know . . . O.K. and all that. But all the same, I don't see what I can do."

He ignored my half-heartedness. "Good. That's a bet, then. We'll start our joint investigating right away. There nothing like a flying start . . . if you doubt me, ask Gordon Richards. Have a squint at this, will you, Maturin?"

He pointed to *The Times* "Agony Column." I followed the direction of his indicating finger. "Read that, Maturin."

I read. This is what he pointed out to me:

"Victoria 9. Section E. 123. Subsections W.T. and F. Grey and Silver.

"When modest water blushed so red
At maiden <u>RIPENING</u> into Life
There came to Man's most ancient head
The spell of Royal Edward's wife.
The worst is not. The best shall be.
For in the dregs lay Infamy."

"'The best shall be,'" I repeated dazedly like a man coming out of a trance. What were these but the words that Philippa had just used?

"Well, Maturin," he asked me, "do you find anything interesting in that? Or aren't you good at acrostics?"

For the life of me, I didn't know how to answer him. Outside the phrase I have quoted—the words were meaningless to me. They were completely incomprehensible to me. I wasn't going to give away Philippa's sentence at the outset, at any rate, so I steered one of my habitual middle courses, as equidistant as I could conveniently get between Scylla and Charybdis. I shook my head blankly.

"Gibberish, isn't it?"

He grinned at me. "Depends which way you look at it, old son. You mustn't compare it with the 'Recessional,' you know, in the light of a purely poetical effort. It's not a poem. Oh, no! Although the first line proper shows, I think, that the author knows his Dryden. What would you say it was yourself?"

"Haven't a glimmer."

"Come now. Surely you can project a suggestion? Try to satisfy the examiners somehow."

"What is it, then—something new in the way of advertisements?"

"No more an advertisement—as you mean the words to be used—than an effort at poetry. No, Maturin, that's a message—nothing more and nothing less."

"A message," I echoed after him.

He nodded.

"If it's a message," I went on, "as you say it is, it would take a hell of a time, I should imagine, to decode it. I'm afraid that I shouldn't—"

He shrugged his shoulders. "Again—that depends. I flatter myself that I've already been able to knock some sense out of it."

I was amazed at this statement. He was confident, but by no means spreading himself. "You haven't let the grass grow under your feet, then. What's it all about?"

He laughed. "Can't tell you that, quite. With any certainty, that is. But I'll say this. It affects your lady friend, whom I interviewed a few moments ago, and it may very possibly affect *you*."

He spoke nonchalantly, but was ready, I felt certain—when the occasion came—to assess the measure of my surprise.

"Me?" I said incredulously. "How on earth do you arrive at that conclusion?"

"Well—if not you, your ill-fated cousin. I'm not sure yet which, but it's one of you, and of that I'm positive."

I knitted puzzled brows. "Explain, Bathurst, please."

"Delighted, my dear Maturin. Look at the third word of the second line of the verse proper. The word that for some reason, obscure to the casual reader, is printed in capital letters and also underlined. Got it?"

"Yes," I replied; "you mean the word 'ripening.'"

"That's it—'ripening.' The word that has been included in the text purposely so that it should catch and rivet the reader's eye. What we may call the 'key' word. Anything strike you about it?"

I thought hard. "Only what you have said. The form in which it is printed. What else can strike me?"

His eyes held mine. "If you were asked for a synonym for 'ripening,' what would be your answer? What would be the answer to that question of ninety-nine people out of a hundred?"

"Maturing," I answered readily—I had almost written "unthinkingly." And on the heels of my speech the truth rushed at me.

"Curtail, as the puzzle-mongers are wont to say—and what have we?"

"Maturin," I answered; "how perfectly dense I was all the time."

"Exactly—about the word being 'Maturin', I mean. I wasn't agreeing with your self-criticism. I wouldn't be so hard on you as that."

He smiled at me again.

"Now that is why I stated that this message is intended for either you or your dead cousin. Suppose—in the first place—we regard it as your legacy, as he isn't able to receive it? Half a minute, though . . ."

He paused and a different look came on his face.

"What is it?"

"I've just thought of something else—but we'll let it slide for the moment. Let's go into this message a little more closely. Are you on?"

"Suits me," I replied.

"Well, you may guess that directly I glanced at the paper, the 'Maturin' touch about the affair intrigued me immensely—so much so, in fact, that I at once began to look for further indications. I didn't have to look either very long or very far. Take the line—'The spell of Royal Edward's wife.' Of whom would you think—ordinarily, that is—from the description—'Royal Edward'?"

"Edward the Seventh," I responded promptly, "without a doubt."

"I should *include* him, certainly, but I think that I should be forced to consider other Edwards as well. You know what I mean, Maturin. You can *think* of the idea better than I am able to explain it to you. There would be a comprehensive, embracing sort of thought at work, and, besides 'the Peacemaker,' I'm almost positive that I should think of the more famous Edwards and their queens. There would be the first Edward—the old 'Hammer of the Scots,' the third Edward, of Crecy and Poitiers renown, and the sixth Edward—of Prayer-book reputation. *And their queens*, let me repeat! Excessively important, this latter, for it brings us, by a natural association of idea and logical sequence of thought to the wife of Edward III—Philippa of Hainault. Does that name hold any interest for you, Maturin?"

His eyes were relentless now and I thought immediately of the girl's recent distress and realised how true was Bathurst's indictment.

"You're right," I muttered; "you must be. It's all so significant."

"There's much more to come. I haven't finished yet, by a long chalk. Let us take the preceding line. 'There came to Man's most ancient head.' Bit of a poser that—what?"

He rubbed his hands in pleasurable anticipation of his explanation.

"I can't get anything out of that," I conceded.

"Let me help you. Once again, it's the point of view that's beating you, Maturin. A thousand to one on it. For instance, what are you understanding by 'Man's'?"

"Mankind, I suppose. What else is there?"

He chuckled.

"There's an island, I believe, situated in the Irish Sea which, by a strange coincidence, is almost equidistant from the three countries of Ireland, England, and Scotland."

I nodded. I was beginning to see what he meant.

"You're alluding to the Isle of Man. Well, what of that?"

He repeated the line to me.

"'There came to Man's most ancient head.' Now what would you understand by 'most ancient head'?"

I wasn't at all confident that I understood anything, but I wasn't, by nature, a jibber, so I had a go at solving Bathurst's problem. I fear, though, that I was by no means optimistic of success.

"One of the old kings of the island, I suppose it means, doesn't it?"

"No. Not that. Try again, Maturin."

I thought a bit more, but eventually shook my head in despair. Any other solution seemed beyond my power.

"I'm afraid I'm perfectly hopeless. Help me out."

"Try your Latin on it, man. Work on the word 'head'—that's what I did. You may then find the clue."

I did as he had bidden me. "Caput."

An idea came to me.

"The old 'capital' of the island, do you mean?"

"You're hot now, Maturin. Burning your fingers almost—and the old capital of the Isle of Man was . . ."

"My dear fellow," I said to him, "you over-rate both my knowledge and my intelligence. Don't forget that I went to a public school. I can remember two towns of the Manxmen—Douglas and Ramsay—mainly, I think, because the railways run excursions there. Oh—and a third—Peel. Any one of these three may have been the ancient island capital for all I know—and equally may not have been. Candidly, Bathurst, I don't know. What's the answer?"

"None of the towns you have mentioned was the old Manx capital, Maturin. The ancient capital was Castletown, on the south coast of the island. So you see we have, in addition to our 'Maturin' association, both 'Philippa' and 'Castletown.' Not quite the correct patronymic, but as near as the senders could get, and near enough, don't you think, Maturin?"

There was a queer look on his face.

"I suppose it is," I replied, completely off my guard. "The accumulation of significance certainly can't be ignored."

At that moment the truth hit me . . . there was no reference to *"Windmill"* here. Anthony Bathurst had known all the time who Philippa was. I looked at him . . . and he looked at me . . . whimsically, rather. I'll swear that he knew what I was thinking. And then, suddenly, my brain seemed to clear and I began to see things in a truer perspective.

"Bathurst," I said impetuously, "I'm going to tell you the truth . . . every word of it as I know it."

"Why the hell couldn't you have done that in the first place, you blithering ass."

I grinned . . . for some inexplicable reason, what he had said sounded good to me.

Chapter XIX
PHILIPPA KEEPS AN APPOINTMENT
(Lance Maturin's story continued)

ANTHONY Bathurst listened to my story with infinite patience. When I had finished, he turned to me critically.

"And I suppose that you'll tell me, if I ask you, that you withheld all these vital particulars for the sake of Miss Castleton's *beaux yeux*? Yes?"

"Of course I did. What else could I do? What would any decent man have done? I had given her my word, hadn't I? Put yourself in my place. What would you yourself have done had you been situated as I found myself?"

He made me no reply.

I continued therefore. "Besides, consider what a remarkable story it is. It seems too extraordinary altogether—and a good many people simply wouldn't look at it. I don't know that you could blame 'em, either."

Bathurst shook his head.

"When your honour's clean, my boy, the truth's always the best. If you don't believe me, let me draw your attention to the wise words of one Robert Burns on the subject of tangled webs. However, we're out of the wood now, from that particular standpoint, and that's a great comfort."

"Going back to this message," I said, tapping the newspaper—"what other meaning have you knocked out of it?"

To my surprise somewhat, he seemed unconcerned at my question. At any rate, he returned me no immediate answer. I repeated the question.

"You give me credit for too much ability, my dear Maturin. I'm neither psychic nor telepathic, you know. It's my invariable habit to glance through the various 'agonies,' and I achieve a fluctuating measure of success. I must confess, though, that I draw any number of blanks. With regard to this particular 'agony,' all else that I would be prepared to assert at the moment, with any confidence, is that Miss Castleton is requested to keep an appointment at Victoria Station at nine o'clock in the evening."

He paused.

"The assignment," he proceeded, "can be to-night, to-morrow, or, should she fail to put in an appearance on either of those evenings, the night after. Those data are moderately simple to understand. You are able to follow me all the way there, surely?"

"I think I am. The place and the time . . . and the three evenings. To-night's Wednesday . . . and the Thursday and Friday naturally follow in the three given letters. Half a minute, though, why nine o'clock in the evening and not in the morning? I don't see how you can be so absolutely certain of that."

"*Section E,*" replied Anthony Bathurst, "Had the assignation been for nine o'clock in the morning, I fancy that we should have read 'Section M.' What do you think yourself?"

I looked at the paper.

"I think that you're probably right. May I do a spot of unravelling now or shall I be stealing your thunder?"

"Not a bit of it. Have a go, laddie, by all means. Nothing would please me better. What else have you dug up?"

I preened my mental feathers.

"Well, if your premises be correct, and I see no reason to doubt this, the question must arise as to how the two people, Philippa and the messenger—the person she has to meet—are to recognise one another when they arrive at the rendezvous. If they ever do find one another that is . . . before now I've seen one or two people assembled at Victoria . . . at least two. Therefore, so that she may be recognised without difficulty, Philippa will wear something in silver and grey. Thank you, my dear Watson, but after all . . . elementary."

I grinned. Then I crashed. My deductions were despised and rejected.

Bathurst shook an uncompromising head.

"I don't think so, Maturin. In fact, I'm as certain as I pretty well can be, over a matter of this sort, that the phrase 'grey and silver' has reference to the person whom Miss Castleton will meet and not to the lady herself."

"Why?" I demanded. "For what reason? You *must* have one."

"Let it remain at that for the present. You mustn't expect me to give all my secrets away at once. After all, it's best part surmise—there's no definite signpost there, as it were."

I shrugged my shoulders at his refusal.

"Very well, then. You're an old hand at the game and your judgment must be better than mine. What about the two lines with which the message finishes? They worry me, rather. What's wrapped up in them?"

He gestured impatiently towards the newspaper. "I can't answer that. I may permit myself to indulge in certain conjectures, but an inch beyond that I'm not prepared to go. My actual knowledge is so limited, you see. For instance, I've never set eyes on your cousin in my life, and know next to nothing about him. Quite frankly, the news of his death came as no surprise to me. There was a precedent. A very ugly and disturbing precedent. But you remember that, no doubt?"

He paused and looked up at me interrogatively.

I denied the suggestion.

"No. I'm afraid that I don't follow you. I knew Lancelot fairly intimately, of course, but he never favoured me with anything like his confidences. Neither did I him. We didn't expect such a condition of each other."

"Then you have never heard of Alan Erskine?"

"Never. Who was he?"

"Erskine was a colleague of your cousin's in the Diplomatic Service. It was confidently anticipated by those best qualified to judge, that he had a brilliant career in front of him . . . just as your cousin was presumed to have. Erskine disappeared . . . again—as your cousin did."

Bathurst paused once more and turned to me with extreme deliberation.

"And the dead body of Alan Erskine was taken from the Scheldt . . . again—as your cousin's has been. How, therefore, can I be surprised, Maturin, at this last turn that events have taken?"

These facts concerning Erskine opened my eyes considerably. It came home to me then that we were against something or somebody much bigger than I had previously imagined to be the case.

"What does it all mean?" I asked him. "How on earth does Miss Castleton touch on all this? It's incredible that a girl of her social—"

Bathurst interrupted me.

"If I knew that, Maturin, I should probably know all that needed knowing."

He began to pace the room . . . hands deep into pockets. Backwards and forwards I watched him go . . . head thrust forward . . . eyes alight with the concentration of mental striving. I learned afterwards, when my acquaintance with him had developed somewhat, that this attitude was a favourite trick of his. Suddenly, and without the hint of a warning, he swung round on me . . . fiercely almost.

"Which night will she attend the rendezvous?"

"Which night?" I echoed.

"Yes. Which night will this Miss Castleton of yours keep the assignation?"

I fenced with him. In the first place, I wasn't enamoured of the idea at all. Who was this person at whose bidding she must keep appointments?

"How do you know that she will keep it? How do you know that she has read and understood the message?"

"I don't know it. But I think this: that you know that she has! Otherwise you would have argued more about it when I first discussed it with you. Tell me, Maturin, I'm right, am I not?"

I yielded the position.

"I think so. I saw her with the paper in her hands, and since then I've heard part of that message from her own lips."

Instantaneously he became all eagerness.

"Which part, Maturin?"

"The best shall be. Simply the bare statement—nothing more."

He rubbed at his clean top lip.

"H'm. She said that, did she?"

He fell to thought again before returning to the attack with his previous question.

"Well—you didn't answer me! Which night will she go, Maturin?"

"How can I possibly tell you that? How do I know for certain, even, that she will go at all?"

"Tut, tut, Maturin. You know her better than I do. Psychologically, I mean. Assuredly you know by now how she reacts to contingencies and emergencies?"

I became wary.

"Why do you want to know? After all—is it so frightfully important to us when she goes—to-night, to-morrow, or Friday?"

"Yes—in one way—most important! To me, that is. I won't say 'to us.'"

"Why? Explain, please."

"Because I am going, too! And I had almost hoped . . ."

"What?"

"That you would accompany me."

He eyed me shrewdly.

"Never," I declared with vehemence. "That's one thing I'll never consent to do. I'm not going to spy on that girl."

He was imperturbable.

"I wasn't aware that I had asked you to. I presume, though, that you are prepared to protect her?"

"Protect her? Do you think it will come to that?"

He shrugged his broad shoulders.

"Who knows? I think that it may. We're arrayed against the forces of evil, Maturin. Surely you've realised that by now."

He watched me anxiously—but I made him no answer.

He proceeded.

"Let me make a bargain with you, then. If Miss Castleton comes into the open and asks you to accompany her, I'll promise to keep out of it. If she does not come with me, so that we may be on hand should our services be needed. Say what you like, Maturin, Monsieur Raoul de Verviac isn't exactly mother's blue-eyed boy."

His reference to de Verviac was clever and perfectly timed, for it stung me into acquiescence.

"I agree," I said semi-reluctantly. "It's true that we may be able to help her. And I think she'll go to-night. If I know her as I imagine I do, Philippa won't stand for delay."

He nodded.

"Then our opinions coincide, Maturin . . . Miss Castleton doesn't hesitate, neither does she waste time . . . when decisions have to be made and plans formed."

Once again he paced the floor of the library.

"Tell me, Maturin," he said at length, "during the time that you were with her, did you ever hear Miss Castleton mention the word ' Apostle' or the word 'Matthias'? Think carefully, please."

"Never," I answered emphatically. "I'm absolutely positive of it."

"Have you ever heard Fawcett use either of the words?"

"Never."

"Hilleary?"

"No—neither of them."

"Your cousin?"

"No."

Bathurst offered me his cigarette-case.

"Smoke, Maturin? Tobacco sometimes stimulates the brain. Although our mental processes can never be absolutely static, concentration and the logical transition of thought are, at times, problems for the best of us. One thing, however, emerges clearly from the mist. It seems to me that I must return to Antwerp. To that city on the Scheldt . . . that river from which are taken the bodies of young Englishmen."

I accepted a cigarette and we lit up.

"At once?" I queried of him.

"Soon, I'm afraid. Directly I have a full acquaintanceship with Miss Castleton's next move. For which, if I'm any judge, I don't think we shall have to wait too long."

The words had scarcely left his lips when I saw the handle of the door turning. Philippa Castleton stood on the threshold.

"May I come in?" she asked.

I beckoned to her.

"Please do. Do you want me? Are you better?" She nodded to my latter question.

"Yes. I'm feeling all right now . . . Rudolf."

She smiled shyly and continued.

"I wanted to ask you something. How are the trains in these parts? I must go to Town to-night. While I've been upstairs, I've thought of something that's most terribly important to me. It's made me change my mind about something I was going to do. Something that was worrying me. I want to be at Liverpool Street not later than half past eight. How soon must I leave here?"

I caught Bathurst's significant glance in my direction and deliberately turned away from it.

"Then let me come with you," I declared to her. "Then you won't have to worry about anything. I'll see to all your arrangements for you."

She shook her head decisively.

"No. Thank you. It's sweet of you to want to, but you mustn't—please understand, won't you?"

"In that case, then," I returned coldly, "seeing that my offer has been rejected, I must consult the A.B.C. Half past eight, you said, didn't you?"

I turned to walk to the bookcase.

"Will you be coming back here to-night?"

I put the question with assumed nonchalance. It distressed her. She came and placed her hand on my arm.

"I don't know. I can't say. But I will if I possibly can. If I don't . . . come back . . . you won't think that I've let you down, will you? And you won't worry about me? Because, if I thought that, I should be very unhappy."

As she spoke, I noticed that Anthony Bathurst slipped quietly from the room. I saw, too, something else . . . tears in the eyes of Philippa Castleton.

Tears that I was not privileged to wipe away. Bathurst's words flooded my brain. "Which night will she go? . . ."

Chapter XX
TWISTED THREADS
(Lance Maturin's story continued)

WHEN I had found the time of her train and given her the information that she wanted, I told her to let my mother know of this new turn of affairs. When she gave her word that she would, I excused myself to her and sought Anthony Bathurst.

"Well?" he queried. "We were right in our assumptions, weren't we?"

I noticed his use of the plural. "What does it all mean, Bathurst?" I asked. "The whole damned business is getting on my nerves. If only I knew what she is hiding from me . . ."

He intervened. "Coming with me, as we arranged, Maturin?"

"Yes. I am. I'm in the business now, for good or ill. The latter probably."

He cocked a quizzical eye at me. "In love with the little lady, Maturin? Is it as bad as all that?"

I reddened at the pointed question. Then nodded. "Like hell," I answered.

He whistled. "I'm sorry. I was afraid so."

I turned sharply. "Why sorry? Why afraid? What do you mean?"

He came and patted me on the shoulder in a thoroughly pally sort of way.

"I'm sorry because I'm afraid that you're going to be hurt—that's all. Somehow I don't think you're going to be the prince for your princess, and in that event your case may be a sad one. Any old how, be prepared for squalls."

"You're pessimistic," I returned. "More so than I am. Yesterday, I might have agreed with you. On the whole indeed—*should* have done. But to-day, my dear Bathurst, my stock has very definitely risen, if you only knew."

He shrugged his shoulders. "Yesterday! That covers a lot sometimes. 'But yesterday the word of Caesar might have stood against the world.' I hope I'm wrong, then. For your sake.

I never care about seeing a decent chap hit too hard in that particular way. I've been through the mill myself and know quite a lot about the geography of hell in consequence. What train is she catching?"

"The 5.21. It's not a fast train. But it's the only one. She'll have to change. What do we do?"

"We shall be in front of her, Maturin, by the time she gets there. My car's here. I came from Harwich in it. I'd arranged for it to be there to meet me when I came off the boat. It's a pretty powerful bus—we shall be in town before Miss Castleton, easily—if we leave at half past five even. I'll tell you what, Maturin—drive her to the station in it—you yourself—and pick me up afterwards. There's a sporting gesture for you. Then you'll see the last of her before she leaves."

My wound seemed to be doing nicely, so I accepted his offer and, when the time came, drove Philippa to the station. She was very silent, and I caught her mood. Mere commonplaces were the sum total of our conversation until the train came in and she gave me her hand to say good-bye. I waited purposely to see what she would say to me, for, with a tilt at Fate, I had bought her a return ticket.

"*Au 'voir*, Rudolf . . . and thank you once again—for everything."

"I don't want you to go," I whispered . . . but before I could say any more the train began to move, and from the window of the compartment she squeezed my finger with her gloved hand.

"I must," she said softly. . . . "It's my destiny. . . . You wouldn't have me a coward, would you?"

I shook my head and waved to her . . . kept on waving until her train was lost to sight. Then I drove the car back to find Anthony Bathurst, and surrendered the wheel to him.

Our drive through Essex and the East End of London to town was uneventful. Bathurst chatted to me quite joyously—but never mentioned the matter nearest to my heart. The Chrysler justified all that he had said about it and behaved itself perfectly.

"Where are we making for?" I asked him. "Victoria or Liverpool Street?"

"The latter, laddie. We shall be there a good ten minutes before Miss Castleton's train is due in. You shall watch the barrier . . . but be careful that she doesn't spot you when she comes through. I don't want that to happen. If I'm any judge she'll take a taxi to Victoria. That taxi will be followed by this car . . . containing you and me—us twain—my dear Maturin."

I carried out his instructions . . . to the letter. The Colchester train arrived in good time and, standing well back from the barrier, I waited till I saw Philippa Castleton come through. Without the slightest hesitation, she hurried out of the station and, just as Bathurst had predicted to me, walked quickly up to a waiting taxi-cab.

"Victoria," I heard her direct the driver . . . and almost immediately, as her car drew away, Bathurst and I followed on behind in the Chrysler.

When she reached Victoria she dismissed her driver; and, leaving Bathurst's car under care that had been quickly volunteered, we followed her into the great terminus. She made for that part of the station that is fed by the corridor that leads from the Underground. But Bathurst and I soon saw that she had no settled plan, for she began to walk up and down . . . scanning intently the faces and the wearing apparel of the countless passers-by. Backwards and forwards we watched her go. Then, to my own secret dismay, I noticed that it was only in the men whom she encountered that she had this interest. To the women and girls whom she passed she was completely indifferent. It was obvious, from the movements of her, that she was certain that she was keeping an assignation with a man.

It was past nine o'clock now, and I could see from the quick way in which she was turning her head that she was becoming uneasy at her inability to find the man whom she had come to meet. Suddenly Bathurst caught me by the arm and drew me to the side of the bookstall from which we had been standing but a few yards away.

"Look here, Maturin," he said, "I've an idea. I'm going to suggest that you and I divide forces. We may do better that way. If Miss Castleton's looking for a needle in a haystack, there's no reason that I can see why we should wear out our fingers as well. You stay here where you can keep Miss Castleton under observation. Don't let her out of your sight, whatever you do. I'll have a scout round on my own."

I was quite prepared to fall in with the suggestion, although I was unable to see what good Bathurst could do on his own. But whatever I thought mattered not a whit, for things began to happen. Bathurst had taken scarcely two steps away from me than he was back at my side.

"Look," he said to me, "Miss Castleton has found her man. Over there."

I looked across the heads of the hurrying people and saw that what Anthony Bathurst had said was true. Philippa Castleton was in earnest conversation with somebody. A man, of course. His back was towards me, but by edging a little to the side I could see that she was looking up into his face with undisguised interest . . . almost eagerness in fact. All I could see of her companion was that he was a man of fine physique and dressed in conventional dark clothes.

"Well, Maturin," said Bathurst, "was I right?"

I was unable to resist the temptation of a thrust at him. "Neither the grey suit nor the silver hair."

His reply was a good-natured grin.

"Aren't you hitting me below the belt, laddie? I don't think I suggested anything of that nature. If you wait a bit longer, it's just on the cards that my meaning will be plainer to you. Give me a chance, 'O sternest of my critics.'"

He laughed again and I felt rather humiliated.

"Watch them," he continued, "in case they—Hallo—they're moving off somewhere. Quick—come with me, Maturin. Somehow I don't think they'll go very far. Hold on. Don't walk too quickly. We mustn't get too near."

I obeyed him. And again he was right. Philippa and her male escort crossed to the refreshment-buffet on the far side of the station and disappeared through its swing-doors. I was on the point of darting in after them, when Anthony Bathurst's hand arrested my further progress.

"Wait a minute. We can't go in there, Maturin. It would be impossible to do so without being spotted. The space in there is limited. I know the place well."

"What do we do now, then?" I queried.

"Wait until they come out . . . and eventually separate. They will for a certainty. Then, I think, we'll have a word with the gentleman. He may not talk, of course . . . we must be prepared for that . . . on the other hand I may be able to stimulate his elocution. One never knows."

"How?" I demanded.

His reply surprised me. "Murder's an ugly word, Maturin. To all of us island people. And I can't forget that Rawlinson and I worked in double harness."

"You know what you're doing—I don't doubt—but when you connect Philippa Castleton with the murder of Rawlinson, you're a pain in the neck to me."

He was imperturbable under my assault.

"Yet twisted threads may be disentangled, Maturin. By patience and perseverance—or by a stroke of good fortune even. And what may look like one thread, turns out to be two—or even three—when the unravelling process has been completed."

He paused . . . to proceed again almost immediately. "I'll tell you something now, Maturin. Your lady friend will return to Trueloves this evening. That should please you."

"How do you know that?" I returned eagerly.

He laughed. "I don't know. It's a prediction on my part, based on what I saw of her during that little interview of which we were spectators just now. You see if I'm not right."

It didn't sound very convincing to me, but I was beginning to have faith in him, and the words put heart into me. Thirty-five minutes passed before anything happened to interest Bathurst and me. I have never known time take so long to pass. Once or twice I saw that he glanced anxiously at his wrist-watch.

"They've been longer than I anticipated," he said, "but I don't think that they should—"

He checked the words on his lips, for we both saw that Philippa was coming away from the buffet. To my surprise, rather she was unaccompanied. She looked straight ahead of her and turned, after a few paces, to make her way from the station. My feet and my impulse were eager to follow her, and I suppose that my face betrayed the fact. For Anthony Bathurst shook his head at me sympathetically.

"Don't worry, Maturin," he said. "Miss Castleton is *en route* for Liverpool Street . . . and her ultimate destination, for this evening, at any rate, is—as I told you—the hospitable roof of Trueloves. Beyond that, I refuse to join the prophetic ranks. Come with me quickly."

He walked rapidly to the door of the refreshment-lounge and I followed him. There was a brief moment, as we crossed the threshold, during which he covered the apartment with a quick and comprehensively sweeping glance.

"There's our man," he said to me curtly. "At that table over there. Do you see him? Right at the end. Couldn't be better. There's nobody particularly near him. We're going to have that little chat with him before he leaves here. Even if it means him missing his train. We'll go over now. Come along, Maturin."

He advanced towards the man he had pointed out to me and I followed him once again, in dutiful resignation and curious as to what would transpire. As before, the man of our interest had his back to my approach. But when we came almost abreast of him and he turned his face in my direction, I was unable to repress an exclamation of astonishment. For the man whom we were so eager to talk to—the man whom Philippa had met before our eyes—was the man who had run down the platform at Antwerp to catch a train . . . when Philippa and I had sat in it . . . the man whom she had not known then . . . of whom, by implication, she had denied knowledge . . . but whom, although she had not seen him since, she evidently did know and recognised now . . . Alec Paton.

Before I could say a coherent word, I heard Anthony Bathurst addressing him. So instead of putting my oar in, I listened, as usual, to the eloquence of Mr. Bathurst.

"Good evening. Forgive my intrusion . . . but would you be good enough—"

Bathurst's opening gambit met with instant interruption. Paton, disregarding the man who was speaking to him, pushed back his chair from the table, to stare amazedly at me.

"Maturin," he exclaimed, "by all that's wonderful! What the hell are you doing here, man?"

I never had cared much for the blighter . . . although he was a big, hefty man, he had a soft unctuous voice which irritated me beyond measure . . . and now, after having seen him with Philippa in the circumstances that I have described, I disliked him even more. Besides, the memory of Dorothy returned to me directly I had come face to face with Paton, which fact, naturally, didn't tend to make matters any better.

Bathurst intervened. There was a light in his eyes. "I had no idea that you knew this gentleman, Maturin. Had I known it I would have asked you to introduce me. Perhaps I'm not too late for that, even now?"

I'm afraid that I wasn't too gracious over it, but I acceded to his request at once.

"Alec Paton," I said with scant ceremony, "and this is Anthony Bathurst."

Bathurst bowed. Paton looked a bit puzzled. The three of us sat down and Bathurst called a waiter and gave an order. The first moment that Paton's attention relaxed, and he turned his head, Bathurst looked at me with a lightning-like movement and put his finger to his lips.

"I expect Mr. Paton is wondering what all this means. Very naturally, too. I must explain myself. It is only fair that I should do that."

He took out a visiting-card and scribbled something on it.

"There is my card, Mr. Paton."

Paton picked up the card that Bathurst had placed on the table. He read it carefully as the waiter arrived with the drinks. I saw his forehead develop a frown. But he lost little of his composure.

"Acting in conjunction with Scotland Yard, eh, Mr. Bathurst? Well, that's most interesting, but at the same time I must confess that I fail to see how it concerns me."

Bathurst looked at him critically.

"I showed you my card, Mr. Paton, in order that you might be able to judge that my business is important . . . that I'm not here, for instance, to collect your views on esoteric Buddhism. I hope that you will consent to give me a little information on a most serious matter. I am investigating the murder, in Antwerp, of the late Chief-Inspector Rawlinson."

I could have sworn that Master Paton flinched at the mention of the name. Certainly a spot of colour flaunted itself on his face. But he smiled sweetly at Bathurst and in that soft ingratiating voice of his replied with a question.

"Really. But why do you come to me? I never saw the man Rawlinson in my life."

Bathurst came to grips with him.

"I want your help, Mr. Paton. I will be perfectly frank. In the matter of Lancelot Maturin . . . of the Diplomatic Service. Incredible though it may seem at first blush, I have a theory that Maturin's disappearance . . . and Rawlinson's murder, may be *not* unconnected. Let me put it a little differently. That the murderers of Rawlinson, and the people responsible for Maturin's vanishing . . . may very well be one and the same. There you have the reason why I have approached you, Mr. Paton. A reason, too, that you will appreciate."

Then a surprising thing happened. To me, that is. Paton became a changed man . . . self-assured and complacent to the nth degree.

"I'm sorry," he said confidently, "but you've come to the wrong man. You're mixing me up with somebody else. I'm afraid that you've had your trouble for nothing."

Bathurst was unperturbed. "Whom should I have sought, then, Mr. Paton?"

Paton shrugged his shoulders. "Oh, Lord—ask me another. Haven't the ghost of an idea. I'm pretty sure I'm right, though."

He was cocksureness itself.

Bathurst looked at me. There was the faintest indication of a fluttering eyelid in my direction.

"Surely we haven't missed a sitter, Maturin? This gentleman almost suggests that we have. Are you sure that this is the man who met Miss Castleton, or have our eyes deceived us?"

We were at close quarters now. Paton was unable to restrain his emotion. If nowhere else, it showed in his fingers . . . they twitched nervously.

"Look here," he said, with an ugly note in his voice, "my business with Miss Castleton is no concern of yours. So keep your feet off that path, my friend . . . otherwise you may get them trodden on . . . and I'm no light weight, I assure you. Get that into your head."

Bathurst made no reply . . . but drummed lightly with the tips of his fingers on the surface of the table. Paton decided that he would spill some more.

"I'll trouble you for no interference at all, Mr. Bathurst. Understand that once and for all. If you must spy, spy on somebody else . . . not on me. What is more, I don't see any purpose in prolonging this interview."

Paton rose. Anthony Bathurst did likewise. He had the height advantage of about an inch. I watched the two of them . . . nerves tingling, and I will confess that nothing would have given me greater pleasure than to see A.L.B. sock him a fourpenny one on his fat jaw. Bathurst looked him straight between the eyes.

"But yours isn't the only point of view, Mr. Paton. You forget that. Strange though it may seem, to one of your temperament, you are not the only chilli in the jar of piccalilli. Even though you may rely for protection on the power of the silver and grey."

He paused, but only for a brief moment.

"The worst is not, the best shall be."

Paton stared at him incredulously, but he forced his incredulity into subjection and once again his manner completely changed. He even attempted the adventure of a smile—of the sickly variety.

"Mr. Bathurst," he said silkily, "perhaps I spoke too forcibly just now. But you must admit that I had a certain amount of reason on my side and just a little provocation. As you hinted a moment or so ago, I hold the privilege of special protection. You were right."

As he spoke, he turned back the lapel of his coat and I caught a fleeting glimpse of the silver greyhound that was attached thereto . . . another score to Anthony Bathurst . . . "grey and silver." Paton went on.

"But I can tell you nothing whatever that will help you. Lancelot Maturin, unhappily, is no longer missing. I rather wonder that your own knowledge of affairs doesn't extend as far as that. You seem well informed on most points. Maturin's dead body was taken from the river Scheldt only a matter of a few hours ago. So, you see, I'm in a position to give you no help at all. My business with Miss Castleton was on an entirely different footing. It was of a peculiarly private nature, and I can assure you that it had nothing to do whatever with the matter of your investigation."

Bathurst thoughtfully caressed the ridge of his jaw.

"Thank, you, Mr. Paton. I accept that statement in the spirit in which it is given."

He resumed his seat.

Paton followed his example.

Bathurst's hand went to his breast-pocket.

"There's just one more thing that I should like to show you. Rather a quaint object in its way . . . but I'm afraid that it not only has a unique history but also a sinister significance."

He produced the carved spoon that he had shown to me in my father's house at Trueloves. Before Paton could make any comment, Bathurst rattled on.

"This spoon, Mr. Paton, came from the house where Inspector Rawlinson was murdered. And I'm at a temporary loss to hit upon either its meaning or its extrinsic value . . . for I am certain that it possesses both."

He flashed a quick look at Paton and I saw the latter's jaw stiffen.

"An Apostle spoon, eh?"

Bathurst nodded.

"Seems like it, doesn't it?" he said cheerfully.

Paton's cheeks flushed . . . he tried hard to affect supreme nonchalance . . . but the finer sensibilities of his nerves, for just a split second of time, proved too much for him . . . and he surrendered to them to betray his particular interest. Then he pulled himself together and endeavoured to retreat.

"Came from Antwerp, eh? Curious."

He fingered the spoon. "Can't say that I've ever seen one like it. Still, there's nothing in that. I don't cut much ice as a globe-trotter. Most of my work is covered by the British Isles . . . and chiefly by our own bright little, tight little island itself. As a matter of fact, I've never been in Antwerp in my life."

This barefaced lie was more than I could stand. Forgetting, almost, that Anthony Bathurst was with me, I turned to the speaker with blazing indignation.

"That's a damned lie, Paton, and you know it," I said, "for you were in Antwerp the very night that Rawlinson was murdered. You left for Brussels by the—"

His face worked convulsively as the full meaning of my words came home to him.

"Who told you that?" he cried angrily. "What rogue or fool—"

"Neither," I returned vehemently. "I had no need of the information. I happened to see you in the train myself . . . and I'll tell you something else, Paton . . . I wasn't alone when I saw you, either."

He rose, spread the palms of his Lands on the table, and glowered down at me.

"I have never had much opinion of your intelligence, Maturin," he said, "and I have still less now. But I'll give you something to remember. 'Fools rush in where angels fear to tread'—and let me tell you you've done some rushing. Your blood be on your own fat head. Good night."

Turning quickly on his heel, he strode away from us.

I jerked myself to my feet.

Bathurst placed a restraining hand on my arm.

"Let him go, Maturin," he said. "There's no point in following him. I fancy that we have learned from him all that we are likely to learn. But what do you make of that last line of the 'agony' now, laddie? 'For in the dregs lay Infamy'?"

He chuckled without waiting for my answer.

"I think I'll go back to my flat, Maturin. You go home and make love to your Miss Castleton. Keep to-night's little expedition secret, but, if you care to, remember me very kindly to her."

He rubbed the side of his cheek.

"I rather think that you'll find her just a wee bit disappointing . . . but don't fret over that, laddie . . . women are moody and inconstant creatures at the best of times. And they give their love, usually, to their sons, Maturin. Never forget that. To the son of their womb."

CHAPTER XXII
THE DEATH OF SCHOONBEKE

THE news of the discovery of the dead body on the railway track between Eeckeren and Cappellen was sent through to Anthony Bathurst from New Scotland Yard by his old friend Chief-Inspector MacMorran as soon as the Yard itself knew of it—Sir Austin Kemble himself issued the instructions. MacMorran carried them out. Let it be stated at once that this quick transmission of news was at Bathurst's express request. He had interviewed the Commissioner as to developments and the Commissioner had paid attention. For there were points about this last affair that very definitely put it in the category of the unusual and abnormal. It was proved beyond the vestige of a doubt that the dead man had been first drugged and then deliberately tied to the rails . . . before the train had done its work.

The lengths of cord found at the side of the track and the marks on the man's wrists were conclusive.

The body of the man, however, was not so mangled as might reasonably have been expected considering the circumstances of his death, and the Belgian Police representatives identified it without undue loss of time as that of Leopold Schoonbeke—the infamous ex-burgomaster of Vilvorde who had been released from prison but a few months previously after serving a sentence for a series of criminal offences the unspeakable nature of which can only be hinted at here. It is enough to say that for sheer obscenity his crimes were almost unparalleled.

When Anthony Bathurst answered MacMorran's 'phone call, and heard the first words of the communication, his mental powers came to their finest pitch, for he realised that his anticipations had been true and exact . . . it must be whispered that he had been expecting something of this kind for some days now.

At the other end of the 'phone, MacMorran could tell that Anthony was all excitement.

"Schoonbeke, you say, MacMorran? Yes . . . yes . . . I remember the Vilvorde case well . . . I've still the cuttings of it, as a matter of fact. He was a man in the early fifties. I rarely destroy anything of that nature. Do you know what it all means, Inspector?"

He listened while MacMorran expressed his doubt.

"I'll tell you, then. Just listen to this, you old villain. Svenhardt went in the spring of last year. . . . Busigny in the following autumn. . . . Whitsbury this last spring . . . and now Schoonbeke in the autumn again. Observe the calendar regularity with which the flies crawl up the window. The two per annum business. Number five is obviously due to be bumped off next spring. Do you get me?"

"Aye, Mr. Bathurst. It's a strange business altogether. If I weren't so busy myself on other things I'd come and give you a hand. There's nothing I'd like better. All I can do now is to wish you luck . . . and good hunting. For poor old Rawlinson's sake. He was one of our best men and his place will be hard to fill. I'll be saying good-bye."

MacMorran rang off and Bathurst stretched, his lithe length in an armchair. He thought hard . . . hands thrust deeply into pockets . . . eyes closed. The panorama passed across his mind. An embezzler, a bankrupt and forger, an abortionist . . . and now a wretch of vile memory. Spring, autumn, spring, autumn. . . . No dagger . . . no revolver or gun . . . no knife . . . no poison . . . but a series of rather fantastic routes to the Styx . . . sinister shufflings from the mortal coil . . . to that bourne from which no traveller returns. Svenhardt, veins opened with pieces of broken glass. Busigny, hanged by the cord of a dressing-gown from an old beam in a disused barn. Whitsbury, burned to death—his funeral pyre a baker's oven. Now Schoonbeke. First drugged and then tied to the railway lines near the Cappellen golf course. Look at it how you would, there must be some bizarre truth to be dug from this depth of disorder.

Despite all the similarities of disrepute, there was, nevertheless, a one great and almost startling *disparity*. Svenhardt, the first of the murdered men, had been an extremely rich man. A man who had fattened himself on the granaries of others . . . on the harvests of the poor and needy. But the remaining trio, Busigny, Whitsbury, and Schoonbeke, as far as Anthony Bathurst could tell from the points of ordinary knowledge that were in his possession, hadn't a bean with which to bless their cursed selves. Also—strange, thought Mr. Bathurst, in his task of concentrated consideration.

He rose from his armchair and went to his telephone . . . asked for MacMorran again. He was soon in touch. The Scotland Yard Inspector listened to him with the most careful attention. Mr. Bathurst's opening remarks were excessively lengthy. MacMorran replied with caution.

"You're asking me a pretty big question, Mr. Bathurst. I shall have to think hard. *Anybody*, you say?"

"Anybody more or less obscure. Nobody terrifically in the public eye. That won't suit me. Yes . . . the Discharged Prisoners' Aid Society . . . that's it. I'll hang on, if necessary. What? Very well . . . right-o."

After a moderately long period of waiting, Bathurst could hear MacMorran at the other end again. This time it was Anthony who listened so carefully.

"What name?" he asked eventually.

MacMorran supplied the name. "Eric Chalmers."

"Oh, good . . . couldn't be better . . . yes . . . I think that I can recall the case. A pretty poisonous business all through. In the East Midlands, wasn't it? A young doctor? Being released at the end of the month, you say? D'ye know, MacMorran, we'll make him a present of a few days. Yes . . . yes . . . don't worry about that part of it . . . the Home Secretary shall exercise his prerogative of clemency . . . I know that the Commissioner will agree and fall in with the idea generally."

Mr. Bathurst developed enthusiasm.

"Damn it all, man—he must! See him at once, of course. Oh . . . by the way . . . will you see to the Press part of it? Especially as regards the Continental papers. Let it be broadcast thoroughly . . . photographs as well . . . the bait will be swallowed all right, if I'm any judge . . . I remember Chalmers' particular reputation, you see. It will be too attractive to be resisted. Take my word for it. They'll jump at him, if we dangle him cleverly enough. Anyhow, we'll await events, MacMorran, and see what the fruit of my idea's like. We can't lose by it. You know where the proof of the pudding lies. Bye-bye. Remember me kindly to the old man."

CHAPTER XXIII
BIRDS AND THEIR PLUMAGE

IN LESS than a week, Mr. Bathurst's trap had begun to achieve success. Consider what happened in a street of the city of Antwerp.

A tall man standing at the bar of the Taverne Suisse turned suddenly at the sound of his name.

"I am Lisle Malfroy," he said, "but I fear that you have the advantage of me. I can't recall that we have ever met before."

The man who had addressed Malfroy with such *bonhomie* grinned with consummate craftiness.

"And yet, Mr. Malfroy," he returned with a spice of sycophancy, "we *should* know each other. Birds of a feather have a certain reputation, you know. We should be dreadfully disappointing to the world at large if we failed to live up to the reputation. So much is expected of us."

His voice seemed to hold hints . . . and veiled suggestions. Malfroy was direct.

"Come to the point, do. Who are you?"

"Compared with you, Mr. Lisle Malfroy, but an ambitious amateur. Have no fear of me, though . . . I admire you tremendously. You disposed of an uncle and aunt. I've only wanted to . . . for more years than I can remember. I shall never forget a turkey that wasn't basted properly, and my uncle's remarks thereon. But that's a Christmas reminiscence of mine and it won't interest you, my dear Malfroy. This is not the time for either chestnut stuffing or cranberry sauce. We will get back to your own exploits. Let me see—what was it about you that I admired so much? Oh, I know—that touch of the sherry . . . and the suggestion of the tin of salmon . . . as a medical man myself in the true descent of Neill Cream, I appreciated them both tremendously."

Malfroy was cold. "One moment. You haven't yet told me who you are. Am I to understand that you are a doctor?"

The man handed Malfroy a piece of paper. It was a newspaper cutting.

"Although not a Lisle Malfroy in the championship class of crime, I'm important enough to have my dial in the paper. That's yours truly. Good likeness, don't you think?"

Malfroy read the description and looked hard at the photograph. He laughed cynically as he took in every line of the man's features.

"An excellent likeness, indeed. I see that I have the honour of addressing Doctor Eric Chalmers of Kettering, and of particularly unsavoury memory."

"I like the way you put it," returned Chalmers, returning the cutting to his pocket. "By no means a catholic quality, there's a warmth about you that appeals to me. Every man's the better for it. What will you drink, Malfroy? Give it a name, man. Good wine or a fantastic poison of your own?"

He laid his hand on Malfroy's sleeve.

"Pardon me . . . my choice of words was somewhat unfortunate. I deeply regret the use of that last substantive. I must be more careful. Name your beverage, my dear fellow."

Malfroy, fully recovered, and as cool as a cucumber now, did as he had been requested. Chalmers smiled and ordered in duplicate.

"Your health, Malfroy," he toasted. "May you evade the menace of the years."

Malfroy imitated the action. "Thank you. And yours. Though the encounter to me, at least, is entirely unexpected, it is none the less pleasurable."

He drank. "Now you must allow me to return the compliment. The same again, I presume?"

Chalmers, with set face, nodded his approval. Malfroy waited for the drinks to be served and then pushed one across to Chalmers.

"And I presume, too, that you haven't scraped , acquaintance with me in order that we may gratify our respective thirsts and toast our delightful personalities. Once again, may I request you to come to the point, Doctor Chalmers?"

Chalmers drank . . . slowly and deliberately. Then he replaced his glass and turned coolly to his questioner. His voice found seriousness.

"You are right, Malfroy. Perfectly right. I had a set purpose when I first spoke to you. Like you, I am a desperate man . . . ready for a last tilt at Fortune and a last wrestle with Fate . . . caring not how heavy are the stakes."

He paused to watch Malfroy's reception of his statement. Malfroy made no sign. His handsome face was impassive . . . mask-like in its serenity . . . it might have been hewn from marble. Chalmers, a little disconcerted, perhaps, at his failure to evoke response, continued.

"As a result of this desire on my part, I have become interested in a certain number, Malfroy; a number with a sinister reputation . . . the number thirteen."

Malfroy started. Chalmers was quick to press home this first advantage that he had gained.

"I can see that you are beginning to understand me. Malfroy. I find that fact, at any rate, grateful and comforting. You were about to—er—observe . . . ?"

Malfroy ordered a further supply of drinks; the interview looked like lasting longer than he had anticipated at the first onset.

"Before we proceed further—who introduced you?" he asked curtly.

Chalmers wagged his head mysteriously and put a finger to his lips.

"No names, no . . . you know the rest, Malfroy, I don't doubt. But the last week of my stay . . . in what we will call my Government hotel . . . when I was a guest of His Majesty King George the Fifth—God save him—was devoted, from information received, mind you, to consideration of that number thirteen. After my—er—lengthy . . . vacation . . . it came as a boon and a blessing. It's astonishing how kind some people are."

He paused again.

"Particularly striking, those carved spoons, I thought . . . especially in these days of futuristic tendency."

Malfroy looked at him suspiciously and was on the point of verbal contribution, when there came usurping interruption. A third man joined them—with a boisterous vivacity. He nodded cavalierly to Malfroy and ignored Dr. Chalmers.

"Good evening, Monsieur Malfroy. My salutations." He raised his glass. "*A toi.*"

Malfroy seemed to come to a sudden decision. "For once, de Verviac, your arrival is distinctly opportune. Let me introduce you to this gentleman who is with me. I have an idea that you may find him interesting. M. de Verviac, Doctor Chalmers. Doctor Chalmers, M. de Verviac."

Malfroy was punctilious.

De Verviac raised his eyebrows . . . there was a suspicion of insolence there. He smirked. Chalmers' lips came to ugliness . . . and antagonism.

"You should know each other," went on Lisle Malfroy. "You should have much in common."

He turned to the doctor. "Show M. de Verviac what you showed me, Chalmers. He will be equally interested."

Chalmers hesitated . . . he became excessively wary . . . defensive and on guard. He looked from one to the other of his two companions. And he still hesitated. Malfroy saw and interpreted his diffidence.

"You need have no fear, Doctor Chalmers. I intended, by the phrase that I used, to make that clear to you. M. de Verviac is also interested . . . like I hope to be . . . like you, possibly, hope to be . . . in the activities of that disreputable number that you mentioned just now. So that you are quite safe in treating him exactly as you were prepared to treat me."

Chalmers gave way . . . albeit reluctantly. He delved in his pockets again for the newspaper cutting that he had shown to Malfroy and handed it silently to de Verviac. That consequential gentleman made ostentatious parade with the paper. He glanced at the photograph and then ran his eyes with an exaggerated impertinence over Chalmers' face. What he saw from the comparison seemed to satisfy him, for he then turned his almost dainty attention to the description of Chalmers that the cutting gave him. Again, he appeared to derive satisfaction. He read on with added zest.

"Excellent, my dear Doctor," he said at length. "I misjudged you. Now that I realise who you are—and what you are—I welcome you with open arms. Like myself, you would be an ornament in hell. When we pass over, you and I, they'll run cheap excursions on the Styx to welcome us."

He smiled and showed a gleam of teeth. Then he turned to Malfroy.

"And an aspirant for the big stakes—eh?"

Malfroy nodded.

"I thought so," continued de Verviac. "I am seldom wrong. Well—and why not?"

There was a gleam in his eyes.

He shrugged his shoulders.

"For myself, I adore it. The tang . . . the swift, sharp struggle . . . the doubt . . . the conflict itself! It is more to me, I think, than freedom. That is why I stay . . . apart from my materialistic soul . . . and its natural avarice."

Malfroy cut in. "There is no arrest yet . . . for the Rawlinson murder . . . that cursed English girl seems to have got clean away."

De Verviac laughed softly. "Don't call her that, my friend. Foolish perhaps . . . to refuse what the gods sent her. For she was very lovely . . . she had allurement. Even I—Raoul de Verviac— honoured her by desiring her. That in itself tells a story. Listen to me, gentlemen. If the police came to me, I could tell them much that they would give their heads to know. The man that killed Rawlinson . . . might have had another scalp in his belt . . . a greater scalp, by far, than that of a damned policeman. It grieves me to think that I've never found a name to give the dog. Ah, well . . . he must remain anonymous."

The soft laugh was repeated. Chalmers shook his head.

"I am bewildered. May I ask what all this means? I confess that I—"

Malfroy—strangely disturbed—checked him.

"You've been in 'stir,' my good fellow, you are not *au fait* with the latest happenings. Don't worry about that. You will find that the present will sufficiently cater for your needs."

Chalmers looked ugly again. Malfroy caught his arm.

"Keep your head and don't be a fool. Otherwise the big stakes will hold no interest for you. Haven't you sense enough to see that? The Rawlinson murder happened a fortnight ago . . . while you were—er—detained. It had nothing to do with . . . us."

His eyes held a wealth of meaning. He went on again.

"Rawlinson was—"

Then he stopped with an abruptness that caused both de Verviac and Chalmers to gaze at him fixedly. Malfroy had turned to look at something.

The door of the Taverne Suisse had opened and a man entered . . . followed by another. The first wore the uniform of a sergeant of the Belgian Police. The latter was a stout man . . . clean-shaven . . . with the far-seeing steel-blue eyes of a lover of the sea. Curious glances were thrown in their direction, but they came placidly through the people until they drew unconcernedly abreast of Chalmers, Malfroy, and de Verviac.

Sergeant Pauwels—the first man of the two—advanced to the bar. He spoke in English to his companion.

"What will you have?"

The stout man turned to answer the demand . . . and the turning gave Chalmers a full sight of his face. With a quick movement and a quicker imprecation, the doctor side-stepped Malfroy and began to walk rapidly away. It seemed that the memory of an urgent appointment had awakened in him. But, unfortunately for him, he was a matter of seconds too late. His quickness of bodily movement had defeated itself. It had called attention both to him and to his haste, and on the stout man's face there gleamed a glance of surprised understanding and recognition. He deliberately interposed his body and barred Dr. Chalmer's further escape.

"Hullo? Hullo? Pardon me, Sir, but I rather fancy that we have met before."

Chalmers scowled uncomprisingly. "I don't."

He attempted to move away, but the stout man stopped him.

"Come now, surely we're old acquaintances?"

Chalmers drew his shoulders back—an ugly twist to his lip.

"I was never an acquaintance of yours, to my knowledge. And I don't know that I've ever wanted to be. Neither of yours nor of any other 'busy'! Your rotten trade makes no appeal to me. . . . I like you and your kind at a distance, and then not so much that you'd notice it."

The stout man had himself under perfect control and smiled at Chalmers' vehemence.

"Steady, man, steady. I can well understand you having the views that you have. Because you've good reason to be prejudiced. All the same, you know me all right, and don't you deny it."

"I don't know you," returned Chalmers venomously, "and that's flat."

The blue-eyed man shrugged his shoulders. "Have it your own way."

De Verviac and Malfroy watched his face intently . . . he appeared to be so sure of himself . . . he impressed them against their wills. They wondered what he would say next. They hadn't long to wait. He went on.

"But if you don't know me, as you assert so aggressively, you must allow me to say that I know you. You're Doctor Chalmers, of Kettering, Northamptonshire, England. Will you deny that, my friend?"

"Why should I?" flashed Chalmers.

The stout man smiled again. "Well now, you mightn't think it . . . but I thought you might be a wee bit ashamed of it."

"Well, I'm not. Now you know. And let me tell you this. If you're under the impression that you can barge your way in here and—"

The other man raised his hand . . . a business-like-looking bunch of fives, if you observed it carefully.

"Now, now, Doctor Chalmers. . . . I'm not standing that sort of thing from you . . . threats from you won't cut any ice with me. You're the wrong side of the fence to hand them out. I know you, you see, which makes all the difference! For I pride myself on knowing a damned bad egg when I see one . . . well—with the next man."

Chalmers wilted obviously under the scourging. Most of his braggadocio melted like snow beneath the sun. He changed his tone.

"You take an unfair advantage of me," he complained. "I come into a place for a drink, as a peaceful and law-abiding citizen, and without the slightest warning—"

An icy voice cut him summarily.

"Do you remember the 'Ram' in Northampton the night that 'Punch' Martin lay at death's door with double pneumonia? When you opened that bag of yours and took out a test-tube . . ."

Chalmers' face went the colour of cream.

"Don't tell me you're Sergeant Chenils of the—"

"Chief-Inspector Chenils now, Doctor Chalmers, if you don't mind. Give the devil his due."

His face changed . . . his manner with it.

"And while I'm here, Doctor—and old lag—and I'm not in this country joy-riding, let me tell you—I'll be warning you. As far as what's happened in the past goes, we'll give it a miss. You've served your stretch for that and no bill need be paid twice. And if you go straight, my lips'll be all buttoned up for good. But go crooked, and get on the cross again with your own private brand of original sin bottled in hell itself . . . and I'll swear I'll make Belgium a damned sight too hot for you! So get that . . . and good evening to you."

He walked to where Sergeant Pauwels had been standing all the time and tossed off his drink with the quick tilt of the hand and steady balance that proclaimed the master.

"Come, Sergeant," he said curtly. "Let's get away from here. I don't care for the atmosphere. I'm an aristocrat . . . I was born and bred near Wapping Old Stairs . . . that makes a fellow rather high-hat, you know."

The two men went as quickly as they had come . . . guardians of law and order who seemed somehow to have lost their way for a time and then surprisingly found it again.

Malfroy eyed de Verviac. The latter returned the compliment. Then they eyed Chalmers . . . and de Verviac at the same time rubbed his hands.

"My friend," he whispered gently, "have you read the papers recently?"

"With regard to what?"

"Maturin—the young Englishman who was found in the Scheldt . . . the second one of his kind. Have you read about him?"

"What?"

"He was shot before his body got into the water."

He spoke softly, but he pointed to his temple . . . with significant drama.

"Through here. The doctors, so the papers say, have found the hole that the bullet made."

Malfroy betrayed but little concern. All that he did was to shrug his shoulders.

"He is dead. That is enough. How he died . . . what does it matter? The destination is what counts . . . as for the route . . . my dear de Verviac!"

De Verviac nodded. "You are right. Still, many things this evening have pleased me. It is rarely that such brilliant testimonials fall into one's lap. Doctor Chalmers!"

The man addressed came nearer, De Verviac probed him. "You spoke of the number thirteen . . . of the brotherhood of Matthias . . . him upon whom the lot fell . . . he was chosen by ballot, if you remember . . . and you spoke, too, of big stakes. Bend down a little, Doctor Chalmers . . . please."

Chalmers bent down. The gigolo whispered in his ear.

Then he put a question. "Do you understand?"

Chalmers nodded. "I think so. To-morrow evening, you say?"

De Verviac nodded. "To-morrow evening—at a quarter past seven."

"The Quai Van Dyck?"

"S'sh," de Verviac dropped his voice. "Turn down by the Hansa Huis . . . then three doors from the hotel that overlooks the Scheldt. Come with Malfroy. I am as certain as a man can be of these things, that the victor on the last occasion *will* take his prize. That means two vacancies. Serviatti and I will do the necessary. You may be lucky . . . who amongst us knows? Don't forget, too . . . Matthias . . . the thirteenth."

CHAPTER XXIV

THE LEAGUE OF MATTHIAS

DR. CHALMERS had been standing at the corner of the Quai Van Dyck for a period of two minutes before he was joined by Lisle Malfroy. On the latter's face there was a contemptuous sneer.

"Must you be so early? I'm not aware that I am late, and I positively loathe impatience."

"I am neither late nor early," returned Chalmers curtly. "I am merely punctual. I am a devout believer in the habit of punctuality."

"Your only virtue, I presume," rejoined Malfroy; "your one ewe lamb of virtues. No wonder you cling to it so tenaciously."

"Your judgment is marvellously accurate," replied Chalmers . . . "and yet the condition of possessing one isolated virtue must be better than that mean paltry state of having none at all. You will remember, my dear Malfroy, that in the country of the blind, the one-eyed man is king. God—how you must shiver."

Malfroy made no answer. As instructed, they swung round by the Hansa Huis. Chalmers turned to look at its allegorical figures in bronze. Malfroy was bitter but still silent. This doctor's quality of cold cruelty impressed even him. It seemed impersonal . . . almost mechanical.

"Where do we meet de Verviac?" asked Chalmers. "You mustn't forget that I am a child in these particular things."

"Don't worry. He will be there. At the appointed place. So I understood from him. And don't you forget that I know almost as little as you do with regards to the details of procedure. Not a child therefore . . . children."

Chalmers stared at him.

"Supposing Schoonbeke had not been—" he stopped abruptly.

A woman, in tattered dress and with spirits-tainted breath, lurched against him and pushed her face into his. Malfroy drew back with a sharp exclamation.

"Don't talk so loudly, you fool. Who knows who anybody is in this quarter of the city? At this hour especially."

He anticipated a torrent of verbal sarcasm from Chalmers, but, to his astonishment, there came, instead, an expression of agreement.

"You're right, Malfroy . . . I was indiscreet to mention names. And it's a damned funny thing—now that I come to think of it . . ."

He paused in reflection.

"What's a funny thing?" demanded Malfroy imperatively.

"Why . . . that woman. I've an idea that I've seen her before . . . more than once, too . . . she reminds me of somebody . . . still, we won't worry over that."

It seemed to Chalmers that Malfroy was shivering.

"If the man, whose name you so foolishly mentioned just now, had not been . . . you know what I mean . . . we should not have been wanted . . . yet. De Verviac would not have mentioned the word 'vacancies.' That's what you implied, isn't it?"

Chalmers nodded.

"It is obvious that you know something."

"A little. Very little." Malfroy's response was reluctant. "New Apostles are elected . . . from time to time . . . sometimes one . . . sometimes two . . . never more, though, than two at a time. I have been fortunate enough to gather those facts. Oh—and something else. When there are two elections, the alphabetical order of their names is taken into consideration. For example, from the numerical point of view of the League membership, I shall be junior to you . . . if our applications are successful. And the junior member, the thirteenth apostle that is, always draws the numbers. That's about the sum total of what I know."

Chalmers was mastered by the strength of his curiosity. "Who told you all this?"

"De Verviac. My reputation as a poisoner represented the strongest of invitations for his confidences. I was as welcome to him for pure companionship as the flowers in May. He invited me to the comfort of the Apostolic fold with open arms."

Chalmers looked across the waters of the Scheldt. He and Malfroy were on the right bank of the river . . . close to them were huge warehouses, a railway and a roadway. The roofs of the dock sheds, both north and south of the Steen, were laid out as terraces, with cafés on them, and, for the looking, there were to be had magnificent views of the river, at its finest by the light of evening, and of the city itself. Proud vessels lay right alongside the quay . . . ships of all nations, at their moorings or berthed in the various docks.

Rawlinson had been right. Quays, docks, sheds, warehouses, dark patches and sinister shadows. All of them imprisoning grief, vice, ecstasy, and even mysticism.

Three doors from an hotel that overlooked the river, Chalmers and Lisle Malfroy stopped. Before a warehouse that, externally, looked eminently ordinary. Chalmers took command. "Here?" he queried.

"I suppose so. According to de Verviac's direction. Knock on that door. That's our next move."

Chalmers needed no second bidding. He rapped on the door with his knuckles. Quietly and excessively smoothly, it opened to them. A man in a black velvet suit stood there on the threshold.

"Whom do you seek?" he demanded. He spoke in French.

"Matthias," answered Chalmers.

"The thirteenth Apostle," added Malfroy.

The man in black stood back courteously, but with some degree of austerity, to give them admittance.

"You will go straight through and up the staircase . . . there is a light . . . it will enable you to see your way perfectly. At the end of the corridor, you will come to a door covered with green baize— there are brass studs on it. You will remain outside that door until you receive further instructions. I can promise you that you will not be required to wait for an unreasonably long time."

Dr. Chalmers, of the East Midlands and unsavoury reputation, walked towards the lighted staircase. Lisle Malfroy followed him. They ascended. At a sharp turn of the flight of stairs, they found the corridor and eventually faced the door which the man in the black velvet had described to them. Neither spoke. They waited in silence as they had been directed. A quarter of an hour passed—a part of time that was absolutely and perfectly silent.

Suddenly, and without the slightest hint of warning, the studded door opened and a man with a quivering, creased face—the flesh of which hung in loose pouches and folds—beckoned to them to enter.

"Who were you?" he demanded in French again.

Malfroy was quick to notice the use of the past tense.

"Eric Chalmers." Chalmers was abrupt.

"Lisle Malfroy." Malfroy was eager.

"Whom do you desire to become?"

"Matthias. The number we know not." The answer came from Chalmers. Malfroy, however, to be on the safe side, repeated both the name and the phrase. The man at the door hurled a third question at them.

"When shall it be? And when was it?"

Malfroy hesitated perceptibly, but Chalmers was in like a flash—crisply and confidently.

"On the Saint's own day. On the twenty-fourth day of the second month."

"Enter then and be silent . . . until the time to speak comes. You will be informed when that will be."

Malfroy and Chalmers entered the room. It was brilliantly lighted and sumptuously decorated and furnished. There were present eleven men . . . and on the face of each were the unmistakable stamp and impress of evil. A thoroughly representative squad of the Devil's Own Brigade. Immediately he looked round, Chalmers picked out a big chair at the farther end of the room. It was upholstered in crimson velvet. Somewhat to his surprise, this chair was unoccupied. Malfroy's eyes were darting hither and thither and his observations were just as keen. Bearing in mind that the eleven men were seated, every one of them, Malfroy and Chalmers walked towards two chairs at the side of the room, which were vacant, and seated themselves. For an appreciable period of time there was a dead silence. The two newcomers knew without a doubt that they were facing a battery of physical examination . . . rigorous . . . searching . . . soul-stripping almost, in its relentless intensity. Suddenly the sinister silence of the room was broken. A man rose from his chair. Malfroy and the doctor recognised him. It was Raoul de Verviac. Like the others, he spoke in French—very rapidly and with a suggestion of breathlessness. Despite these conditions, however, his enunciation and articulation were perfect.

"*Messieurs et camarades!* The chair was to Nijegaard. But he has exercised his right and departed from our brotherhood. As the victor of the previous contest, I claim the chair. Who disputes?"

There was no answer to the claimant question. None spoke. None moved.

"Who supports?"

Ten men rose from their seats as one. De Verviac, with the superb swagger of the Gascon, made his way to the big chair at the end of the room.

"*Messieurs et camarades,*" he cried. "Be seated, please."

Ten men obeyed. De Verviac himself remained standing.

"Nijegaard." He passed his hand across his eyes. The gesture was ominous.

"Schoonbeke." He repeated the gesture. The ten men did as he had done with studied and meticulous imitation.

"Chalmers," he cried. Then he raised his hand above his head and the extended hand held a carved wooden spoon . . . the spoon of an Apostle!

"Malfroy." There followed, from him, an exactly similar movement.

"*Attendez . . . messieurs, s'il vous plaît.*"

Malfroy and Chalmers strained their ears . . . their zest to hear every word was burning . . . acute . . . superb. For they realised what was taking place. De Verviac was introducing them. He was their sponsor . . . how appropriate the word! Chalmers could hear the details of his own infamous career being described in glowing terms to this pack of men. He heard the array of adjectives that de Verviac employed to the architecture of his dishonour. De Verviac supplied with unsavoury and disgusting relish the details of the encounter with Chief-Inspector Chenils at the bar of the Taverne Suisse of which he had been witness and auditor. De Verviac was an orator . . . a most able advocate of Barabbas. He pointed the career of Chalmers with infinite verbal adornment, and then, with a magnificent peroration, came gradually to an artistic conclusion. He turned to Doctor Chalmers.

"Monsieur," he demanded softly, "you will be pleased to support my humble words on your behalf. Your credentials!"

Chalmers understood what was required of him. He handed up the press cutting and photograph which he had shown to Lisle Malfroy on the occasion of their first meeting in the Taverne Suisse. De Verviac walked from the red chair and passed the paper from hand to hand . . . it travelled slowly round the circle of craft and crime. Each man who looked at it not only read it avidly, but turned his glance on to Chalmers himself. Occasionally there were sinister noddings of approval. Chalmers bore these searchings scrutinies with nonchalance . . . why shouldn't he, he whispered to himself . . . they knew now, of a certainty, that he was as evil as they. Chalmers half chuckled at the realisation. In time, the papers travelled back to de Verviac, who placed them on the curved arms of the big chair . . . and started to declaim again.

This time it was Lisle Malfroy who found himself the subject of the speech. De Verviac was a trifle quieter in this his second of eulogy. Quieter, but with an attack no less convincing and effective. Eventually the moment came for Lisle Malfroy to imitate the example of his associate and to furnish his certificates. He passed them up, just as Doctor Eric Chalmers had done before him, and they, too, went their way along the ranks of rogues. The faces that had surveyed him and assessed Chalmers now surveyed and assessed him . . . until his papers found themselves back to de Verviac. That gentleman placed them with those of Chalmers on the arm of the red chair.

Then, standing erect, he called in a shrill voice: "*Messieurs et camarades* . . . your hands and badges! Shall it be Chalmers?"

The ten men to whom he had made the appeal again stood as one . . . right hand raised above head . . . and in the raised hand of each a carved wooden spoon. De Verviac turned. "Dr. Chalmers," he declared almost intimately, "your election to the League of Matthias is unanimous . . . your number, which you will retain until our next meeting, will be twelve. Our rules will be read to you within a few moments."

He began ceremonial again. Raising his voice to the shrill tone he had used before, he made his second appeal.

"*Messieurs et camarades*, your hands and badges again . . . shall it be Malfroy?"

Again the ten men raised their hands and spoons in the token of their acceptance and approval.

De Verviac addressed Malfroy.

"Lisle Malfroy," he announced quietly. "Your election to the League is also unanimous . . . and your number until we meet again, will be the number of Matthias himself . . . thirteen. It is a very privileged number."

The last sentence was almost whispered.

"And as I told our brother who is now number twelve, the rules will be read to you in a few moments."

The thirteen Apostles settled down in their seats.

De Verviac, from his chair of presidency, read the rules and commitments of the League. For twenty minutes his eager fanatical voice commanded the interest and attention of his hearers.

"There only remains," he said, "the fresh allotment of the numbers from one to eleven . . . occasioned by the biennial admissions, discharges, and—er—removals. They will be as follows:"

Malfroy leant forward in his chair, eagerly impetuous to hear every detail of the procedure and every syllable that was spoken.

Chalmers, as always, was cold and calculating. His number was twelve. Sufficient for him was that evil. Dr. Chalmers had never believed in journeying to meet trouble.

De Verviac was speaking again.

"The draw for the next contest will now take place. I will call upon the thirteenth Apostle to come forward to the chair of ceremonial and draw the two numbers . . . the numbers of the twain . . . between whom the conflict and the secret shall he."

Lisle Malfroy understood what he was expected to do.

He licked dry lips, clenched his hands . . . remembered his reputation . . . and walked steadily towards the President. De

Verviac held out to him a silver goblet, shaped, so it seemed to Chalmers' eyes, like a chalice. Malfroy thrust in his hand and drew out a square of paper. In a breathless silence he unfolded the square with trembling fingers.

"Number one," he announced quietly.

De Verviac took the paper and examined it eagerly. If Malfroy expected articulate response, he was disappointed. Not the vestige of a sound disturbed the room . . . overhung by its clinging canopy of evil. Malfroy searched de Verviac's face, extended his hand again and drew out a second white square. Again he went through the process of unfolding.

"Number thirteen," he declared in a voice husky with emotion. When he had delivered this second paper square to de Verviac, Malfroy swayed like a tree not yet to strength . . . as a quivering sapling that is shaken by a mighty wind.

De Verviac repeated the two numbers in a voice that all could hear, and the soul of Chalmers shrivelled within him at the smile that twisted the speaker's face. For Chalmers' mind contemplated problems. But a few days ago, let it be remembered, he had been in a very different place!

Why had Malfroy himself secured the devilish allotment that might have been his own . . . or, for that matter, have gone to any other of the grim thirteen? Fate, he decided, had not only dealt the cards, but had also named the suit that should be called trumps. These were the thoughts of Dr. Chalmers when he noticed that de Verviac was beckoning him. He pulled himself together and advanced to the ceremonial chair. De Verviac bent his head and began to speak. . . .

CHAPTER XXV
MALFROY CHOOSES HIS GROUND

ANTWERP, the boat that on a previous crossing had borne Lance Maturin, Philippa Castleton, and Anthony Bathurst from the city of the same name to the quay at Parkeston, now carried

Lisle Malfroy. The man who, to twelve other lawless men, was now known as the thirteenth Apostle.

For a reason best known to himself, he had turned his back upon the city of Antwerp and was travelling hot foot to the shores of England. As far as he could ascertain, after the closest consideration of the matter, he had at least twenty-four hours' start of his adversary. Just enough, in his opinion, to make matters interesting. "Number One plays Number Thirteen." His plans had been hastily arranged. He knew that only too well. But a sound plan, prepared though it may have been with amazing speed, should be a better proposition, in the end, than an unsound plan upon which a wealth of time and care has been expended. None knew the truth of that better than Lisle Malfroy. He had learned that lesson in the academy of experience. Raoul de Verviac might well be a master of craft, but he would find that in Lisle Malfroy he had a foeman worthy of his steel and stealth.

On the boat, Lisle Malfroy kept religiously to his cabin, and spent the better part of the time in the careful examination of certain papers that he took from his suitcase. What he found in them seemed to afford him a considerable degree of satisfaction, for, when he replaced them, he fancied his chances in the battle of wits with de Verviac even more than he had previous to reading them.

As the boat approached the English shores and Harwich, he went on deck and took stock of his fellow voyagers. He hit against nothing calculated to cause him the slightest uneasiness. A man . . . a big fellow . . . glanced at him shrewdly and somewhat critically . . . . but nothing happened beyond that. Generally keeping well away from him, Malfroy was nevertheless able to hear, on one occasion, one of the officers address the man as Paton. After that incident, Malfroy avoided him, and Paton, on his part, betrayed not the slightest interest in Malfroy's doings.

The boat ran alongside Parkeston Quay after having made an excellent passage. Malfroy disembarked and, without as much as a glance over his shoulder, walked quickly away from the landing-stage—to a car that had obviously been awaiting his arrival. He gave an address to the chauffeur which the latter repeated in tones that betokened some surprise.

"'The Ingots,' sir?" he queried. "Why, that's the—"

Malfroy gave the address for the second time . . . roughly and impatiently. The chauffeur stared insolently. The knot of quayside loungers who had gathered round, recognised antagonism and evinced interest . . . a matter of this kind, if it developed properly, brought a spice to life. The news spread and the group received additions.

"I don't know that I need any observations from you concerning my destination," declared Malfroy frigidly. "Kindly drive me according to my directions."

The chauffeur shrugged eloquent shoulders and accepted the inevitable. The captains of industry who had watched the spurt of flame . . . only to see it die down and burn out . . . turned away disappointed and returned to their task of doing nothing. The chauffeur scowled and swung himself into the driving-seat.

The car drew away. Lisle Malfroy was *en route* for his destination. An hour after he had left the quay, he shrank back from the window of the car . . . to avoid the sight of a man walking towards it. The man was Lance Maturin . . . whom Malfroy had no wish, at that moment, to meet. Delay meant danger and complications, both of which were best avoided. He smiled grimly as once again he surveyed the situation as he saw it. But even in the moment of his smiling . . . matters were coming rapidly to a head . . . for the best of reasons . . . Raoul de Verviac was hot upon his track . . . number one against number thirteen . . . seconds out of the Ring!

CHAPTER XXVI
CHIEF-INSPECTOR CHENILS INVESTIGATES

CHIEF-Inspector Chenils watched the retreating figure of Dr. Eric Chalmers, and deliberately slackened his pace, so that he saw it turn into the Quai Van Dyck. Chenils remembered the encounter in the Taverne Suisse, rubbed the line of his jaw with the back of his hand and thought hard. Every moment now, his problem was becoming more acute, and, acting under instructions recently received from headquarters, he was on his way to the Hôtel de Lutèce . . . the hotel that had housed Hilleary, Fawcett and Lance Maturin when they had stayed in the city of Antwerp . . . at the time of the murder of Inspector Rawlinson.

Outside the hotel, Chenils, according to arrangement, was joined by Sergeant Pauwels. The two men entered, and the reception clerk who gave them his attention listened to them assiduously. Pauwels was curt and immediately made his meaning clear.

"I understand your requirements," said the reception clerk. "I will see if I can find the manager. It is plain that you must have an interview with him."

He went on his way. Pauwels and Chenils kicked their heels. After a time, the manager of the Lutèce came to them. Pauwels repeated his statement. The manager showed signs of apprehension. The last people wanted in an hotel are the police. Always . . . that is a *sine qua non*. Give an hotel a bad name and . . .

"There is no trouble, I trust?"

His voice was almost querulous in its anxiety. Pauwels shrugged his shoulders.

"There has been. That is enough. You have not forgotten the murder of the English detective Rawlinson in the Rue du Sacré Coeur, have you? Well . . ." The manager spread out his hands, palms upwards. "I have not. How can one? The matter created too much of a sensation to be forgotten so quickly. But that is nothing to do with this hotel, Sergeant. That should not have brought you here."

Sergeant Pauwels rubbed the side of his nose.

"Ah! Who can say? At any rate we are here now to make certain enquiries. It will be the time to talk when we have done that. Will you kindly turn up your register of guests on that particular date?" He handed the man a slip of paper which he took from his pocket. Pauwels proceeded.

"That is the date of the Rawlinson murder . . . I expect that you have already noticed that."

The manager went a shade paler at Pauwels' words, but nodded. He produced the hotel admission register. The interview took a new turn.

"Now, friend Chenils," prompted Pauwels, "tell him what you want."

Chenil's steel-blue eyes lit into a keener interest. He ranged himself at the manager's side.

"You had three guests here that day . . . three young Englishmen they were. They'd been staying here, I think, for some few days before the Rawlinson murder. Their names were Fawcett, Maturin, and Hilleary. You've got 'em there, I suppose?"

The manager ran his finger down the various names in the book.

"Yes. Here they are. As you said . . . Fawcett . . . Hilleary, and Maturin. Yes . . . they're the three. Ah . . . that reminds me of something . . . something that you might very well call peculiar."

Pauwels and Chenils pounced simultaneously.

"Oh—in what way? Explain."

"I will, Sergeant. Mr. Maturin was the young gentleman who left us so suddenly. There was an evening when he did not come back to the hotel. His belongings were left here. It was strange . . . something unexpected must have happened to him. His two friends saw to his things when they left here, and also, of course, settled his account. But of Mr. Maturin himself, we never saw so much as a glimpse again. He went out and never came back."

Pauwels and Chenils nodded approval. The news was to their liking . . . for the best reasons . . . they knew the truth of it. Chenils put cheese into trap.

"That evening . . . when Maturin failed to return to your hotel . . . was the evening on which Inspector Rawlinson was murdered. Here in Antwerp. Do you realise that?"

The manager became a bundle of nerves.

"I do now. I confess that I hadn't done so before. I scarcely—"

"Do you mean to say that you had never connected the two events?"

"Never. Not for one instant."

"I see. H'm! It didn't suit you to, I expect. Well . . . that's as far as we can go with the man named Maturin. But he's only one of the three men who were located here. Let's have a look at number two . . . the man named Fawcett."

The manager seemed a little surprised.

"Mr. Fawcett? What of him?"

Pauwels, from the stronghold of his knowledge, listened eagerly to this exchange of question and answer. Chenils had been primed . . . and it was essential that the manager should be tested. If he rang true twice, there was the overwhelming probability that he would do the same on the third occasion.

"Can you tell us if this man Fawcett slept here on the night of the Rawlinson murder?"

"Mr. Fawcett?" The manager repeated the name and rubbed his cheek. Then he turned away and beckoned to an underling.

"Knopp."

The stout porter came quickly up to him. Chenils heard sharp sentences. A question. Then the reply supported by curt explanation. Another question. A second reply. The manager—his name was Lambelet—came back again to Chenils and Pauwels.

"I have enquired of the porter," he announced—"the porter who was on duty on the night in question. And there is something strange about it all. Mr. Fawcett slept here, in the hotel, for part only of the night of the murder. He came in very late. It was well into the morning, in fact. Knopp remembers him coming in quite clearly. Also, Knopp says . . ."

Lambelet showed signs of hesitation. Chenils endeavoured to assist him.

"Well . . . what else does Knopp say?"

Lambelet found words.

"That Mr. Fawcett appeared strange and by no means at his ease. He looked ill . . . 'dazed' was the word that Knopp used to me. Knopp asked him, so he tells me, if there were anything the matter . . . if he could get him anything . . . but Fawcett shook his head, refused Knopp's offer, said that he felt all right, was only tired and that he was going straight to bed."

Again Pauwels exhibited symptoms of approval. For, once more, Lambelet's story bore the guinea-stamp of truth. Chenils tried his third attack.

"Now for the third member of that little holiday expedition—the man named Hilleary." He affected carelessness. "Hilleary. Let us examine him as we have examined the others. Did Hilleary sleep in the hotel on the night in question?"

Lambelet turned and spoke to the porter again. There was no responsive volubility on this occasion, however. Knopp seemed to have little or nothing to say. The manager was inclined to argue . . . and eventually came to expostulation. To no avail. Knopp was taciturnity itself. He had taken up a position and he meant to hold it.

"You don't know," argued Lambelet.

"No."

Chenils heard Knopp say something more.

"The *femme-de-chambre*."

Knopp shrugged his shoulders. Lambelet surrendered the information that he had obtained from his subordinate.

"Knopp tells me that Mr. Hilleary did not sleep here that night. That is all he will permit himself to say. For further details, he refers me to the chambermaid."

The manager looked up interrogatively. Pauwels nodded.

"We must see her, Inspector," he said. "That is certainly indicated."

"I agree."

Messengers were despatched. The chambermaid became one of the party. She was taxed . . . demands were made upon the storehouse of her memory. The woman in her came to her rescue and their service.

"I can answer that," she said quickly—"your enquiry about the gentleman. Mr. Hilleary did not sleep in his room on the night you mention. He came in just before breakfast-time. I know that because I had gone to his room to tidy up as usual, and I was in his room when the door opened and Mr. Hilleary came in . . . and told me to clear out. That's the kind of thing a girl like me remembers."

She tossed her head, in a reminiscence of indignation.

"There you are, Pauwels," said Chenils, "what did I tell you? Three of 'em . . . Fawcett, Hilleary, and Maturin. All stayed in this hotel, had been here for some days, but on the night that Rawlinson was put out—mark you—every man jack of the three is somewhere else! Make what you like of it—but it's damned funny. You can pay your money and take your chance, but it looks to me like a damned arrangement. Mr. Bathurst *saw* Fawcett, you say?"

"Yes. He was with me when we picked him up."

"Did he say much to him?"

"H'm—they chatted together a bit. Your Mr. Bathurst asked him certain questions—natural questions—and the young man, Fawcett, told his story. You know what the story was, Inspector. . . . I told you the other day."

Chenils was puzzled. More puzzled than he had been before. More puzzled even than he cared to admit.

"Have you checked up again on that fellow de Verviac's story?" he asked of Pauwels.

Pauwels shook his head. "Not again, my friend."

"Why not? I think that he might tell us a lot more than he has. He was in the house—remember—on the night of the murder. Mr. Bathurst is positive of that. Have another go at him . . . that's my advice . . . as soon as possible."

"Not so simple as it sounds, Inspector Chenils."

Chenils turned and surveyed Pauwels critically.

"What the hell do you mean, Pauwels? What's crawling over you? Let's have it."

"Nothing. But there's a difficulty that you don't appreciate, my friend."

"What's that?"

"I can't get at our friend de Verviac . . . to check him up again, quite so easily as you seem to imagine."

Chenils stared. "You can't? Why not? What's happened?"

"De Verviac has disappeared. According to one of my best men—Rombouts his name is—de Verviac has slipped through my fingers and has crossed to England."

"In that case, then," said Chenils, "you and I, Pauwels, need not stay in the Hôtel de Lutèce any longer. For friend de Verviac will discover what many people have discovered before. That it's a much simpler matter to get into my country than to get out."

He turned to go—and Sergeant Pauwels followed him.

Chapter XXVII
GATHERING CLOUDS
(Story told again by Lance Maturin)

I GOT back to Trueloves, on the night that Philippa had met Paton at Victoria pretty late. My first enquiries elicited the fact that Bathurst's prognostication concerning Philippa's return to my home was bang on the mark. I hunted round for her and eventually discovered her in the music-room. All that my mind reacted to, with any degree of efficiency, were the last few words that Anthony Bathurst had addressed to me.

"Go home and make love to your Miss Castleton, Maturin. I think that you'll find her a wee bit disappointing . . . but don't fret over that . . ."

I hated playing a part to her, but Bathurst, in his wisdom or otherwise, had left me no option. I assumed the mantle, therefore.

"You are back, then?" I exclaimed with a feigned surprise. "I hope to God that everything is all right."

She turned her head away from me and then slowly signalled the affirmative.

"You don't seem over-enthusiastic about it," I supplemented . . . waiting to see if she were on the point of telling me anything. But I was destined to be disappointed—she was silent. I stabbed again—more deeply this time.

"I understood that when you went away, that your destiny was at stake . . . you say now that everything's all right . . . but instead of being happy, as one might expect you to be, you're troubled and—if I may presume so—unhappy."

She forced a smile to her face.

"Don't worry over me, Rudolf, I'm not worth it."

Bathurst's words came to me again, as I assured her.

"I can't help worrying over you," I said fiercely. "You see—I love you."

"I know you do—and it's very sweet of you."

She laid her hand on my arm.

"And the knowledge of that love of yours should make me happy, shouldn't it? But sometimes . . . it doesn't. Everything's all wrong, Rudolf . . . and I can't help it."

The tears came to her eyes.

"Why?" I intervened. "What do you mean?"

"I can't tell you, my dear. And if I could, it wouldn't make you any happier. And I'm ever so worried, if you only knew. Sometimes I wish I'd never asked for your help . . . that I'd let de Verviac have his way with me. It might have saved an endless amount of trouble."

I shivered—for the hint even of these things singed my soul. Philippa went on.

"At any rate, I should have saved you pain . . . and that, I think, at the present moment, would be my heart's delight."

This was spoken with sweetness, and I cried my joy aloud to her.

"You love me, Philippa! You must—to say things to me like that."

I tried to take her in my arms, but she resisted me.

"I don't know, Rudolf . . . yet. If only we had met before . . . before those other things happened about which I told you . . . there would have been no doubt about it. But, as it is . . . I don't know."

My jealously of her previous lover flamed in my soul again.

"Can't you possibly forget?" I cried desperately . . . deliberately trying to force the truth from her. "Can't you remember how he treated you . . . how he deserted you . . . left you to starve and die, for all he knew or cared?"

To my amazement, her eyes were shining.

"Don't, Rudolf," she said, "that hurts a little, you know. And it's unworthy of you."

Suddenly, her mood changed and she became a different creature.

"Oh . . . let's be happy," she cried, "while we may . . . we've got each other now . . . let's forget everything else in the world. Put something on the gramophone . . . there's a dear lad."

I accepted her mood.

"What shall it be?"

"Take a chance, Rudolf. Take the first record you find. I'd like to persuade myself that it will have a message for us. I'm a weird little beast, you know . . . full of omens and superstitions. . . . Daddy always said that I was half-pagan and must have learned to spell from the Sibylline books."

I put on the record and let it revolve . . . caught her hand and listened eagerly for what would come. There followed the little interval of rotation . . . I looked across at the girl whom I had learned to love.

"If you were the only girl in the world . . ."

After a time . . . "I would say such wonderful things to you . . . there would be such wonderful things to do."

The girl looked away from me . . . but her eyes were soft and sweet. The record ran to its finish.

She found another mood.

"Now another one, Rudolf," she cried gaily. "Pick it from anywhere just as you did that one. Don't choose anything deliberately."

Again I obeyed her. I waited as I had waited before. The words and the music came to us.

"Sometime soon to be . . . there's a lover's moon to be . . . I want you to kiss . . . for there must be two to kiss."

My companion's voice broke into the melody.

"Twilight soon will fade . . . I'll meet you at the masquerade . . ."

I deliberately attuned my spirit to hers.

I returned the words to her.

"Lady dressed in jade . . . hold me tight at the masquerade."

She held out her hand to me . . . was coming towards me . . . speaking. . . . "I have a fancy, Rudolf . . . that you and I *will* meet at a masquerade . . . perhaps it will be the last"—when I heard the stir of voices and the bustle of feet. I stopped the gramophone so that I might the better listen. There were people at the front entrance. I heard my father's voice welcoming them—whoever they were.

I heard, too, another voice raised a little higher than the others.

It was a voice with which my ear was familiar, and I motioned to Philippa to be silent.

"Listen," I said to her, "there are visitors come to Trueloves. It's over-late for chance callers and I'm a little puzzled. I've heard a voice that I know very well."

I went to the door of the music-room and opened it at a comparatively happy moment—for I encountered my father on his way to find me.

"There are two friends of yours here, Lance, extra special friends, my boy. They tell me that they couldn't exist any longer without news of you."

His eyes twinkled. "I told them that you were rather busily engaged, but even that delicate hint failed to assuage their curiosity and they insisted on coming along. Extraordinarily complimentary to you, you know, my boy—say what you like! A rare tribute of friendship. I question whether anyone would fuss over me like it—at all events I should feel very bucked if one did. But come on out and speak to them. I'll do my best to entertain Miss Windmill."

Even then, I was at a loss to identify the visitors, and I sailed out, racking my brains as to whom they could be and still unable to place the voice that I seemed to know so well.

A second later, revelation came to me.

For there, waiting for me in the hall, with out-stretched hands and grinning faces, were Fawcett and Dennis Hilleary.

And under my breath I cursed them for having come between me and the precious moments of Philippa. But for courtesy's sake I went to them and lied.

Chapter XXVIII
THE FOLLY OF WISDOM
(Told by Lance Maturin)

HILLEARY and Adrian Fawcett were, of course, incredibly glad to see me. They said they were, which is conclusive. I hadn't looked upon either of them since that evening when Hilleary had shepherded us into that place of the scarlet flare and the trouble had started. I gave them such explanations as I considered necessary and expedient, but all the time I felt that Hilleary's eyes were tenanted by the little devil of doubt. He had always been a deep 'un, had Master Dennis!

About Fawcett, however, there seemed to hang the aura of a change. He wasn't carrying his usual mood of super self-confidence; he appeared to much less certain of himself than I had always known him. However, I had little time to amplify my diagnosis, for Hilleary was pressing me for further details of my escapades on the night of our separation.

"I knew it was an affair of the heart," he declared with mock gravity, "and I fended Fawcett off, whenever he opposed the knight-errant notion."

Here he paused to fling a curious glance in Fawcett's direction, and then made a remark that caused me to start with surprise.

"That Rawlinson murder was a queer business, Maturin! You've read about it, old man, no doubt? What did you make of it?"

"Not a lot, I'm afraid," I answered him—"had too much to think about, for one thing. My hands have been pretty full."

"To say nothing of your arms—eh?"

I saw Hilleary watching me carefully as he spoke, and felt rather relieved when Fawcett came in.

"My condolences, Lance," said the latter quietly, "if it's not too late—on the death of your cousin. I saw a paragraph in one of the Belgian papers. It hinted pretty strongly at foul play. I'm always sick when I hear of a fine career cut to ribbons."

"Thanks, Fawcett," I returned—"er . . . come along and let me introduce you to Miss Windmill."

I took the two of them along with me to the music-room.

"Philippa," I said as I entered—the guv'nor had gone, evidently—"here are two men to see you. They're two of my greatest friends, if you want to know, and they've come miles to enquire after my health. From Antwerp, as a matter of fact."

At the name of the town, the colour left her cheeks. "Miss Philippa Windmill," I announced . . . "Adrian Fawcett . . . Dennis Hilleary."

She bowed.

"Incidentally," I continued, "they've seen you before, though you may fail to remember them."

I saw Philippa square her shoulders, as though bracing herself for an ordeal.

She answered with dignity. "You do me an injustice, if you only knew . . . for, on the contrary, I do remember this gentleman . . . and this other gentleman—well—I remember him very well indeed."

At my father's invitation, Hilleary and Fawcett stayed at Trueloves that night and for several nights. A couple of bedrooms were prepared for them and it was well past one o'clock on the first night before we all turned in. Days passed uneventfully. One morning during the following week I got down to the breakfast-room fairly late. For me, that is. I am usually an early bird. When I arrived I could see, from the condition of the sideboard, that several of the others must have been down before me and have acquired savoury worms.

I helped myself to some slices of Scotch ribs and then to a spot of veal-and-ham pie, and actually—as it happened—breakfasted alone—which was another unusual occurrence. I came to the conclusion, as I approached the finish of my meal, that I must be the last boy in school. I looked in the billiard-room, poked my nose into various places where merchants most usually did congregate—with no luck at all—and then decided that I'd stroll out somewhere. For it was a glorious morning that called to me incessantly and made *Te Deum* in one's heart!

The walk that I took was one that I had loved ever since I first knew it. We had come to Trueloves in the winter of a year. I had first taken this walk on a Saturday about a week before Christmas . . . the date, I fancy, had been December 17th, and the day had been heralded by a most marvellous morning sky. Colours of copper, amethyst, dull red, and purple had vied with each other in the preparation of a shepherd's morning. Everybody whom I had passed predicted torrential rain, but for once the celestial portents were wrong, and there followed one of the most exquisite December days that I have ever lived . . . that I shall ever live, I think. This is how the walk went:

Up the slope by the side of Trueloves until I hit the road where stood the red house that belonged to Colonel Womersley. Along by the grounds of the house, until I reached the footpath that led to Latiman and Braddock. Across the main road till I reached that glorious wood of old elms underneath which, at the bottom of a verdant slope, stirred the lazy waters of the Shess. Then up to the fine of hurdles planted slant-wise by the side of the old church, with its Tudor Mausoleum, down the hill to the hostelry known as the "Huntingdon Arms," and past the old cottages until I hit the road again to the old railway arch and Trueloves. It was a beautiful road, this. A road that bore the spirit of England.

With long stretches of green on either side of it. So unlike the corners of most foreign fields.

It was a windless morning as I walked now. The waters of the Shess rippled only at the occasional jump of a questing fish. The sun was veiled in mist. In the world of haste and flux, this little corner of the county of Essex was a symbol of stability and repose. I stopped by the cut trunk of an ancient elm, that had been hewn by the arms of man into a trysting-seat for lovers, faithful and unfaithful, and, from my altitude, looked right down at the Shess water. There was a stretch of it that I could just see between a line of trees. As I watched the river, and tossed my thoughts to and fro, I suddenly heard the throb of a motor-boat.

Unthinkingly, almost, I turned my head to watch for the boat's coming. For a time, it was invisible. The noise of its approach was the only evidence of it that my senses knew. But at last it came speeding into sight. There were two occupants of the boat. Even from where I was, my eyes picked this fact out easily. As the boat swept past the belt of trees that I mentioned . . . my heart came almost to a standstill . . . I rubbed my eyes . . . to no avail . . . I couldn't alter the truth or banish the bitterness . . . the girl in the boat was Philippa . . . the Philippa who held my heart. The man, I was unable to identify, for Philippa was between him and me. All I could see was, that, judging from his sweep of shoulder, he was a man of fine physique. Then I saw something else as the boat sped by. Philippa was talking with extraordinary vivacity . . . pointing her remarks with quick impulsive hand gestures and head movements.

The motor-boat passed out of the range of my sight and left me there by the old tree trunk . . . for the better part of two hours. In time, I pulled myself together and walked my way, the prey to bitter musings. Where had Philippa been that morning? With whom was she now? What was the end of it all going to be? These questions hammered at the portals of my brain.

I had walked on for a couple of hundred yards, I suppose, and reached the old farmhouse that lies close to the railway arch. They serve refreshments in its front room. Teas and such like. New laid eggs, biscuits and honey. You eat them overlooked by pictures from Christmas annuals.

Just before I came abreast of it, I saw a man push open the gate and walk up the road a few paces in advance of me. And I clenched my fists at the sight and cursed him . . . for the man that walked the road in front of me . . . was Raoul de Verviac. I began to hasten, in the hope of overtaking him, when something else happened that caused me to pull up short in my tracks. I was not the only person after de Verviac! A tall woman in a red dress came out of the wood to his left and fell in behind him . . . stealthily and furtively.

CHAPTER XXIX
THE WORLD STANDS STILL
(Story continued by Lance Maturin)

IT IS my desire that my readers should visualise with accuracy the entire situation. Consider it as it was De Verviac in the van, the tall woman behind him, and I bringing up the rear—the woman, if you like, the ham between the two slices of bread that made up the human sandwich. De Verviac was so intent upon his way that he seemed perfectly oblivious to the fact that he was being followed. We went past the narrow lane that led down to Trueloves, past the embankment that skirted the railway line, and then straight on again for at least another mile. At the Hawkridge sandpit, with its treacherous waterpool, de Verviac turned, and, as he turned, I became suddenly aware of his intended destination. This realisation came to me in a flash. He was making for "The Ingots"—the house that had been my cousin's—about another half-mile beyond. I was proved to be right, and when he reached the swinging-gate of the field that separated "The Ingots" from the road, the woman between him and me drew away from the possibility of his observation and crept well to the left of the road into the cover of the hedge. The bend of the road hid her now from the man in front, and, knowing that I was less happily placed, I lay full length along the dank bank of an unpretentious ditch.

De Verviac turned for the fraction of a moment, threw a careless glance behind him, passed through the gateway opening and started on his journey of crossing the field. For a time I stayed where I was. I was waiting to see what the woman in the red dress would do. Now that the risk of being seen was lessened, because de Verviac had left the road, and in order to see better myself, I stood up. Please understand that the woman was about a hundred and fifty yards in front of me. As I came to the standing position again, I was destined to receive yet a further shock.

A slim graceful figure ran across the white width of road and attached herself to the tall woman who had crouched into the cover of the hedgerow. I knew instantly who it was—and again I marvelled! The girl was Philippa Castleton! To my utter amazement, she seemed to know the woman, for a quick snatch of conversation passed between them. Indeed, it occurred to me very forcibly, from the condition of the encounter as I saw it, that this meeting was no chance happening, but had been brought about by definite arrangement. They talked together, and opinions clashed, I think. Because Philippa caught the woman's hand, and, to my idea, as I watched that distance away, began to plead with her in regard to something. At all events, the tall woman shook her head repeatedly, and eventually I saw Philippa shrug her shoulders in a kind of silent resignation and surrender her cause as a bad job.

The woman patted Philippa's cheek with a curious touch that almost suggested proprietorship, turned through the gateway, entered the field and began to approach "The Ingots." But she approached not by the route of the main path, but by skirting the side of the hedge and working towards the house in a sideways direction. For some little time I stayed where I was. Philippa was my primary interest, and I naturally wanted to see what her next move would be. She walked up to the gate, opened it, and went into the field—and then I lost sight of her. I deliberated for a while, and ultimately made up my mind to investigate matters generally. One thing stood out clearly as I surveyed the situation. I had no love for Monsieur de Verviac, and little confidence in his behaviour as a gentleman. Also, there was a second point. I was curious to discover the reason of the tall woman's interest in him. Her sudden entry into the cast puzzled me. I therefore made my way quickly down the road and into that field that lay against my cousin Lancelot's house.

Of the woman, or of Philippa, there was now no sign. They might have been spirited to other realms for all that there was to be seen of them. For a reason that I can't adequately explain, when I came to the broad part of the field-path which fed "The Ingots," I started to run . . . and as I ran I thought of that first

Easter morning and of "the other disciple who did outrun Peter," and come first to the empty sepulchre.

Lancelot's house was a comparatively small one—of Tudor design. It had been there for centuries, naturally, and he had been able to purchase it, for renovation and modernising, for a mere song. I had always loved its old oak beams, pine floorings, and quaint gables, and as I came close to the door at the front I wondered, now that he was dead, to whom it would come. The main door was open. It yielded immediately to my push. The lounge-hall, in which I found myself, was small but luxuriantly furnished. You could see Lancelot's deftness and certainty of touch in everything there. Beneath a modern ceiling it was crossed by two massive oak beams. Here it had been rebuilt, but Lancelot had insisted that the beams should not be touched. The panellings and floor were of polished pine.

A chamois-skin rug lay across the floor and candle-sconces glittered on the mantel.

As I crossed the threshold, that strange and inexplicable feeling which at times we all endure took possession of me—the idea that I was under intimate observation! I looked cautiously round, therefore, before I moved very far.

I could see nobody . . . and I could hear nobody.

I strained my ears in an attempt to hear the staircase creak . . . or to catch a sound of any movement in one of the other rooms. To no avail. The house, with its rooms, for all the sound it or they knew, might have been empty, save for my unworthy self. And yet . . . just previously . . . I had seen three people . . . on their respective ways here. . . .

Suddenly, I became aware! At the leaded window-pane there bulged a heavy curtain that hung from top to floor. The moment I looked at it, I understood the *fontem et originem* of my feeling of uneasiness. For somebody was hiding behind that curtain! I endeavoured to measure with my eye the lines of the concealed form . . . was it de Verviac? But I discovered nothing that brought me any real satisfaction or uncertainty. Another idea came to me. Walking noiselessly to the curtain, I knelt down in front of it and gently turned a fold of it to one side. To disclose a brogue, on a foot by far too small, too shapely, and too slender to be a man's. Then I knew the truth. Behind that curtain stood the girl I loved. I think she must have shivered when the curtain-length stirred over her feet because the hanging folds trembled just a little as I looked at them . . . but she gave me no other token that she was conscious of my presence. I turned away . . . doubtful . . . uncertain . . . seeking her reason for this concealment.

The tranquillity, the repose, the almost deathly quiet of poor old Lancelot's house worried me . . . if only for the fact that they were so totally unexpected to me. Again I cudgelled my brains. Three people had crossed the field in front of me. Where were they? Other questions darted from the secrecy of their hiding-places, and began to torture me. From whom did Philippa hide? Where and who was the man who had been her companion in the motor-boat that I had seen on the Shess but a short time before?

Within the space of a split second I had my answers. God help me in the telling! I understood the slight movement of that curtain that hid Philippa. For the moment, I was more than either startled or surprised—I was frozen with horror.

Between cream-coloured ceiling and oaken beam, stretched along the latter's brown length, I saw the body of a man . . . serpentine almost in its sinister suggestion. The glint of his eyes and the curiously quick movement of his limbs told me that it was de Verviac. It was at this moment—forgive me, sweetheart—that I made my fatal mistake. For this reason: I heard the slightest of sounds behind me . . . turned almost imperceptibly . . . and saw, standing at the front door, the tall woman in red.

But I had taken my eyes off de Verviac, and this fact had given him his chance. In an instant, with incredible swiftness, he had dropped from the beam. On to his clever twinkling feet. I saw him raise his hand. I saw the tall woman rush towards him . . . and then I cried aloud, for to my unspeakable and eternal agony I saw Philippa throw her dear body in front of mine . . . just as two shots came spitting from de Verviac's revolver. Philippa held my hand and sank slowly on to her knees. There came a rush of feet past me . . . the feet of de Verviac and another, but it meant nothing to me. Except for the girl in front of me I was unconscious. The world stood still! As I knelt by her side, my darling still clutched at my fingers, and with my help tried to buoy herself up. The effort was in vain . . . her hurt body was unable to obey her brain. She sank to the ground again and the tears ran unchecked down her face. I pillowed her head against me as best I could. That it should have to end like this! She spoke . . . and I put my ear to her lips. When she saw me come closer to her, she smiled a little, and my stricken soul tore at its bonds as I gazed down at the white face below me.

"Rudolf" . . . she whispered very softly and with some difficulty . . . "I haven't long to stay with you, my dear . . . but there's something that I want to tell you. Something . . . first of all . . . for which I want your forgiveness, and then something else, for which I want you to thank me. I think that it will make you happy. Listen."

I put my arm round her and supported her.

It was clear to me that her strength was ebbing fast.

"Listen, I know that I was ready to give another man my body . . . forgive me for that, my dear . . . it has hurt me ever so much to hurt you, but I had promised him, you see . . . but understand . . . there's this as well . . . you are the only man to whom I have ever given my soul. Pleased? Try to be, for my sake."

I couldn't speak . . . for I choked with pain and bitter suffering. I just nodded to her what she wanted to know, and kissed the dear lips and glorious hair that I had learned to love so well. Then she pulled my fingers down to her lips and held them there . . . pressed hard . . . for what seemed a long while. I gave her the loving comfort of my arms. My tears had stopped now . . . but my soul was burnt and tortured and writhed in hell. Words came from her lips in snatches. I listened to them. She was back to the days of her girlhood. Back to worship, I thought, in her father's church at Longbarrow. Yes . . . the festivals of the Church's year were rioting in her dying mind . . . "Christmas," I heard her whisper. "And out of the East where the old gods are, Caspar, Melchoir, Balthazar . . . For the light of a star in the darkling sky . . . Palm Sunday . . . the Sunday next before Easter . . . Ride on, ride on, in Majesty . . . The Angel Armies of the sky

. . . Look down with sad and wondering eyes . . . To see the . . . Harvest. The valleys stand so thick with corn that even they are singing . . . Evensong . . . Just before Advent . . . A dark afternoon in November . . . Where in joys unheard of . . . Saints with Angels sing . . . Never weary raising . . . Praises to their King . . ."

Her voice trailed off, and minutes, I should think, passed in silence. Nothing mattered to me. Nothing at all, for I knew that the end was near. She rallied . . . the last flicker of the dying light.

"Kiss me, Rudolf," she said . . . and I put my lips to hers . . . for the last time.

"Always?" she questioned wistfully, sweet pleading in her eyes.

"Always," I answered . . . "always, my sweet! Winter and Summer—Present and Absent—all through Life—and Beyond."

She smiled . . . "I was sure of that, my dear. Take my hand-kerchief . . . keep it . . . with my chain . . . they will remind . . ."

I took the tiny square of cambric from her hand as she died . . . and I have it to this day as I have her chain. They're mine, you see . . . nobody else's . . .

I left that place of death and went out to seek de Verviac. And I walked without thinking. Without trying to think . . . blindly . . . for I knew that I should come upon him.

That same evening, just before sundown, the dead body of Raoul de Verviac was found in the wood of ancient elms that slopes down to the Shess water. Vicious finger-marks on his throat showed that he had died from strangulation . . . that he had been strangled by bare hands. When I heard that he had been found and how he had been found, out of the frailty of my humanity . . . my soul magnified the Lord . . . may I be forgiven!

CHAPTER XXX
ONE OF THE THIRTEEN
(Told by Lance Maturin)

THERE is something that I feel that I should say here, in order that I may be excused the deficiencies that there must be in my telling of what followed. And that is this: I have little heart to write another word. When Philippa went from me . . . everything else went with her. Please understand that! Anthony Bathurst 'phoned to us the news of Verviac's killing. I told him of Philippa's love . . . and of her death. He didn't seemed too surprised at what I told him, but sent me comfortable words that were intentioned to my help. Words that, I think, I shall never forget. I told him, too, of what we were doing . . . how and why Hilleary and Fawcett had come to Trueloves.

"My dear chap," he said, "I know the extent of your grief . . . may it pass from you . . . as soon as God wills . . . try desperately to remember that there are the claims of the living . . . de Verviac's dead . . . and to-night you shall know who killed him and also who killed Inspector Rawlinson."

I put the receiver down with a grim and bitter smile . . . as though I cared who had killed whom. The day crawled by on hands of pain until about a quarter past eight—when who should arrive at the house but Paton.

When he came in he asked a question that astounded me.

"Is Anthony Bathurst here?"

Now Bathurst was the very last man for whom I should have expected Alec Paton to ask. I told him so. But he seemed unperturbed, and replied that there was little doubt that Bathurst would arrive before very long. While he was talking to me, Fawcett and Hilleary turned up, and I introduced the three of 'em to each other. Scarcely had they settled down, when Paton's words were proved true. My 'phone went again. It was Bathurst at the other end.

"Is that you, Maturin? Well, let me fix up something with you. Listen . . . That's understood, then . . . I'll be with you as soon as I can. Oh . . . and, Maturin! I know you're not too fit at the moment . . . so I'll warn you. Be prepared for a tremendous shock."

I replaced the receiver wonderingly.

"You're right, Paton," I told him with little ceremony. "I must congratulate you on your powers of perception. Bathurst will be here shortly."

He replied after the same manner. "I told you that he would. I wasn't speaking out of the back of my neck. I've had reliable information. I'm in the position to get it."

Then there came a period of waiting; none of us seemed at ease. Fawcett made one or two attempts to force the issue. He supplied the commonplace conversational *hors-d'oeuvres*, but they seemed lacking in savour. Hilleary gave the talk a topical turn.

"Any arrest for this local murder?"

"No," returned Paton quickly; "and there won't be, either."

I flashed a question at him. "Why not, pray?"

Paton set his lips and shrugged his shoulders.

"Well?" I demanded, with scant courtesy, I'm afraid. "You've made a statement. Won't you, or can't you, support it?"

Paton sensed my hostility and stuck out his jaw.

"I can—but I don't think that I will. My past indiscretions have not been altogether lost on me. Perhaps I've already said too much."

"That kind of talk annoys me," I declared—"It's so futile."

Hilleary flung me a reproving glance. But I was like Gallio—I cared for none of these things. I became bitterly provocative.

"Especially considering what Bathurst has just told me."

"What's that?" queried Fawcett.

I enjoyed every moment and every phase of my petty triumph.

"That when he comes here he will announce the name of the man who killed Rawlinson . . . and the name of the person who strangled de Verviac."

You could have cut the silence! Hilleary fidgeted in his chair. I could tell from his manner that he desired to say something, and at last it escaped him.

"There's a rumour down in the village—I heard it at the station, as a matter of fact—that de Verviac was killed by a woman."

I saw Paton start. I was certain that Hilleary's statement was unwelcome to him. Fawcett started an argument.

"She must have been first cousin to an Amazon, then. The man was strangled by bare hands. I should have thought it would have required—"

Paton looked anxiously at his watch. His whole demeanour puzzled me. It was so unlike the Paton of ordinary.

"Look here, you chaps . . . I'm a bit worried, if you only knew. I came here by appointment . . . under instructions, if you like, and I'm not quite sure if plans haven't miscarried. If they have—"

I checked him abruptly.

"What on earth do you mean, Paton . . . that you came here under instructions? As far as I know, Trueloves still belongs to my father . . . and failing him . . . my name also happens to be Maturin. I'd hug you if you explained."

He looked at his watch again. Hilleary and Fawcett remained silent. Then Paton gave me the impression that he'd arrived at a decision.

"Look here, Maturin. There's a hell of a lot that still remains to be explained. You've told me that you saw me in that early train from Antwerp. The train to Brussels. Well, I'd like you to know this. I went across there to help your cousin . . . who was in grave peril."

Fawcett and Hilleary were listening eagerly.

"Well?" I queried . . . "What about it? It's late in the day to talk of that, surely? Rawlinson's dead, de Verviac's dead, my cousin's dead . . . and somebody else . . . has gone to join them."

My voice was husky, and I cursed at the sign it showed of impotence . . . God . . . to what was I coming?"

Paton watched me. I went on with my indictment. "So that you don't seem to have achieved much, Paton, do you?"

"How do you mean, Maturin?"

"Isn't it sufficiently obvious? Or must I repeat myself?"

"You mean that I was unable to save any of the four that you named?"

"Exactly. Sticks out a mile, doesn't it?"

Paton shook his head. "We've never been on the best of terms . . . Maturin . . . for good reasons, no doubt . . . but for once, you do me an injustice."

"Is it possible? I'm learning things."

Paton flushed a dull red. "I'm endeavouring to make allowances for you. Let me tell you that you're making it extremely difficult for me."

I was about to reply, when I heard the door behind me open to admit somebody. Paton was facing the door, but Hilleary, Fawcett, and I had our backs to it. We three turned simultaneously. There, on the threshold, stood the tall woman in the red dress whom I had seen on the road, behind Raoul de Verviac, and later in my cousin's house, "The Ingots," when . . . my world had come to its standstill. The door was closed.

"Good evening, gentlemen," said a well-remembered voice, and three of us looked up in astonishment. Paton's embarrassment had given way to something like satisfaction.

"I must apologise," went on that familiar voice, "for coming upon you like this, but I have had little time to assume a more reasonable costume."

The figure in red crossed to me . . . with purpose showing in every movement.

"I must thank you, Lance, for all that you have done for me . . . I know something of it . . . and for her."

Then I knew the naked and amazing truth. This woman who had come to us was a man . . . more than that—he was my cousin Lancelot . . . whom we had mourned as dead those many days. He gripped my hand . . . and I think, in that moment of our joy, there was also sorrow . . . and that we sorrowed in communion for love of the girl we had lost.

Chapter XXXI
BATHURST GATHERS THE FRAGMENTS
(Story continued by Lance Maturin)

I SHALL never know if I spoke coherent words to him. There was a big lump in my throat that dried everything up . . . all that I can remember is that I just held his hand and went on shaking it.

After a time I pulled myself together and did the conventional honours, introducing Lancelot to Fawcett and Hilleary. Now that I had a better opportunity to look over him, I noticed that he appeared tired and pale, and that his face bore the signs of a great sorrow. At the same time his clean-cut features and blue eyes were splendid auxiliaries to his impersonation.

We all waited for him to tell us more—for God knows there was much to explain! But he spoke first to Paton. "Isn't he here yet? Bathurst, I mean?"

"Not yet."

Lancelot looked at his watch with a gesture of annoyance. "He's late."

The words had scarcely left his lips when there came the last staggering shock of this amazing drama . . . to others . . . if not so much to me. There was a tap on the door, and before anyone of us could be quick enough to get across to open it, there entered to us Anthony Bathurst himself.

My cousin jumped to his feet in astonishment.

"Dr. Chalmers," he declared, his voice thrilling to the measure of his surprise, "what is the meaning of this unwarranted intrusion? You have no right whatever in his house, and I consider your presence here an insult and an impertinence. If you have anything to—"

The man whom he addressed came forward and they met face to face in the middle of the room. There was a gleam in the newcomer's grey eyes.

"You've got me all wrong, you know, my dear Maturin. I'm not really Dr. Chambers . . . my name is Anthony Lotherington Bathurst."

You don't often see Lancelot discomfited, but you saw it all right this time.

"Bathurst?" he gasped wonderingly.

Bathurst nodded. "Yes. I'm Bathurst, believe me. You see, I wasn't Chalmers any more than you were Lisle Malfroy. We happened to be working the same idea. I confess, too, that I picked up the dodge from you. It seemed to me that it was the only way to arrive into the inner circle of those old friends of ours, the Apostles."

A slow smile twisted over Lancelot's face. For the moment he forgot the pain in his heart. Bathurst's revelation had driven it away.

"By Jove," he muttered . . . "so you hoist me with my own petard, do you?"

"I was forced to. I couldn't see any other satisfactory way of getting to close grips with the problem. You must understand I'd promised Rawlinson . . . more or less . . . to see the thing through. You came into my affair, of course, because of Erskine?"

My cousin nodded.

Bathurst continued:

"I 'phoned Mr. Lance Maturin this evening that I intended to come along here . . . a personal call from Paton had made that imperative, and, amongst other things, I promised him that I would disclose who killed Rawlinson and who strangled de Verviac."

Anthony Bathurst paused. I felt that that pause held an immense significance. I saw, too, that Fawcett clenched his hands round the sides of his chair. Bathurst turned again to Lancelot.

"Erskine, I take it, was the first man of your staff to evince an interest in the League of Matthias?"

"Yes. That's right. He was my particular chum in the Service, and he let on to me two or three little pieces of news. When those devils got him and chucked his body into the Scheldt . . . dear old

'Nudger' . . . it was up to me to carry on from where he had left off just as you have done with regard to your pal Rawlinson. My 'disappearance' was arranged . . . I had orders to that effect from my chief, and all our plans were laid with the most rigid care and efficiency. Not the slightest risk was taken . . . not a soul was put wise as to what was being done, and the strictest silence was enforced, not only upon me but also upon the man who part-nered me. But the whole business, from my own personal point of view, came at a most inconvenient time . . . for I was on the verge of marrying . . ."

My cousin stopped. I saw him wrestle with his grief . . . as I grappled with my own.

"But my service had to come first . . . my lips were sealed . . . and the girl who waited for me suffered the agony of the belief that I had deceived her. An agony that was the more bitter, seeing how near we were to our wedding."

"One point," remarked Bathurst—"it's occurred to me before, as a matter of fact. In what way did the League of Matthias specially concern the higher 'Intelligence'? I must confess that I've been a trifle puzzled over that. Beyond the fact that it traf-ficked in murder and sudden death, I haven't been able to—"

My cousin nodded again "I see your point, Bathurst. But it came about in the first place through Svenhardt. Svenhardt was as unscrupulous as the Borgias were cunning, and he had in his possession certain vital information about a German attempt to re-establish the Hapsburgs, which he had promised to hand on to us . . . for a price, of course. When Svenhardt passed out in such a ghastly way . . . his veins were opened by pieces of jagged glass . . . we were exceedingly interested . . . the significance of the crime couldn't be overlooked, and we naturally desired to know whys and wherefores."

Bathurst motioned to him. "I see. That explains much. Go on, please."

"Well . . . I 'disappeared.' The Press advertised it. The last person apparently, whom the Apostles need consider then, was Lancelot Maturin. A week after my 'disappearance' I was at my wit's end as to the best way to proceed. All I had to help me were the few scraps that 'Nudger' Erskine had spilled to me. They weren't very illuminating, I can assure you . . . either singly or accumulatively. Well, when I was right down in the mouth and as worried as hell, I had a stroke of luck."

Fawcett was staring at Paton, but the latter never batted an eyelid. Lancelot resumed his story.

"According to what Erskine had told me, the district round the Quai Van Dyck had been under his direct suspicion. He had been almost certain that in some way it was linked with the Matthias League. So I made myself as disreputable as I could and loafed round there—for days on end. It was dead easy. The docks and ships and sheds meant that any amount of people were passing to and fro daily and nightly. There happens to be a deserted shed right at the end of one of the blocks, and one evening, when it was raining cats and dogs and I was glad to crawl in anywhere for protection, I went into it . . . to discover on the dirty flooring the body of a man. He was dead . . . shot through the head . . . and by his own hand. A note on the boards and the revolver that he still held told me this beyond question. Well . . . you've probably guessed his identity. There were letters on him . . . one that positively thrilled me to read . . . a newspaper cutting and a visiting-card. He was Lisle Malfroy . . . the man who had recently been twice tried for murder . . . to be released on a Crown *nolle prosequi*. . . . I shall never forget the ghastly time that I spent in that shed down on that dismal quay."

My cousin paused for a moment.

"As I shall never forget, either, other things. It rained in torrents, the wind howled round the shed, and there was just enough light to see the corpse on the floor. You heard me say a moment ago that I found one letter on Malfroy that thrilled me. When I read it, I knew that God Himself had directed my steps into that disused shed . . . and I thought of Erskine . . . and of a girl in England who would neither see him again nor hear his voice again."

A little gasp came from Fawcett. He was following Lancelot's story as though his life depended on it. My cousin gave him a quick glance and proceeded.

"This letter that meant so much to me was signed by a man who called himself Raoul de Verviac . . . which was the one definite name that 'Nudger' Erskine had mentioned to me. More or less, it was an invitation to Malfroy to join the infamous League. It had grown very dark now in the shed, and as I read the letter by the light of three spluttering matches, the obvious idea began to germinate in my mind. Were I Malfroy, and Malfroy, Maturin, there would be a Malfroy that would ruffle up the spirits of that League and put the fear of God into every one of their cursed souls. There was a doubt, though, that I had seriously to consider. How far had Malfroy gone with his negotiations? Had de Verviac and he met . . . were they acquainted with one another? I struck another match and looked at the date on de Verviac's letter. It was the date of the same day. This looked a lot better to me. It eased matters considerably. A thousand to one, I argued, that Malfroy hadn't moved in the matter at all, but had decided to blow out his brains as a more agreeable alternative. Then occurred my second stroke of luck."

Lancelot rose and walked to the mantlepiece. He surveyed the ring of us.

"The photograph?" queried Bathurst.

My cousin nodded. "Yes. The Press photograph of Lisle Malfroy. Fate had played into my hands. It was the picture of a clean-shaven man, taken in profile, under a broad-brimmed hat. Collar, tie and clothes all followed the traditions of convention. Dozens of young men of my acquaintance could have answered to it with a fair amount of confidence—at any rate, without the anticipation of serious criticism. So I took my life in my hands—I'm speaking literally—and crossed the Rubicon. I dressed myself in the dead man's clothes, and took everything that he had possessed, including his revolver. I dressed that corpse in my clothes, gave it several things that would serve to identify it as Lancelot Maturin, waited until well past midnight, until it was pitch dark, shoved the body on my shoulders, crept out of the shed, and dumped the body of Lisle Malfroy in the Scheldt. I was therefore, gentlemen, from that moment, committed to my adventure. From now onwards, there could be no retracing of my steps . . . I couldn't go back."

There came a long pause which we all of us respected. Lancelot lit a cigarette. He was silent for what seemed an appallingly long time. There wasn't the vestige of a doubt that he found himself in the throes of a poignant emotion.

"Would it help you Maturin, if I tried to fill in a few of the blank spaces?" queried Bathurst with kindly intention.

"It would help me tremendously, my dear fellow. For at the moment I have neither wit, nor words, nor worth."

Lancelot smiled sadly.

"You went to de Verviac the next morning?"

"Yes. Went slow for a time, until I knew everything was all serene. He accepted me as Malfroy, the man whose name had been sent to him for his sinister League. The man to whom he had written. I met him afterwards, by appointment, in Mother Rasmussen's house in the Rue du Sacré Coeur."

"And you left with him your Malfroy credentials?"

"Yes."

"Sit down, Maturin," said Bathurst to my cousin, "for I'm coming now to the killing of Rawlinson, and I want to be sure of . . . every one of my points."

He looked round the room at each one of us.

"The house of Mother Rasmussen, that evening, became the centre of a circle with various radii reaching the circumference. Miss Castleton, who lodged there, had employed the help of Lance Maturin . . . against the blackguardly de Verviac. They went there and de Verviac arrived later, as he had intended to, all along. Besides them, there were Inspector Rawlinson and . . . er . . . I myself. I was disguised as a woman, but I'm afraid the masquerade wasn't the artistic piece of work that yours was, Maturin."

He glanced at my cousin. Lancelot shrugged his shoulders with apparent lack of interest. Bathurst made no further comment but continued his story.

"Besides the people I have mentioned, there were three other people in the Rasmussen house. They arrived at various times. I will name them one by one . . . and attempt to supply the reasons that took them. Number one was Lancelot Maturin . . . who was curious, in his character of Lisle Malfroy, as to whether Monsieur de Verviac was the actual murderer of his colleague and friend . . . Alan Erskine. Am I right in my assumption?"

Lancelot nodded. "Quite right. I had scarcely let him out of my sight for days."

"Thank you, Maturin. You got away from the house, of course, when I was seeing to Rawlinson. Number two was Adrian Fawcett."

Fawcett went a paler shade.

"You were there," said Bathurst, turning towards him, "because you were curious as to the reason that had taken another member of your party there. In other words, you followed that person there. In the dark, not knowing who you were and never dreaming probably of your presence in the room, that man gave you a nasty welt on the head. The shots you had heard scared you . . . you guessed that there had been foul play . . . so you concocted a story to account for your being there and to white-wash, if necessary, any of your friends who might be implicated. Well . . . any criticisms?"

Fawcett looked round wonderingly, but shook his head at Bathurst's question.

"No. You're about right as far as I'm concerned." Bathurst proceeded imperturbably. "Number three . . . of our unexpected visitors . . . was Dennis Hilleary . . . who, anxious for the welfare of Lance Maturin, had followed him and Miss Castleton to Mother Rasmussen's . . . gone back to the hotel for a revolver . . . perhaps . . . and started out again for the Rasmussen rendez-vous. Followed by Fawcett, who had seen him depart. It was Hilleary who had the scrap with Fawcett in the dark . . . each thinking the other 'the enemy.' And, like Lancelot Maturin, he got away before I had time to get the police there." Bathurst turned to him. "Yes, Mr. Hilleary?" Hilleary nodded, but the colour had drained from his cheeks and he looked like a man who feared what was coming next. Bathurst approached his triumphant moment.

"Consider the stage, then, as it was now set. Lance and Philippa upstairs. . . . with de Verviac. Rawlinson and I, in the kitchen at the back of the house. Near to us, Mother Rasmussen herself. Downstairs, too, in the rooms to the right of the stair-case, down which de Verviac came running, Maturin, Hilleary, and Fawcett . . . not one of whom knew that the two others were there. De Verviac had a start. Rawlinson ran towards him and called upon him to slop. I was just behind the Inspector. When de Verviac reached the front door, after dropping the Malfroy news-paper-cutting, he turned . . . revolver in hand. Rawlinson, with desperate courage, ran on, and, as he ran, he was shot down."

Bathurst paused. "But, if my theory be right, the bullet that killed him *was* intended for de Verviac and was fired by *you*, Mr. Maturin."

He turned to my cousin. "Am I right?"

Lancelot buried his face in his hands. "God forgive me . . . yes. He ran right between us as I fired. From my little revolver. I had given Philippa one exactly like it. I told de Verviac the story this afternoon . . . just before I lifted my hands and strangled him."

Bathurst rose and, with a gesture of sympathy, patted my cousin on the shoulder.

Chapter XXXII
"AND THE LOT FELL UPON MATTHIAS"
(Story concluded by Lance Maturin)

"I TOLD Paton that I should meet you here to-night. I knew that the time had come for the whole story to be told." As he spoke, Lancelot looked up. He continued.

"The night that Rawlinson died, I went to Brussels. Paton followed me. I still had to get de Verviac, and I had lost my big chance. So I had to go ahead with the Apostles' business. And I felt that . . . in some obscure way . . . that didn't hold the hint of a risk . . . I must let Philippa know that I was alive. You see, she always knew my code word 'ripening,' and that gave me the idea. Paton tells me that you read the meaning from my *Times* 'agony'?"

Anthony Bathurst nodded. "That gave me the first glimmer of the truth. 'The worst is not. The best shall be. For in the dregs lay Infamy.' Those lines told me a lot. I thought I detected the identity of Malfroy in that drowned body, and how you had contrived the change of identity. Out of that, I hit on my own plan of becoming Dr. Chalmers. I realised that I, too, if I wanted the entire truth, must get into the secret council of the Apostles."

"How did you work it—the Chalmers' touch?"

"Chalmers—the real Chalmers—was due to be released in about a month's time. I obtained that information from the 'Yard.' His record of crime was such that I knew—if they were properly primed—that the ' Apostles' would jump at him. Paragraphs appeared in all the Press by arrangement . . . *and my own photograph.*"

"The altercation with Chenils was . . . a bluff, then?"

Bathurst grinned. "Stage managed for de Verviac's personal and especial benefit. A command performance if you like. Look at the testimonial it gave me. There was no doubting my infamy after that."

My cousin gave him a quick glance of admiration.

"By Jove . . . your coolness all through was marvellous. You amazed me when you instantly replied with the date of St. Matthias's Day. You know how I arranged to get de Verviac, of course?"

"I think it would be as well, Maturin, if you told the others, first of all, the full functions and history of the League. Don't you think so?"

"Perhaps I had better. Some of it's conjecture, but the main facts are true enough. If you disagree with anything I put forward, pull me up."

"Agreed," said Bathurst.

Lancelot became more animated than I had yet seen him.

"The Apostles' League was initiated by Svenhardt, the banker. There is little doubt that the two years that Svenhardt spent, hunted and a fugitive, after he fled from Christiania, turned him into a homicidal maniac. Not an ordinary homicidal maniac, but one—mark you—with over a quarter of a million of money. To be precise, an amount of two hundred and sixty thousand pounds . . . money that had been stolen from rich and poor alike. When his brain went, he was in Antwerp. Here, he had got into touch with de Verviac and put before him the initial details of his bizarre scheme. Like so many of the more daring criminals, Svenhardt, in his earlier years, was a man of professed religious principles, and when he went to de Verviac, I have been told that one sentence from the New Testament had fairly burnt itself into his brain. It had become a mad obsession with him."

"May I interrupt?" intervened Bathurst. Lancelot nodded.

"May I have a shot at that sentence?"

"Of course. What do you think it was?"

"And the lot fell upon Matthias," returned Bathurst with quiet impressiveness.

"My congratters, Bathurst. You are absolutely right. Svenhardt's lust for money . . . now satisfied . . . had turned into a lust for excitement. In effect, Svenhardt's scheme was something like this. He and de Verviac collected eleven men . . . to whom life meant nothing. Men of unspeakable reputation . . . of broken career . . . men to whom suicide was, in most cases, the almost inevitable and even welcome finale. You will remember many of them if I give you their names. Busigny, Dr. Whitsbury, Nijegaard, and Schoonbeke. To these men, whom they enlisted one by one, they presented the scheme of what Svenhardt was determined to call the 'League of Matthias'."

My cousin paused in his narrative and lit a cigarette. But I noticed that his hand was unsteady. The strain of the last weeks was beginning to take toll of him.

"As nearly as I can establish it, Svenhardt's bloody mind parented the following grotesque tournament. The 'League' was to meet twice a year. At each meeting, two names were to be drawn . . . by lot . . . just as Matthias had been chosen to fill the place of the Iscariot by the glorious company of the authentic eleven. Of the two drawn opponents, one had to kill the other.

But by no lethal weapon, mark you. Each knew his antagonist . . . they were each in the open as it were . . . it was quite fair from that point of view. Consider the stakes! To the loser . . . death! To the winner . . . twenty thousand pounds! There would be, of course, thirteen struggles . . . until the money of Svenhardt's fund was exhausted. A comfortable reward, gentlemen, for a desperate, ruined, or broken man. Added to which, the victor, if he so chose, could leave the League and spend the remainder of his evil days in affluence."

"One moment, Maturin," Bathurst interposed again. "I imagined that the general idea was something of that kind, but I confess to being a trifle puzzled with regard to the League's finances. Who held the money?"

"The money was lodged by Svenhardt—not in his own name, of course—at an Antwerp bank . . . to the credit of 'The Matthias League.' Erskine had verified that fact. Five 'overseers,' as they were designated, were appointed at the preliminary meeting, and no money could be withdrawn except by the bankers honouring the signatures of four of them. If one 'lost' a tournament, or left the League, another was appointed at the next meeting."

"I think I see. Svenhardt went out first round, if I may use the term, didn't he?"

"Yes. As luck had it. De Verviac got him. And de Verviac, with his illimitable supplies of devilry and bestial cunning, found his baptism of murder so easy . . . and effortless . . . that he stayed in . . . although victorious . . . he persuaded himself that there were other 'twenty thousand pounds' prizes that he always had the chance of pulling off."

"You, of course," remarked Anthony Bathurst, watching my cousin steadily, "as Lisle Malfroy, the night you and I were initiated, 'seeded' the draw? That was my impression, at least."

Lancelot nodded nervously. "Oh—yes . . . yes. You see, I went to get Raoul de Verviac . . . to make absolutely sure that he was the man who had killed 'Nudger' Erskine . . . and for other reasons . . . that I need not go into here. I had the numbers '1' and '13' in my palm before I drew. I knew that I must be '13,' and I knew that '13' was the Apostle who always drew the numbers.

I had wormed certain information from de Verviac, and, in addition, an Apostle spoon, and I had in my mind, too, what Alan Erskine had told me. Also I knew that de Verviac would be number '1.' Nijegaard, after murdering Schoonbeke, took his bonus . . . so the right of the chair reverted to the previous victor, de Verviac, who had burnt Whitsbury in a baker's oven in the Quai Van Dyck."

My cousin put his face into his hands and sank into silence. Bathurst asked another question.

"When vacancies occurred . . . after a claim, as we'll call it, by a murderer . . . they looked round for likely recruits. Yes?"

"That's right. That's how they drew their line on Malfroy."

Bathurst chuckled. "I thought so. That's why I thought Dr. Chalmers would commend himself to their tender arts. Well—they're finished altogether now. The Belgian authorities rounded up the whole lot of 'em last night. I was able to supply most of the identities, and their own personal reputations filled in whatever blanks there were."

This time it was my turn to ask a question. "How did you come to solve the mystery of Rawlinson's death, Bathurst?"

"Well—I was lucky, perhaps. But I reasoned in this wise. Your cousin was alive. I read that from the Maturin cryptogram, and I toyed with the idea that he was wearing the Malfroy mantle. The 'Malfroy' clues, that I found on the staircase of the house in the Rue du Sacré Coeur, and the spoon in the room, suggested to me that he *might* have been the man in that room. Then something else struck me. Something of vital significance—this! Rawlinson had not been killed by *any* of the League. Rawlinson had been killed by a shot. To the members of the League—revolvers were taboo. So I cast round for the truth. The idea came to me suddenly—when it did come. And it fitted beautifully. I was there when Rawlinson was killed, don't forget. The shot had been fired at de Verviac . . . and the Inspector had run in between de Verviac, and the person who had fired. It was the only possible solution as far as I could see, for Hilleary and Fawcett seemed to be merely on the fringe of the affair."

He turned to my cousin. "By the way, Maturin, I'll see the Commissioner to-morrow and put one or two matters right for you. Sir Austin is seeing Dr. Castleton, too . . . the Bishop of Longbarrow. You may rely on my discretion in the matter of the inquests. 'Intelligence' has already been to work, and there'll be but little trouble."

Lancelot rose and came to me.

"Good-bye, Lance. We'll mourn together . . . perhaps she'll understand. Let's hope so."

The tears showed in his eyes as he turned away from me. I pulled him back . . . caring naught who heard.

"Tell me," I said to him. "I'm not sure . . . were you there when de Verviac shot . . . at me? Did you see him when she . . ."

He nodded, "I saw it all, Lance. I was almost at your side. I thought he was firing at me. Nobody could have told for certain that he meant to fire at you. I saw you go to her . . . so I went after him . . . and got him."

"Tell my people what you would like them to know," I said to him.

Can I ever forget the grateful comfort of my cousin's words? I think that I repeat them to myself at the every rising of the sun and the going down of the same. Consider the sweet truth that they held for me. He was at my side when de Verviac fired. Only a few yards away. The shots that left the revolver might have been meant for him . . . or for me. Nobody could have told for certain. . . . And Philippa, my glorious girl, had made her lightning choice and put her dear body between those shots and me. Not between those shots and Lancelot. Not between those shots and . . . Mine was the life for which she gave her own!

Oft-times of an evening, when the day is dying and almost dead, I throw open the window of my bedroom and whisper of her to the silent trusting darkness. To the darkness that holds so many secrets and which comforts so many sore and troubled hearts. This brings me the only happiness that I shall ever know . . . and I knock the ashes from my pipe on to the sill, close the casement, and whisper, "Good night, Philippa."

There is something else. On each first of May, the day that the calendar has given to St. Philip, I take that walk of mine along the banks of the Shess . . . until I come to the place where I had been standing, when Lancelot's motor-boat came into my sight on that morning . . . when the world stood still . . . and there I murmur to her the last words that I ever spoke to her . . . with the fancy that she is looking down upon me and hears them again . . . "Winter and Summer . . . Present and Absent . . . All through Life and—Beyond."

Oh—God! Is there room in your heaven, my sweet?

THE END